Berthed at the largest pier in New York, the *Normandie* was shrouded in ice, sleet and smoke . . .

In the glare of the floodlights, forty-three fireboats and trucks battled the flames, whipped to a hurricane by the high winds off the Hudson River. In the freezing February weather, the crowd of onlookers watched as the gray wartime paint put on her sides blistered and ran.

Suddenly an explosion ripped apart the third funnel on the ship's superstructure. Thrill-seekers pulled back in terror. The great ship rolled over, her sides scraping against the concrete pier. Two tugs still valiantly tried to upright her. Thirty thousand spectators pushed forward to watch the *Normandie*, largest, fastest ship in the world, die. . . .

THE SINS OF WAR

A Novel by
John Rester Zodrow

PUBLISHED BY POCKET BOOKS NEW YORK

This novel is a work of historical fiction. Names, characters, places and incidents relating to non-historical figures are either the product of the author's imagination or are used fictitiously. Any resemblance of such non-historical incidents, places or figures to actual events or locales or persons, living or dead, is entirely coincidental.

Another *Original* publication of POCKET BOOKS

POCKET BOOKS, a division of Simon & Schuster, Inc.
1230 Avenue of the Americas, New York, N.Y. 10020

ISBN: 978-1-4516-1414-5

First Pocket Books printing October, 1986

10 9 8 7 6 5 4 3 2 1

This book is for Gina
and Joshua, who keep me
flowing.

I wish to thank Bill Grose, who opened his arms once again; Pamela Dorman for her thoughtful editing and "icing the cake"; George and Virginia Rester, whose enthusiasm and wonderful cooking nourish both spirit and body; Caryn Spencer for attention to detail and the extra mile. And Jeanne Bernkopf for her friendship.

THE SINS OF WAR
is based on a true story.

I

INFERNO

I came into a place void of all light,
which bellows like the sea in tempest,
when it is combated by warring winds.
                    —The Divine Comedy
                    Inferno, canto III, 28

1

ONE DAY IT WAS ordinary life. The next it was like living on Mars.

Trains and planes were all booked by the military. Gas was rationed, so you stayed home for your entertainment. It wasn't uncommon for men to work eighty-hour weeks. Women joined the work force and the whole family grew gardens to feed themselves. Nearly every mother's son became Government Issue. People were stunned by the atrocity of Pearl Harbor. Eighty-five million went to movies every week to escape the weird realities or bar-crawled and danced until they collapsed from fatigue at night, only to rise early in the morning and go back to the task of filling the president's request for seventy thousand warships and one hundred thousand tanks.

Turning twenty now was like turning thirty in peacetime. Everything became compressed. Nobody walked. America was losing a war everywhere. And nowhere more dramatically than in New York City.

February 9, 1942
New York Docks

IT WAS OVER A hundred degrees and the hold was filled with smoke from the welders' torches down on level seven of the great ship, so at first no one noticed the fire.

Nick Remington lifted his face bucket and glanced at his friend Joey Stumpo working nearby. Some sixth sense was tickling him. Why weren't the exhaust fans working? Stumpo, mistaking his look for fatigue, shot a thumbs-up in encouragement and went back to welding his toilet seat to the metal floor.

A few days ago this level on the giant luxury liner *Normandie* had been divided into elegant bedroom suites. Now after removing all walls they were installing showers, heads and row after row of metal bunks in the hangarlike area. The facilities were needed to accommodate soldiers bound for the war in Africa.

Nick turned back to welding his metal head to the floor. Again he fought the urge to panic in this tightly constricted, airless place below the water line. Claustrophobia, he told himself. Never liked tight rooms. Wouldn't do to make a scene down here. Taking a deep breath, he adjusted his face mask down over his chiseled face, concealing most of the curly black hair with its few touches of gray.

As the sparks flew, the familiar lines danced with them.

> *"There is no greater sorrow*
> *Than to be mindful of the happy time*
> *In misery."*

He had always loved Dante's epic poem. Used it in his sermons a lot. Now it haunted him.

4

THE SINS OF WAR

Being in this dank, airless, smoke-filled hold was just another aspect of the hell he had lived in for these past seven years. The war had brought his latest misfortune. And he didn't feel patriotic about winning it, although the white tally board of lost ships erected on December 8, 1941, bothered him. This morning when he came to work he saw "SHIPS SUNK: 117." He did not like to think that German subs ruled the waves just off the coast and that men leaving the shelter of New York Harbor went out to die.

The United States and its allies were losing badly, suffering defeats in Guam, Luzon, Borneo, Wake Island, Rabaul, the Philippines, Netherlands East Indies, Burma, Agedabia, Singapore and the Malay Peninsula. Three months after entering the war, caught offguard by the massive attack on Pearl Harbor, America was frantically struggling to create a military machine strong enough to counterattack her enemies. But to make matters worse, the war had come home to America's soil. Ships leaving ports along the Eastern seaboard were routinely sunk by Nazi U-boats waiting offshore. Millions of tons of war goods were being lost, not to mention the thousands of lives. Sabotage was totally uncontrolled along the docks, adding to the feeling of desperation. Floating mines had been found in New York Harbor. A secret, well-organized effort, loyal to Hitler, was said to be strangling the fledgling armed forces across the seas by denying them supplies. And the navy seemed helpless to stop it.

Here at Pier 88, he was helping modify the largest ocean liner in the world, the sleek *Normandie,* into a transport ship to be renamed the *Lafayette.* She would carry thousands of boys into battle, complete with their own supplies and armor, and would be able to outrun any U-boat. In addition, she was reputed to be unsinkable and fireproof. The *Normandie* was touted by even President Roosevelt as the hope of the day.

5

He threw up his mask and tried to breathe. God, it was close in here today. Where were the exhaust fans, anyway?

Joey was peering at him. "What's the matter?" he yelled over the noise of torches and hammers ringing around them.

"Nothing!" Nick lied. What could he say? A feeling? Something? It must be just him.

"You goldbrickin'?" Stumpo roared, grinning. He motioned to the long line of other welders working down the length of the ship. Everybody was in high gear. "We got a war to win!" Joey punched him, then swiveled down his protective asbestos mask over his smiling, boyish face.

Joey liked to smile. That innocent, angelic face of his, those round blue, reassuring eyes. What would he have done in all this adversity without Joey? What a blessing to have him as a friend. Freshly cast out of the clerical world of the Church as untouchables, he and Joey had settled for the company of themselves.

Two blond men passed through the length of the third level and exited into the parallel corridor that ran the full length of it. In the dim light, it was not obvious that their blond hair was crudely dyed. In the daylight outside it would have been immediately spotted. But hats had taken care of that.

The men were a Mutt and Jeff combo, one tall and thin, the other fat, bowlegged. The fat one said as they paused in the corridor: "There's a stack a trash."

"I only got one left," the skinny, tall one said, checking up and down the corridor. "This'll make an even dozen!"

"Do it and we go! That fuel-oil tank should be goin' good by now!" He was sweating heavily in his new overalls, and streams of water from his forehead were streaking the pancake makeup they had both used to

6

lighten their skin. But as the tall one cracked the flare in half-igniting it, a foreman of the docks came down the stairs. The short, fat one grabbed his partner and pulled him under the steps. Their hands moved to pistols concealed beneath their arms. But the foreman, busy with papers he was studying, continued past, not noticing the smell of the flare in the smoky air.

In a sudden dash, the tall blond man ran with the phosphorus fire to the pile of refuse and stuck it under.

"Fire!" somebody screamed down the line.

Nick started, his worst fear realized. Suddenly there was an explosion deep below in the ship. It seemed to rise up and he could hear it coming up and up, and then the wall that Joey Stumpo and he were near split open. A blast of flames roared out.

Two men near them burst into firebrands. Stumpo and Nick were thrown the entire width of the hold. When Nick came to, he saw his legs were on fire. Quickly he rolled and patted them out. He must have been unconscious only a brief moment. He looked for Joey and saw that the calm order that had reigned on the deck seconds before had been replaced with chaos. There was fire everywhere. Men were fighting to get up the metal stairs. And then he saw Joey get up and try to run, a living flame, his clothes, hair and shoes burning brightly.

Dimly he heard cries of "Abandon ship!"

2

CHARLIE LUCKY LUCIANO paced the warden's office at Dannemora Prison and lit a Lucky Strike Green. The door opened and the warden said: "Your visitors are here, Mr. Luciano." The prisoner, clad in the gray cotton washables of the New York prison system, blew out the match, took a deep drag and spoke as the smoke drove from his mouth: "I'll see Kratto first."

Salvatore Lucania, alias Charlie Lucky Luciano, still owned most of Tammany Hall, and that included the judges and politicians who kept the warden in power. And the warden knew that. He laughed politely. "What about Mr. Costello and Misters Meyer Lansky and Polakoff?"

Whenever Luciano wished not to answer, he pretended not to hear the question. So he turned now toward the window that looked out on the gray, barren fields of upper New York, where melting snow lay in the stubbles. The warden immediately backed out, closed the door, making a little nervous clicking sound in his throat.

In a moment, the door reopened and a slightly-built man in a dark suit entered. Moustached, shaggy dark eyebrows, long slicked-back hair, parted in the middle, he removed his dark glasses and stood waiting. Luciano kept his back to the door, a game he relished, dreamed about, sometimes felt he would dream it for the next fifty years he was sentenced in this shit-hole. If what he had in mind didn't work.

He turned and faced the man in the suit.

"Strip," perhaps the most powerful man after the president of the United States, commanded.

The man obediently pulled off his makeup moustache, threw the dark glasses to the floor and smiled. The coat fell away, followed by trousers, unloosed with a simple tug on black suspenders. Then the shirt opened, dark tie pulled apart and above a slim waist two sleek, hardening dark nipples faced him.

"Ruthie," Luciano grinned in surprise. Each week a different girl from his staff arrived. Ruthie was his favorite.

"Uncle" Frank Costello, Luciano's right-hand man in New York and New Jersey while his boss served his time, entered the warden's office. Ruthie was putting on her moustache. Luciano swatted her on the rear, kissed her, told her he'd see her next time and Ruthie left the room as a man. The warden had actually encouraged the charade. He had no desire to cause a riot with the prisoners seeing Ruthie's heart-shaped ass swish around inside a dress. As Abraham Polakoff and Meyer Lansky came in, the warden left and shut the door behind him.

The first order of business was accounting. Luciano did not trust either the warden or his old enemy, Governor Tom Dewey, not to bug the office. Dewey was, after all, the man who had sent him to prison on charges of prostitution. He checked over the slips of paper Costello handed him in silence. With his photographic memory, Luciano reviewed the take of his casino in Las Vegas, four other regional casinos across the country and his drug operation that stretched from New York to Florida and as far west as Chicago, where

Al Capone's gang took over. Then he accepted the receipts from prostitution. More than one thousand girls working at a hundred houses in New York.

Sending Luciano to prison hadn't stopped anything. He had simply run it, like all the other illegal scams he had going, from Dannemora. Once a week, his attorney, Polakoff, arrived with Costello and Lansky and they did business . . . after pleasure. Luciano was still the kingpin of the entire Eastern seaboard and the most respected *capo* in the United States. With his loyal friends fronting for him, it was like he had never gone away. And everybody was getting rich with him. Only his old pal Vito Genovese, sitting in Naples, was having a shit attack of poverty. He had fled the country when Lucky went to prison. All because he had thought the collapse of his Mafia Family headed by Luciano was certain.

Luciano listened to his profits and studied Frank Costello. Cool. Urbane. Always soft-spoken, never violent. He and Frank went back a long way. They had started as bootleggers, running rum in from Canada. It had been Frank who had always quieted him down when he wanted a hit done on some troublemaker or when he lost his temper. Good old smooth-talking Frank Costello. Not quite Mafia . . . one foot in, one foot out, they always said. But nobody got out of the family. Not alive.

Meyer Lansky, the little red-haired Jew, was speaking now, talking about his plans for a gambling expansion into Cuba. He was smart. Real smart. And lethal. Dutch Schultz had found that out. So had that wily Maranzano and before him that old greaser Massaro. Lansky had done it while Luciano went to the bathroom in Scarpato's Italian restaurant down at the wharf. Joe the Boss never knew what hit him after all that wine and pasta. Three shots point-blank in the face. Old Joe, his mentor. And Meyer Lansky, a Jew, let in on the action, but never into the Family. Luciano's partner now . . . for as long as they needed one another. Lansky, more than Costello, had to be watched.

When Lansky had finished, Polakoff gave a report on the latest progress of Luciano's release from prison. The case was now before the Supreme Court. Dismissal was being requested on the grounds that Tom Dewey, before he became governor of New York as a result of winning the trial against Luciano, had falsified testimonies. Luciano listened and then he said: "Abe, maybe you better leave now."

Polakoff understood, bowed his balding ring of white hair and exited. Luciano lit another Lucky Green, and Costello brought out his English Ovals and tapped one on the box held in his fingertips he had had manicured that morning at the Waldorf Astoria barbershop. Meyer went to the radio and turned it on and began searching for a station that carried the news.

"How can you hack those?" Luciano pointed to the Oval Frank was lighting. "English rolled turds."

Frank laughed diplomatically and said: "They make me smoke less."

The radio whined in and Walter Winchell said: "I am standing here at Pier 88, watching the water play over the giant burning mass of what was once the famed *Normandie* . . . the completely fireproof *Normandie,* it was claimed. A few tugs are still attempting to right the stately lady, once the fastest ship on the seas. She was to have carried our troops to the war front, and no U-boat could have stopped her. This once-proud ship lying now nearly on her beam in the Hudson River cries out for revenge! I say to you, ladies and gentlemen, this is an act of sabotage! Our ships are being sunk by Nazi submarines off our very coastline. We are losing the

11

war! Twenty-seven ships lost in December, another forty in January and fifty so far in this month of February! Something is drastically wrong!"

"Those fucking, no-good *tesoros!*" Luciano hitched up his prison pants, which were string-tied, like pajamas. "Those Germans even put that pig Mussolini in like a puppet to come after our *famiglia.*" He spat on the floor. But he was having a good time.

"Naval authorities have warned that the water the firemen are pumping into her hold will surely capsize this tremendous ship," the announcer went on. "And so it remains to be seen if the *Normandie,* which once personified the beauty, style and spirit of an age . . ." Walter Winchell broke off. "A scoop, ladies and gentlemen—a moment, please."

"What's wrong?!" Lansky turned up the volume.

"It seems," Winchell came back on breathlessly, "that several men—dock welders, we believe—are trapped in the great hold of the *Normandie,* and now we have a new human dimension of tragedy added . . ."

Luciano himself turned off the radio.

3

A BONE-TIRED ARCHBISHOP Francis Spellman stepped from the drab green military DC-3 and hurried toward the front of La Guardia Airport, where he hoped his limousine was waiting. Since his plane was early, no one was there to carry his luggage, but right now he preferred it that way. He gingerly felt his gray stubble. Up for over seventy-two hours now. Wouldn't do to have anyone of note see him bedraggled like this. Oh, the hell with appearances for once, he thought. If anyone had been through what I have in the last three days . . . and then he noticed several passengers hurry past him to their planes and stare at him. He averted his face.

The terrible sense of urgency that drove his footsteps now and gave him courage to face New York in such a disheveled manner was powered by patriotism . . . and ambition, he admitted truthfully. A red hat. To be a cardinal. After all the turmoil of the past few days, he had a solution in his hands: not one he wanted. But he had had no choice but to cooperate with the wishes of Franklin Delano Roosevelt.

From the very beginning, the president's plan had seemed preposterous. Joe "Socks" Minestrone, a local hood who controlled the extortion racket at the Fulton

Fish Market down at the docks, had met a commodore of the United States Navy. The commodore, buying some haddock, had remarked that while the ghetto area suffered from vandalism and general disorder, the Fulton Fish Market was clean, in perfect condition and seemed to have no elements of crime. Later, at a luncheon arranged by Joe "Socks," the commodore was let in on a little secret. The Mafia kept the docks clean.

Unfazed by the truth since he already knew it, Commodore Hahn continued to pursue an idea he had. He allowed he was frustrated at trying to stop the general sabotage on the docks, which was his area of authority. Was it possible to bring in the Mafia to patrol the docks? If every longshoreman had his eyes open, maybe all this destruction could be stopped. And at the moment, any help would be appreciated. The navy didn't even have the slightest idea who were the saboteurs! Joe "Socks" shrugged and said he'd think it over.

When the navy had been presented the idea by Commodore Hahn, the brass balked. They wanted nothing to do with the Mafia and ordered the commodore to drop the scheme. As it turned out, the Mob felt the same way about the navy. Authority and crime just wouldn't mix. But then, somehow, Roosevelt got wind of the notion. The culprit, Spellman surmised, was Hahn himself. The commodore was out of solutions, and his future was obviously going down the drain. So three days ago, Spellman, in his official rank of Vicar General of the Armed Forces, received an urgent request to meet with the president.

Arriving at the Oval Office around four that afternoon, Spellman found Commodore Richard Hahn already with the president. He knew Hahn as a pompous, stiff-necked, behind-the-desk officer, a man frustrated by sitting out the war.

"Thank you for coming up for this little emergency meeting, Excellency," Roosevelt had said, lighting a cigarette which hung at the end of his long filter. "As you all know, we are sickened at the continuing news of our losses in New York Harbor and the growing number of our ships being sunk off the East Coast. In short, America is losing the war because our ports are in the hands of the Nazis. We are beleaguered, Eminence."

"What can be done, Mr. President?" Spellman had asked, wondering just how he, a clergyman, could possibly fit into this discussion.

"Dick here tells me the navy has had little success in stopping the saboteurs. But since the waterfronts are ruled by the Mafia, I had a notion that since they're mostly Catholic you might help."

Normally Spellman had a perfect poker face for just about anything. Someone could have come up behind him and fired a .45 by his ear and he would not have lost his composure. But this . . . coming from the president of the United States! Expecting the Holy Roman Catholic Church to work with gangsters, pimps, extortioners, and . . . murderers! He wondered if the rumors that Roosevelt was a sick man were true.

"I know, I know," Roosevelt said, lowering his observant eyes. "It's outrageous. But without your help, we can't make a go of this. The Church alone has the power to influence the Mafia to help us. And as your commanding officer, I am giving you an order."

Spellman's blue eyes twinkled suddenly. He felt better. A way out had occurred to him. As an American citizen and military official, he had no choice but to obey his president in this matter. But there was still the pope. And Pope Pius was notoriously noncommittal toward everything. The perfect diplomat, he would somehow sidestep the president's request and veto this entire plan.

15

"Mr. President, you have my full cooperation." Spellman played his trump card. "But I'm afraid I'll have to discuss this with my pontiff."

Slipping another fresh cigarette into his holder, Roosevelt smiled in total confidence. "Go see my friend the Holy Father. Tell him what another good friend, Winston Churchill, so wisely said in defining wartime morality: 'If by some stroke of fate the devil came out in opposition to Adolf Hitler, I should feel constrained to cooperate with him.'"

Leaving the White House, Spellman had boarded the military DC-3 which Roosevelt had placed at his disposal. All through the night flight, he had tried to sleep, but could not even manage to doze off. He was counting on Pius to say no, betting on it! But what if he went along with Roosevelt's scheme? Then it would be up to Spellman to implement the plan, and he could not possibly approach a crime boss of the underworld for a favor . . . even if he had accepted a gift of huge bronze doors for the entrance of St. Pat's Cathedral from Frank Costello. Costello was a fervent, Sunday-going Catholic. That was different. That was charity. This, if it ever got out, was his career!

Spellman, driven from Fiumicino Airport directly to Rome, was stopped at several checkpoints by Mussolini's bands of roving *fascisti*. But each time he was waved through once they saw the Vatican license plate and the purple gowns of the archbishop in the rear seat.

Finally, he was shown into Pius' third-floor study inside the Belvedere wing of the Vatican and was greeted by the stout and cheerful German nun who was called Sister Pasqualina. Good friends, they hugged each other warmly. Spellman knew she was very powerful and had great influence over the pope. She had even got Spellman appointed Archbishop of New York. So he told her about the plan. To his amazement, she liked it and thought it might work. Excusing herself,

16

she went into the pontiff's study. My God, Spellman fidgeted, does she think I want *approval* of Roosevelt's operation?! He feared he had made a prime mistake by telling her. In a moment, his terror was confirmed.

Standing before the white-clad and ascetic-appearing Holy Father, Spellman repeated Roosevelt's words. Pius was also a close friend; they had known each other before the war, and even hiked across Europe together. After a moment, the pontiff replied almost casually that he was anxious to keep his relationship with FDR rosy. "You have no need to talk to me," he finished. "Use your own discretion."

It was a perfect move. The diplomat-pope had neither approved nor condemned the plot, but had thrown it back into Spellman's lap.

On the plane home, Spellman sat morosely in his seat, not even trying to sleep. He was beyond fatigue and he could even smell himself, an unusual occurrence since he was normally fastidiously dapper. What to do now? Perhaps let the scheme lie for a while? Let its momentum slow? Roosevelt was very busy, beleaguered by the enormous efforts of organizing a peacetime nation into an armed and warring one. Months could go by. The idea would get lost in the shuffle. Perhaps Roosevelt would forget "Operation Underworld."

But upon disembarking at La Guardia and nearing the curb where he prayed his limo would be waiting, even that solution was canceled out.

Commodore Richard Hahn fell into step with him. A saboteur, he said, had set fire to the *Normandie*. The president was intensely interested in starting up "Operation Underworld."

"Sir, President Roosevelt asked me to relay the Holy Father's answer," Hahn said in his clipped tone.

The game was over. All hands played for the archbishop. He would never be cardinal. "Pope Pius answered affirmatively." Spellman cringed. What was he to do?

"And will you implement our plan immediately?" Hahn pressed as they arrived at the limo. "The Mafia will probably want a deal."

"Of course, Commodore," Spellman said. "I always obey my orders."

"Good," Hahn said as Manny, the chauffeur, took the prelate's bag and stowed it in the trunk. "May we expect you to meet with us tomorrow morning at 0800 then?"

Spellman nodded and dragged himself into the limousine, sitting there like a zombie. He was caught in a vise. Think, man. Think hard. Save yourself!

"Welcome home, Excellency." Manny grinned.

Spellman did not reply.

"Straight home, Excellency? Looks like you need a bath and a little shuteye."

Spellman's gaze was far off. Manny began driving toward the Chancery at Fifty-first and Fifth. Spellman was unusually quiet. Manny thought he might be praying or meditating. He did that sometimes. But as they turned onto Fifth from the Midtown Tunnel, the archbishop suddenly sat forward in his seat and shouted: "Nick Remington! The perfect go-between for this mess! He's working as a plumber . . . no, something else . . . on the docks! Turn here, Manny, get down to the Port Authority. They'll know where he's at. And step on it!"

But as Manny obediently switched directions, Spellman began to wonder. Remington was almost certainly bitter about the Church. He'd never agree to it. But there had to be a way to convince him.

When Manny emerged from the water-stained Port Authority, Spellman roused himself from the stupor he had fallen into. "Where is he? Do they know?!"

"Union says he's working on the *Normandie* today," Manny said.

Spellman grabbed his crucifix nervously, rubbing it as he did whenever he got beyond himself. He knew it made him look old and feeble. But he only did it whenever he was sure no one was watching.

4

NICK HAD SOMEHOW gotten to Joey. He was actually surprised to find himself carrying him like a child in his arms. The fires on his and Joey's body were out. But every step hurt as his muscles contracted. Joey kept humming something softly. It sounded like "Te Deum." In the thick smoke, Nick tried to keep low to the floor, breathing only through his nose. It was roaring hot and he could not see where he was going. Twice he bumped off the wall, dropping Joey, who cried out, but he managed to gather him up. It didn't make any sense. The stairway had to be near. He tried again to picture it in his mind but found he could not hold the image. Absurdly he began counting his paces, trying to measure where the stairs should be. His head bumped a pipe and looking at it in the roiling smoke, he realized he had been walking in circles. The pipe ran above the toilets he had been installing.

Joey Stumpo moaned in anguish. In his state of near asphyxiation, Nick sat down on the floor. He wanted to save Joey but he could not remember now what he had been looking for to do it. His mind seemed as clouded as the room, and he realized he was lost and strangely did not care.

Joey was suddenly wracked by a fierce cough. Nick bent close and in the thick haze, surrounded by crackling flames on all sides, saw that Joey was mortally wounded. He had no face, just swollen, blackened skin, and two slits for eyes.

"Nicky . . ." The voice came from the ruined skin.

He leaned close, or thought he did.

"Absolve me . . . !" he hissed painfully. "You're still a priest!"

Joey's request seemed perverse. But feeling that this was his last act on earth, Nick raised his hand over his fallen partner, Father Joseph Stumpo, his "accomplice" in the scandal that had brought them to this end.

In the spring of 1928, the "million dollar priest," as Nicholas Broderick Remington was being affectionately called, was ordained. Joey Stumpo stood at his side, along with their sixteen other classmates from the Diocesan Seminary of Boston. Cardinal Stamp performed the ordination, and when he anointed Nick's hands, he bent close and whispered: "Talented hands, talented." And winked.

It was well known that Nick was his favorite and was regarded by him as a son. The future "million dollar priest" had raised money easily from all sorts of people. Bankers, little old rich ladies, politicos and the average guy. Everybody loved seminarian Nick Remington. Nick had the touch. Money flowed to him like water from an open spigot. He was magic. Singlehandedly he had organized raffles and bingo and picnics.

At the dinner after his ordination, Nick Remington was secretly pulled by Cardinal Stamp from the room. He led him to the chancery garages and showed him a shiny new black Cadillac.

"You're to be my own assistant, Monsignor," Stamp told him. And with that sentence, in less than two hours after being ordained a priest, Nick Remington rose to the rank of monsignor.

His career rise continued at a meteoric pace.

In the next two years, he raised money for the diocese, paying its many debts, making other prelates in the United States who also carried red ink on their ledgers watch with envy.

Everything to which Nick turned his golden hands seemed to blossom into greenbacks. Municipal bonds doubled when the diocese's pension fund was instructed to buy them. Taxes were mysteriously lowered on Church investment properties. Bankers forgave old debts for the opportunities to seek advice from the genius-priest. Harvard University conferred an MBA in economics on the good monsignor, and he lectured there every fall quarter.

It was inevitable that Rome take notice of Nick Remington. Pope Pius XI, inheriting the money-raising scheme of Pope Pius X in the form of "Peter's Pence," called Nick to the Vatican.

With the infusion of ninety million dollars into the Vatican's treasury by Benito Mussolini, Pope Pius XI explained, people were wondering why the Holy Father needed any more. It did not help that the world's press had reported the ninety million received by the Vatican was reparation by the Italian government for seizing the Church's limitless properties. The dwindling size of "Peter's Pence" across the world showed that the faithful felt the Vatican had enough. And that simply was not true! The Holy Father wanted them to hear about his real needs. That money received from the Italian government was to be used for the future. It would be the bedrock of everything for centuries to come. But Peter's Pence covered the pope's everyday expenses, and it was imperative people understand and keep donating money.

Returning to the United States, Nick looked up his childhood buddy, Father Joey Stumpo. They had grown up as lads in Boston, went to the seminary together and had remained friends as priests of God. Finding him in his new assignment as assistant pastor of St. Anselm's parish in South Boston, Nick told him about his mission.

"I want you along, Joey," Nick said. "There'll be huge sums to handle and there's no one I trust more." Father Stumpo did not relish leaving his people at St. Anselm's. But he saw his friend was desperate.

"Me, a moneybags?" Joey had said. "I can hardly count!"

They crisscrossed the country, visiting Seattle, Los Angeles, Albuquerque, Tucson, Denver, Chicago, Detroit and Philadelphia. Nick took the podiums at Masses and spread the word of Pope Pius XI. Faithful across the nation became suddenly enthusiastic. "Peter's Pence" was an important cause again. And more than seven million dollars flowed into the Vatican coffers.

In Baltimore, Maryland, they were greeted with open arms by Cardinal Timothy J. Manley, an old friend of Cardinal Stamp's. At a special dinner thrown in Nick's honor, Cardinal Manley announced that the Holy Father had informed him by telegram this morning that Monsignor Remington was to become a bishop. The gathering of businessmen and nuns and priests applauded. Cardinal Manley smiled graciously and shook Nick's hand.

"Your work in the vineyard is being rewarded," he told him. "You're doing a much better job than I ever could have."

It was well known that "Peter's Pence" was once Manley's exclusive domain.

"You had your hands full in Baltimore, Eminence," Nick suggested. "No time to go on the road, right?" He wanted to move past this delicate subject. Manley had the reputation of being a hothead whenever he lost—at anything. And Nick's figures made Manley's attempts look pitiful.

"You've got it all!" Manley said, smiling bigger. "You're young, good-looking, smart . . . why, you could be pope someday!"

They both had laughed. But Nick felt uneasy.

Upon leaving Baltimore and arriving in New York City, Nick and Joey settled into a suite at the Drake. Nick was shaving, in preparation for a visit to the New York Diocese chancery behind Saint Patrick's Cathedral, when a heavy knock resounded on the door. He heard Joey answer it and then come into the bathroom.

"Trouble," he said.

"Who is it?"

"Apostolic Nuncio from Washington. Says he's got to do an audit on 'Peter's Pence.'"

"Now?!"

"He's got three accountants with him."

"Well, let 'em check our books. We got nothing to hide!" Nick was pulling on his monsignor's cassock. He had not yet been elevated to bishop, but it was to happen next week when he returned in triumph to Boston.

"I didn't want to tell you this, Nicky," Stumpo said. "But after Baltimore, we're short."

"Short?! That's impossible!"

"I don't know where it went. But there's eighty-four thousand, some odd dollars missing. I was just going over the books again, trying to find where it might have gone. And now these guys show up!"

"No sweat, Joey," Nick said. "They'll see everything's on the up and up. We'll just cooperate with them."

But sixteen hours later, no matter how hard they tried, Nick and Joey could not locate the money.

The next morning, several of New York's muckraking newspapers somehow got wind of the matter and carried front-page accusations that Nick Remington and Father Joey Stumpo were crooks. Cardinal Manley called in person and said he was sure it was only an accounting error and these damn newspapers would go to any length to sell copy on the street corners.

But other papers mysteriously picked it up across the country. In less than twenty-four hours, Rome contacted Nick and informed him the subject of his laicization was being discussed by the Holy Roman Curia. His accuser was Cardinal Timothy Manley.

The news astounded him. Archbishop Model, who ran New York in those days, arrived at the Drake Hotel. He told Nick and Joey that Pope Pius XI was very angry and was insisting that not only were they to be relieved of their positions on "Peter's Pence," but that there was no place in the Catholic Church for thieves. The amount of scandal they had caused could never be undone. The Curia, for its part, had recommended they be defrocked, their names stricken from the Church's records. Unless . . .

"We're listening, Excellency." Joey urged the churchman to tell the rest.

"Unless you go into a monastery and stay for the rest of your lives."

"You tell the Curia to sit on it!" Stumpo had said. "We're innocent and we won't be blackmailed into admitting anything else!"

"Monsignor Remington?" Model asked for Nick's reply.

"Tell the Holy Father, the dignity of the layperson has long been overlooked in the hierarchy of the Church," Nick muttered. "And I'd rather bust my butt on the streets, making an honest living, than hide in a monastery!"

So Rome laicized Father Joey Stumpo and future Bishop Nicholas Remington. A polite way of saying they had been kicked out of their priesthoods.

Untrained for the world, penniless, Nick and Joey turned for temporary help to all the friends they once had in the Church.

Cardinal Stamp, though he gave them five hundred dollars, could offer no further assistance. "You're political anathema," he told them. "Pope Pius XI has got it in for the both of you."

Their families didn't have enough to help them. And the businessmen and priests and nuns they once knew as friends shunned them like lepers.

Their first jobs were pumping gas and washing windshields at a small service station outside Boston. When that station folded, they hitchhiked their way toward New York, working as waiters, honey-wagon cleaners, stockyard attendants and even chimney sweeps.

Finally, when both of them had saved enough money, they attended night classes at the New York Craft Institute and learned to become welders.

Seemed fitting, Joey had said. Repairing, putting things back together. Uniting. Wasn't that what they had been doing as priests before?

"Te absolvo," Nick began, bending over the dying Joey Stumpo and hearing himself say the Latin words of the ritual.

5

THE *NORMANDIE,* BERTHED at the largest pier in New York, was shrouded in ice, sleet and smoke. In the glare of the floodlights, forty-three fireboats and trucks battled the flames, whipped to a hurricane by the high winds off the Hudson. In the freezing February weather, the crowd of onlookers stomped their feet and felt the heat on their faces and watched the famous *Normandie* lurch farther to her port and settle dangerously into the water. The gray wartime paint put on her sides blistered and ran. Seamen, dock workers and mechanics fled down the gangplank to shore. The power on the great ship failed and inside, through the miles of corridors, everything went black.

"Everybody off?" Captain Merser, a broad-faced Irishman in a yellow slicker, roared at his lieutenant as the last of the workers gave up hope and dashed to safety.

"She's clear!" the lieutenant said, coughing up a wad of ash-filled sputum. " 'Cept for those five below."

"Mother of God!" The captain crossed himself in dismay. "They'll never find their way out of that black inferno, not even if the Angel Gabriel took their hands!"

At the far end of Pier 88, a black Cadillac limousine pulled up and was promptly stopped by a New York

City policeman. "You can't go farther," he said to the driver. "Turn it around."

The back window whirred down and Archbishop Francis Spellman, Lord of New York and Vicar-General of the Armed Forces of the United States, thrust his round, moonlike face out. "Afternoon, Officer. Might I have a word with Captain Merser?"

The New York's Finest's mouth dropped open, and instead of answering, he tipped his hat and ran forward to the nearest fire engine. The archbishop settled anxiously back into the car and began to shut the window against the noxious fumes. Before the window closed, a striking young woman, her face blackened from smoke which accented her large, luminous green eyes, leaned her head in. "Archbishop," she said.

"Lieutenant Massaro," he responded, recognizing her from Commodore Hahn's office.

"I hear you got the okay, Excellency?"

"You know already?"

"Received word ten minutes ago from Commodore Hahn." She spun toward the burning ship. "Been here all morning trying to uncover evidence of sabotage."

The fire captain, a short bull of a man, approached. "Cappy," Spellman greeted his old acquaintance from oft-visited sites of tragedy where he offered spiritual assistance, "you know the whereabouts of a Nicholas Remington?"

"Trapped with others down below," Captain Merser reported. "Got the names from the dock foreman a minute ago."

"What level?!" Lieutenant Massaro demanded.

"And who might you be?" the captain demanded.

"It's okay," Spellman said quickly. "Tell her."

"He's on the seventh, we think."

"A man . . . vital to our plans . . ." Spellman added pointedly.

"I know every foot of the *Normandie*." The lieutenant understood what the archbishop meant immediately. "The whole seventh level is one long corridor, no light, no air, broken up by bulkheads and watertight compartments designed to prevent sinking."

The captain wiped at his stinging eyes and focused for a moment on the young woman. She was copper-haired, and her green eyes were bright and hard. But even in her khaki overalls, she was beautiful.

Suddenly an explosion ripped apart the third funnel on the ship's superstructure. Thrillseekers pulled back in terror. Two of the gangways tore off at the pier. The *Normandie* visibly yawed farther to her left. Turning, the captain shouted orders to cordon off the area with police lines. Spellman, mesmerized by the terrible force of the explosion, spun at the last moment to see Lieutenant Rafaella Massaro slip through the mayhem and run up the last remaining gangplank. Several firemen, including the chief, yelled at her but they did not pursue.

"Stop!" Spellman started to cry. But the sound died in his throat. Instead, he uttered a quick prayer.

Picking her way over the hawsers and cables that littered the iced decks, Rafaella made straight for the electrical maintenance conduit shaft at the bow. It was well away from the fire. She hoped no smoke had seeped into it.

She passed a fresh-air shaft and saw dark, oily smoke pouring from it. That was to be expected. She hurried directly behind it to where she knew the electrical shaft door was located. Squatting, she unscrewed the two-foot handle on the iron plate, beneath which all the ship's wiring was exposed. When the lid popped open, she was relieved. There was no smoke inside. Quickly removing her navy flashlight from her pocket, she peered down the length of its twelve stories to the bottom far below and saw only water, sloshing back and forth. Satisfied, she climbed inside and began the long descent down the narrow metal ladder.

Since the ship had tilted, descending the slanting ladder was difficult. She had to brace herself, moving one foot down at a time to keep her balance.

She climbed down past the third level, felt heat through the metal casing begin to surround her. The fire, as she had thought, was spreading upward. She kept going, the shaft growing hotter until the ladder scorched her fingers. The fifth-, sixth-, and seventh-floor levels became increasingly unbearable. She held her breath and squinted at the light from her torch, trying to forget the pain in her bare hands.

As she had hoped, the eighth level was slightly cooler. Chancing it, she hooked her elbow through the narrow metal ladder, being careful not to touch any of the thick wires along the wall, and took its screw wheel in both hands and turned. It would not budge. She cursed in Italian and attacked as she always did when she really wanted something. The wheel spun free. Its metal catch released sharply. But without warning the ship lurched farther to port and her feet swung dangerously off the ladder. In a movement to save herself, she kicked against the eighth-level door and, as it swung open, rolled inside.

Rising, she saw she was in a corridor that led to the newly installed army kitchens. In the smoky beam of her flashlight, brand new stainless steel counters and institutional dishwashing machines indicated she was near a mess hall. The thin, wispy smoke that hung in the air seemed to be thickening.

She began to run down the corridor, stopping only when she was out of the kitchens and into the officers' mess. Reconnoitering her position in relation to what she knew was above on the seventh level, Rafaella Massaro turned and went up an emergency set of steel-holed stairs. The heat began to build as she ascended higher. At the seventh level, she stopped at the waterproof door, designed to control flooding, and saw heavy smoke puffing out like heartbeats through the cracks.

Taking a deep breath, she whirled the wheel, kicked against it and rushed inward. A roar of flames shot above her, singeing her hair. Bringing up her forearm, she covered her face and yelled: "Remington!" She took a step forward and tried to see in the smoke. He was dead. Dammit! All this time wasted!

"Nick Remington? You horse's ass!" she screamed at the man she had never met and who now she knew had stupidly died on her!

"Here . . ." a voice said behind her.

She wheeled, hair smoking, eyes livid with anger, and spotted a huddled form on the floor. Quickly she bent to him, then noticed a corpse nearby. "Remington?" she asked, disappointed.

"Joey . . ." the man, fixed in the halo of her flashlight, said.

Breathing a sigh of relief, she helped him up and saw that he was tall. "You would have to be huge!" she mumbled. She laid him across her shoulders Red Cross style and carried him out the door.

For Nick Remington, half-asphyxiated, it was like a dream. Passing to and from consciousness, he wasn't sure if he was alive or dead. When he had seen the fiery-haired woman burst through the door, he thought he was witnessing a vision. An angel. Or perhaps a heavenly guide come to take him from this hell.

6

THE GREAT SHIP ROLLED over, her sides scraping against the concrete Pier 88 until she listed sixteen degrees to port. Two tugs valiantly tried to upright her. But it was useless. Thirty thousand spectators pushed forward to watch the *Normandie,* largest, fastest ship in the world, die. The groaning, chinking, snapping noises from inside sounded like screams of protest. The spray from the firefighters' hoses sent clouds of steam wafting into the freezing air over the Hudson, and the black smoke rolled low through the streets of midtown Manhattan.

Sitting among the workers who pushed carts stacked with crates toward different ships at the piers on the west side of the Hudson, Fritz Fleckenstein was the first to spot the smoke. He did not work on the docks, but most of his *Bund,* of which he was president, did. The authorities had never caught a single one of the one hundred and fifty of them in an act of sabotage. And in America, though you might be suspect, you were presumed innocent until proven guilty.

The fact the members loved Adolf Hitler meant they were watched. By the local cops. By the FBI. By the OSS. But nothing, not the slightest trace of unpatriotic behavior, had ever been proven. So here the *Bund* was, working side by side with good American citizens. Each with differing views on the war. No crime in America, the land of the free. You had a right to dissent.

Fritz, a short, heavy-shouldered man with a drooping handlebar moustache, had been speaking with his girlfriend, *Fraulein* Hoffman, when he had seen the smoke on the *Normandie*. Delighted, he pushed forward and took a ringside seat on one of the large wharf poles, making room for Hoffman. Some of the other *Bund* gathered around them. All were surprised. The *Normandie* was burning?

"Our lucky day," Fritz joked. He had no idea his expression would prove to be prophetic for his *Bund*.

7

HE EMERGED FROM the emergency room of the Polyclinic Hospital on Fifty-first and Ninth and entered the jostling rush of downtown traffic moving en masse to Queens, Brooklyn, Long Island or wherever else the civilian work force of New York retreated after the day. At the end of Fifty-first, he could see the sun just setting over the Hudson, magnified by the smoke from the *Normandie,* huge and blood red. At the corner he was lucky enough to catch a taxi. What with the shortages and gas rationing, there were fewer hacks running. Maybe the driver felt sorry for him in his cutoff overalls, his naked legs bandaged. Then again, maybe not. This was New York.

"Four sixty-four Tenth," he said as he got in.

"Near Greenwich, right?" The cabbie turned. "Looks like you had a hard day, bub. You in that boat thing?"

Nick laid his head back. He did not feel like small talk. As the cab swung into traffic, he gingerly raised his legs onto the back seat. The injections were wearing off. And despite only first-degree burns on his calves and assurance from the hospital that his lungs, packed with smoke and soot, would in a couple of days be as good as new, he felt terrible. Joey Stumpo was dead.

As they drove downtown, joining the rush hour

34

traffic on the new West Side Expressway, Pier 88, which lay between Forty-eighth and Forty-ninth streets, passed by. He turned and stared at the dying *Normandie,* on her side now in the mud of the Hudson. An ignominious end to the finest ship in the world. *Sic transit gloria mundi.* Like himself. Maybe like America.

For the first time, he realized it *was* really possible to lose the war. Seeing the ship, despite her size and strength, humiliated like that made him realize the United States was not omnipotent, but very, very vulnerable. Three things ran men, Machiavelli had said—greed, fear and ambition. Clearly fear had to motivate this country now.

As the taxi swept past the docks, he could make out ship after ship being loaded by cranes and readied to make up the next convoy. Ancient freighters, paint peeling, some near-derelicts. Stacked to the gunwales with guns, bombs, rations, fatigues, boots, tanks, jeeps, armored cars, parts for airplanes—everything it would take to win the war. And everything that was *not arriving* to WIN the war. Nearly three-fourths of these ships, if the average of the past months was continued, would be sabotaged in harbor or sunk less than one hundred miles off the coastline. For the first time, he felt this was his war too. But he was too old to join . . . thirty-nine. It made him furious to watch the unprotected ships flit by in the gathering dusk.

In the hospital, he had overheard nurses talking about saboteurs that had struck the *Normandie.* If only he could find out who had done this terrible thing and who, as a result, had killed Joey Stumpo! Then he would be doing something to help win this war! But he did not have the slightest idea how to proceed. Approach the navy? Offer *his* services? A neighborhood overage welder volunteers for heroic duty?

Suddenly the taxi was too tight. The walls were closing in on him. Claustrophobia was tearing at his stomach. He felt helpless and needed to get out. Needed to do something! He fought the panic, breathing in slowly, convincing himself he could take in air. He was not buried alive.

When he and Joey were eighth-graders, they had found a mysterious field to play in. His father had said it was owned by an out-of-state speculator who wanted to build apartments on it, but Boston wouldn't give him the right zoning. So it sat there and grew weeds in the summer and piles of snow in the winter.

That summer in 1917, just before school let out, Joey and he had started digging a hole. Just a hole in the ground to use up the excess energies of onsetting puberty. Then one of them had an idea to dig a tunnel at the hole's bottom. And pretty soon, they were carrying up dirt, piling it unseen among the high weeds.

It was their clubhouse. Other kids came, were initiated, and secret meetings were held by candlelight down in their humid cave. It was scary down there, nearly five feet beneath the surface. But that was part of it all. They told jokes and laughed, but there was always that fear everyone had of being below.

It rained that summer. Four inches in an hour. And on the last day of school, on the way home, Nick stopped at the secret cave. He had left some Tarzan comic books down there and didn't want them to get ruined so he lowered himself down into the now slimy hole to the bottom, got on his knees, then eased his head into the cave. He hadn't brought a candle, but in the faint light he saw there was a large puddle gathered already and their club things were floating. The last thing he remembered was that he was reaching for one of the comics when his body was suddenly crushed. Mud rushed into his throat, nose and eyes. His head hurt from the weight and he tried to bring up his hands to push it off. But he could not move his hands; only his legs worked, since they were exposed a few feet behind him. Paralyzed, he fought for a breath. But the plug of mud in his throat jammed up his windpipe. He struggled to swallow it but gagged and nearly vomited. In the suffocating darkness, Nick, unable to breathe, felt his lungs seared with an unbearable fire.

Joey was thinking only about getting home in the rain when he noticed at a glance down their path that somebody's books were lying beside the entrance hole to their secret cave. Curiosity made him turn and stop. Was someone down there now? He thought it might be that twerp Atkinson, whom they wouldn't let join the club.

Angrily he approached the vertical shaft. But as he peered down, he cried out. Only Nick's brown scuffed shoes were sticking out! The cave had collapsed!

People said later that Joey had gone crazy. He was not a big boy, but he leaped down into the hole and began to dig frantically, screaming at the top of his lungs for help. He stopped every once in a while to yank furiously on the shoes. He threw great, wet clumps of earth out of the shaft, clawing maniacally at Nick's legs, thighs, waist—ripping the skin from his own hands until they were bleeding, some of his fingernails torn clean off.

Joey superhumanly tore Nick from his grave. Then, lifting him out of the filthy hole filled with mud and water, he stuck his fingers in Nick's mouth and dug in vain at the mud. Joey squeezed Nick's chest hard. A wad of goo popped out of his mouth like a slimy cork.

Still yelling for help, which had brought people on the block running, Joey began giving him artificial respiration the way he had been taught in the Boy Scouts. Everyone who gathered around thought it was too late. Nick was limp and dead. But Joey never gave up.

Later in the hospital, when Joey came to see him,

THE SINS OF WAR

Nick told stories and laughed about a lot of things. Neither of them mentioned the cave. They were from New England stock. Emotions were weak—and dangerous. Stoicism got you through life better. So Nick never even thanked Joey for saving his life. Never mentioned it. Not a word.

8

It was nearly dark when the taxi pulled to the curb in front of 464 Tenth Street. The entire block was squeezed tight with ramshackle brownstones. Garbage littered the curbs, and there was the smell of something rotting in the air. Brown-skinned kids were smashing bottles against a fire hydrant on the corner.

As Remington wearily climbed out of the Nash cab, he noticed there was a black limousine parked down the street, the driver sitting patiently behind the wheel. The back seat was too dim to see who was sitting there.

Joey Stumpo needed a toast. He would have liked that.

Paying the driver, Nick limped up the steps, past the old woman who never spoke but sat there every night out on the stoop. It didn't matter that it was barely thirty degrees at the moment. If he asked her to go inside, she'd say she needed fresh air. Nodding to her as he always did, he went up the brownstone stairs to his room.

On the second floor, he paused at the door, fishing for his key. He was relieved at finding it. He had not been sure he'd even had any money for the cab. But there it was. The ambulance drivers and hospital personnel had been honest. All effects returned to his pockets.

The door behind him opened. "Rem," Judy said, "you look like hell!"

He turned, tried to smile, but his head was aching now and he really needed that drink.

"What in the name of Mike happened to you?!" She was holding onto the door, her blue cotton dress front unbuttoned to the soft white silk of her bra. And now he wanted her . . . could take her just inside her door! And she would love it. Bury his terror and frustration and disappointment in her.

She smiled, seeming to read his thoughts, and cupped her right breast momentarily. She ran her hand lewdly down her front and, closing on her crotch, made the dress strain and outline that place between her slender legs. But Christopher appeared and wrapped his tiny arms around her thigh. At the child's whining cry, exhaustion swept over Judy's face and she picked up the year-old boy. She suddenly seemed old, frustrated, as needy as he was. Not the fountain of youth in which to immerse himself at all.

"Come in, Rem?" It was pleading.

He found himself feeling sorrier for her than himself. Judy, a kid in her arms, the other probably asleep in its crib. Husbandless Judy. She'd always had eyes for him. Wasn't the first time she'd offered herself either.

"Not tonight," he muttered, which was only partly audible over the child's wailing now.

"Bastard!" she suddenly spat. "Just what the hell's the matter with you anyway? I'm not good enough for you, that it?! You're a fuckin' faggot! The manager thinks so too. You and that goddamn Joey Stumpo. Two queers livin' side by side!" And she slammed the door.

He stood there, momentarily unable to move. Tears

filled his eyes for the first time since Joey's death. It had taken Judy to free the grief he had bottled up.

Instead of entering his room, he went down to Joey's, and found it locked. With a sudden rush of anger, he kicked in the door. Immediately, he regretted it as he slumped down on Joey's bed, holding his aching leg.

After the pain had subsided, he flicked on Joey's desk light and saw the room, despite being threadbare, was immaculate. Joey had made his single bed that morning before going to work. Clothes hung pressed in his closet. The small desk and chair which completed the room's only furniture were polished, wood gleaming.

Only Joey's breviary lay on the bed. Then overwhelmed suddenly with a new rush of tears, he went into the bathroom and returned with Joey's "holiday vice," as he called it . . . a fifth of bourbon. In the two years he'd owned it, the level was down only an inch.

Upending it, Nick drank and picked up the breviary. The Lord giveth, the Lord taketh. He threw the breviary against the wall.

A shadow filled the doorway.

"No way to treat our holy book," Archbishop Spellman chided, picking up the breviary. "And do you always enter a room by kicking in a door?"

"So that's who owns the limo," Nick said, smearing the tears away.

"Got a glass for me, m'boy? I've been on me feet for a long while and I could use a wee pick-me-up." Spellman, with his overly friendly brogue, sat in the chair at Joey's desk. Nick noticed he was wearing just the black suit of a priest. He handed the prelate the bottle, half-expecting the notoriously tidy archbishop to refuse. Instead Spellman took a long pull.

"What are you doing sneaking around here?" Remington asked when the archbishop handed Joey's bottle back.

"Sneaking?"

"You look like a bum. You obviously haven't slept in days and you're not even in uniform. I don't remember you ever favoring common black."

"You used to cut quite a figure in purple yourself." Spellman grinned. "Manicured, barbered. Shoes shined so you could see yourself. I remember." He took another pull on the bottle.

Somehow the thing Remington had missed most when he was cast out of the ministry was not the limo, the vestments, the cuisine, the expense accounts. No, what had driven him crazy was his hands. Constantly blackened with grease, calloused and grimy, they were never clean. His fingernails broken and cracked. Bruised with a missent blow of a hammer. He raised his hands now in the meager light of the lamp and looked at them. "Priests should have soft, plump hands." He shrugged.

Spellman was studying him closely. "Some of us know what really happened that time," he said. "Too bad Pope Pius XI believed the Lord of Baltimore."

Remington took an insultingly long drink from the bottle, then belched. "Tell me one thing. Just why did Cardinal Manley, the most important churchman in America, pick on a lowly monsignor?"

Spellman shrugged. "He resented your position with Rome. It threatened him."

"Threatened?! That's a good one! He made up false charges against me, had me stripped of my office, forced me to make a living pumping gas because I *threatened* him?"

"He was human. Like us all. A mite overly ambitious. You of all people should have come to realize that, Rem, m'boy." Spellman cleared his throat. "You want back into the priesthood? I'm serious."

"I'm not a priest anymore!"

42

"Oh, maybe not on the surface, but once you learn to ride a bike . . . you never forget. And you may not be a member of the active ministry, but Pius can change all that. We do have a new pope, you know."

Remington shook his head. "I can forgive, but not forget."

"Good, good!" Spellman grinned enthusiastically. "An answer I myself would've given! God forgive me. We're rather alike, hey, Rem? We worked together here and in Rome, didn't we? We're both ambitious. And I got a feeling this passive life you're living doesn't suit you." He made a point of glancing about the room. "You know, you get on one of those new highways they're building around New York and watch the drivers. All the people who got old cars or new cheap ones drive like mad! To hell with the gas coupons and the fact it eats up precious wartime rubber! They whiz in and out of traffic, shoot ahead. I always get a feelin' people like that live in the suburbs, where life is safe and secure. They've opted out of the action, Rem. No risk. No confrontations. Nothing there to shake them up. So they drive like crazy to make themselves feel like they're going somewhere. Get that adrenalin goin'! But the ambitious guys, the ones who make things happen? The ones with the Rolls Royces and Cadillacs, you ever study them? They drive slow, Rem. 'Cause they don't need action on the road. They've got plenty of it. They're going somewhere!"

Nick looked up and noticed that old twinkle in Spellman's eyes, the one he got whenever he knew his sermon was working. To scotch him, he said: "I don't drive."

"My point, my point exactly!" Spellman shrugged it off, not missing a beat. Then he leaned forward and came in for the kill. "But, you wouldn't want to end up like your father, would you?"

It was a cruel remark, but calculated to gain the effect Spellman desired in an entirely different way. Edward G. Remington, III, one of Boston's Brahmin, one of the most influential bankers in Massachussetts, had acquired a sizeable following of investors who sought his opinion. He had issued astonishingly successful advice in a weekly newsletter on stocks.

Unfortunately Edward optimistically identified the high-flying stock market of 1929 as a continuing bull market. After the crash, he was ignored in his Harvard club, snubbed by other families and took to drink. One night he drove off the Boston Bay Bridge. Some say it was an accident, but most, including Nick, knew his father had not wanted to live.

And now, "Bishop" Nicholas Remington, once destined for great things, had fallen like his father. He was snubbed by his friends in the hierarchy, penniless, broken. And Spellman had intuitively guessed that Nick secretly feared he would end up like his father.

"Low blow." Nick stood up.

Spellman suddenly leaped up, his head barely to Nick's chest, and pinned his arms in a desperate grip. "This is your deliverance, man! You won't ever get another chance to save your soul! I've got a job for you. A dirty job. It isn't charity! You're going to have to work your tail off and earn back your title. But if you do, if you succeed at what none other than President Roosevelt and Pope Pius XII request of you, I promise to make you Bishop Nicholas Remington!"

"If I do your . . . dirty job, whatever it is, I want something else," Nick said after a long silence.

"Name it!"

"Joey Stumpo is lying unclaimed at the city morgue. He gets buried in hallowed ground, his head close to the church wall at Saint Pat's. Just like the best of

44

priests get. And on his stone, his full, restored title."

"Done!" Spellman promised. "Now, sit. I hate looking up at you. My neck's sore from the darn seat on the plane over from Rome."

And then he told him.

Nick listened carefully. It was uncanny. He would gain a ticket into the war. Become Excellency Nicholas Broderick Remington. And all the time he'd be working to find Joey Stumpo's killers. If ever there was an example of God reaching into his affairs, it seemed it was now.

"For this you should make cardinal!" Spellman took another drink as he finished outlining Nick's job in "Operation Underworld," the code name invented by the navy.

Suddenly the archbishop's casual comment made him wonder. What about the volatile mixture of Nazis, Mafia and navy? Could he handle it? Somehow, he told himself, no matter what lay ahead, he had to. There was no other way but up for Nick Remington.

At ten o'clock that night, Archbishop Francis X. Spellman received a call from President Roosevelt congratulating him that "Operation Underworld" was a go. "Spelly, it is entirely in your hands now," Roosevelt said. "You've made a great contribution to the war!"

When the president hung up, Spellman, despite his drooping eyelids, drafted a memo to His Holiness, Pope Pius XII, then made one last phone call to Commodore Dick Hahn, informing him that the meeting was on for 0800 tomorrow morning and that the navy would not be seeing or hearing from him ever again. Instead Spellman said the man handling the Church's end in this affair was a Father Nicholas

Remington. Hahn, eager to begin, wanted to know what if anything they were authorized to trade in the deal with the Mafia?

"You're on your own, Commodore," Spellman mumbled noncommittally and, hanging up, collapsed still clothed on white satin sheets, specially imported from a little shop facing the Vatican in Rome.

9

COMMODORE HAHN, NEVER a man known to waste time, particularly when a promotion was in sight, rousted Joe "Socks" Minestrone out of a midnight poker game in his office at the Fulton Fish Market and told him he needed the Mafia for "Operation Underworld." What was the price?

Minestrone did not seem surprised at that request and said he would find out and be at the meeting tomorrow at 0800, at 90 Church Street, the navy's headquarters.

When he hung up, Minestrone tipped Ruthie, who, among a number of other things, was keeping the drinks flowing, and excused himself from the game— much to the other players' disgust since he was ahead two thousand. He then got his bodyguard, Lou Asserello, to drive him across town.

At a little past 1:00 A.M., the doorman in the luxurious Majestic Apartments, a modern, tan-colored high-rise on Central Park West, admitted them through the locked glass doors, but only after Minestrone passed a C-note through the cracks. Frank himself answered the intercom buzz and said he would speak to Minestrone. In a moment, the downstairs phone rang.

"It's on," Minestrone said huskily. "They bought it."

"I see, Joe," Costello said. Unlike every other

member of the Luciano Family, Costello never called him "Socks." He hated Mafioso nicknames, thought they were stupid, dreamed up by men without educations. Which was why Don Francesco Castiglia of Lauropoli, Calabria, never was called anything but Frank Costello.

"Next step's tomorrow, Uncle Frank," Minestrone said familiarly and with affection. Everybody liked Costello. He was one of the genuine soft touches in the Family. Except, of course, when you crossed him as the late Vince Mangano had done when he wanted to reorganize all the Families in the nation under himself with the title *capo di tutti capi.*

Frank hung up without further comment. There was no offering of congratulations, no excitement. There never was. The congratulations for putting the deal together would arrive in an "envelope" for Minestrone.

Minestrone gave the doorman another C-note and went home. He had been generous because he knew Costello would hear about it and be ten times as generous with him. No charity involved. Just smart business.

10

At 2:17 that same morning, Fritz Fleckenstein, head of the German-American *Bund,* was awakened in his Brooklyn house from a dead sleep by a ringing phone. Lulu, his German-born wife, quickly got out of bed, walked around to the telephone where it sat on Fritz's side table and answered it. It was what any good German woman would have done for her husband. But as Lulu handed the receiver to him, she whispered: "It's a woman!"

Fritz wasn't too popular with most people, but women loved him. And he knew that his wife suspected he had lovers, which was true. So he said: "Who?! It must be the wrong number!"

When Fritz got mad, he got crazy. He had been called bizarre, revolting, anarchistic, a thief (he'd stolen hundreds of dollars from his own organization), a loudmouth, a crackpot, a wife-beater and a savage.

Police watched him, posting undercover cops at his meetings with the *Bund.* The F.B.I. had tried to link him to sabotage committed on the docks but, like the police, had never succeeded. It *was* hard to believe anyone as stupid as Fritz Fleckenstein, with his rantings and ravings against the United States and his overt loyalty to Hitler, was anything but a mental patient. But that was his best defense. No one could take his

49

threats seriously. That was exactly what Fritz counted on. By being so open, so public, such a marching protester and political mouth, he was dismissed as being a fool. His personality was the perfect cover. And Fritz had practiced the disguise so long, made it such a second nature, that he could act this way when he needed to—even when he was alone with his wife.

Angrily he swung out of bed, took the receiver which his wife had dutifully laid down on his convenience table. No one was supposed to call him at home.

"Hello, who is this? You realize what time it is?!" he shouted to impress his wife. But as he reached over to hang up, a voice said: "This concerns the *Bund!*"

Startled, he brought the receiver back to his ear. He heard the voice say that she knew who was responsible for the sabotage on the New York docks . . . and the ships sunk at sea.

"How did you get my number?! It's unlisted! Who are you, some fuckin' commie? A Jew?!" Fleckenstein began screaming.

But the voice went on, unperturbed. "To show you can trust me, I will give you important information."

"Why are you doing this?!" Fritz squealed.

"Who I am and why I am doing this is not important. What you must know is the navy is mounting a campaign against you called 'Operation Underworld.' The Mafia who control the docks will stop you."

By now, Fritz suspected the caller *was* sympathetic to his cause. "Are you German?" He lowered his voice to a whisper. "You don't sound like one."

"Neither do you. Ready to finish listening?"

Fritz acquiesced in an unusual silence. No one normally shut up Fleckenstein, the "American *Führer,*" that easily. But he was a believer now.

"The weak link in their whole scheme is a priest named Nicholas Remington. He will be at 90 Church Street tomorrow morning at eight o'clock. If he is out of the picture, their plan fails. Do I make myself clear?"

"Hey, you're not makin' a joke?" Fleckenstein softly inquired over the phone. But the caller hung up. Fritz made several quick calls, then dressing quickly, Fritz slipped on the same suit trousers he had worn the previous day at his job. He worked as a CPA at the downtown Manhattan firm of Joyce and O'Brien, which mostly tabulated NYSE market receipts. Fritz pulled shoes on sockless feet, grabbed a cardigan sweater and fled his small tract house, leaving behind a terrified wife who watched from the window and secretly hated him. But she knew no way of leaving him. This big American country terrified her even more.

Fritz drove his 1936 Chevy across the lighted Brooklyn Bridge, deserted in its stateliness, then downtown to Sixth Street, near the docks. He parked in back of the Dimely Soda Fountain and Grill. He knocked five times on the door, one for each letter in "Adolf," and was immediately admitted. Inside were the half-dozen coconspirators he had summoned after listening to the mysterious voice on the phone.

Fritz studied each of his compatriots as they sat gathered around the Formica soda fountain counter. Most of the *Bund* had come over to the States in 1934, before the rise of Hitler. Genuine immigrants. In fact, American officials thought they were escaping Hitler. When they had formed the *Bund,* these immigrants were deemed a bunch of misfits. Now, with the war creating priorities, demanding all energies be channeled to making guns and joining up, the *Bund* still attracted little attention. The loonies at home had dropped through the cracks. Well, what a surprise they'd get someday when they found out. Fritz smiled at his "crackpots."

"I don't know whether to trust that call or not," Fleckenstein said after he told them about the phone conversation. He took the proffered cup of coffee from the proprietress, Mrs. Kuhn, who was in her dressing gown. "But we can't take any chances. There are more than a hundred ships leaving New York Harbor in a convoy in three days and we have to wipe them out! It's the biggest shipment ever overseas! And we don't want any guinea Mafia ruining our plans!"

"Up 'til now," Brautenmeier, a beet-faced, dull man with a heavy German accent, protested, "we have been able to do as we please! We are winning the war! Why should it change now?"

There was a murmur of too-eager assent from the other lieutenants, all in various states of undress. For more than three months, they had operated almost totally *carte blanche*. Oh, they were careful. But there had never even been a close call. It had been strange how consistently it had all come together. Every operation a success. Mines in the harbor, ships wired for radio detection, contrived "accidents" in holds. Almost as if someone was behind it all, allowing it, guiding it, keeping the navy off their backs and out of the way. But when the question was brought up at a *Bund* meeting, Fritz had said it was all because God was on their side. The matter had been uneasily dropped. Yet it preyed on their minds.

"Nothing will change now!" Fleckenstein growled, getting to his feet. "We have been fat, *mein Offiziers*. We have come and gone as we pleased on the docks! It was to be expected as the war heated up the enemy would get tougher. Now they are attacking. Shall we turn and run?!" Dramatically he reached into the rumpled pocket of his trousers and extracted his wallet. Opening it, he took out a carefully folded telegram and reverently flattened it on the soda fountain counter. Every eye fixed on the paper.

"'Congratulations to the *Bund*,'" he read. "'You are all loyal sons of the Fatherland. My spirit is with you, signed Adolf Hitler.'" He folded it carefully again and put it back in his wallet.

"So the battle escalates!" Brautenmeier stood up suddenly. "*Heil,* Hitler!"

"*Heil,* Hitler!" the others shouted, rising to their feet. Even Mrs. Kuhn raised her arm in salute.

"A certain Nick Remington will try and destroy us tomorrow!" Fleckenstein screamed, expertly working their emotions to the climax. "And the Mafia—those criminals—think they can stop our Holy Cause!"

"This priest will not live past tomorrow!" Brautenmeier announced. "And we will certainly sink this next convoy! And if the Mafia comes at us again, we will be ready again!"

"But who made the call to you tonight, *Herr* Fleckenstein?" Mrs. Kuhn was thinking it all over.

"*Ja,* and who set fire to the *Normandie* today too?" another asked. "These are puzzles!"

"It *is* puzzling," Fritz allowed. "But someone did us a great favor by saving us the trouble of burning that troop ship! Perhaps it was an act of God." This brought smiles to the terrorists assembled there. "And perhaps the voice was that of a friend. But," Fleckenstein continued speaking solemnly, "we must be very, very careful. And so we will do our part for Germany, *Ja?!*"

"*Ja!*" the room erupted.

"This priest is a dead man! I swear it!" Brautenmeier roared as he brought his massive fist down hard on the counter, nearly cracking it in two.

11

NICK SLEPT LITTLE THAT night, dreaming repeatedly of a tiger chasing him, each time barely escaping it.

At dawn, he woke in a sweat, stripped off his leg bandages and, throwing on a bathrobe, went down the hall to the community shower and toilet. He walked lightly so as not to awaken Judy. He bathed his aching legs, leaving the skin bright red and itching. After he shaved, Nick hurried back to his cell-like room.

Naked, he opened his closet door and took down a carry-all he had not used for a long time. Unzipping it, he pulled out a folded black clerical jacket, trousers, white collar and rabat. When he was dressed, he stood in front of his sink mirror, filled with memories. The face was older. Harder and more seasoned. Gone was the baby fat and cherubic innocence. But it was the same face. His waist, smaller by two belt holes. He'd have to get the pants taken in.

He told himself everything was about the same. No big, big changes. And then he saw his hands and realized nothing at all was the same.

Pausing at the door, he remembered Judy. He cracked it open and peered out. The corridor was empty. What would she say if she saw him now?! He glanced at his wristwatch. Seven-thirty. Half-hour to make 90 Church Street. He didn't want to be late. Slipping through the door, he ran down the stairs and out to the street.

The old woman was already sitting facing the street, the expression on her face vacant, eyes rheumy.

12

THERE WAS, OF COURSE, nothing on the old brick building at the corner of Church Street to identify the fact that United States Naval Intelligence had taken residence inside. Church Street teemed with maritime insurance brokers, consignment companies and shipping firms. And so here at 90 Church Street, the navy dressed like businessmen, carried briefcases and tried generally to fit in.

When Nick was shown into Commodore Hahn's office on the second floor, which overlooked Church Street and piers 25 through 29 on the Hudson, he again found nothing military. Just typewriters, adding machines, ledgers and row upon row of maritime law books. The front door had said: "Hahn and Marsh, Attorneys." The cover was complete.

Nick sat in one of the plush leather chairs and sipped the coffee he had been served. As Hahn spoke, he sized up the two men before him. Hahn was mid-fifties, paunchy, gray hair clipped short military style, an analytical, yet stuffy air about him as he spoke of the "immense" sabotage occurring on the docks. Nick had a feeling Hahn desperately wanted "Operation Underworld" to be a success. As for Captain Marsh a spic-and-span administrative type, he had been the one to get the coffee when Hahn suggested it.

"At a meeting about two months ago"—Hahn was speaking in his stiff military cadence—"Naval Intelligence was presented with the idea of bringing in the Mafia. I had met a Mr. Joe "Socks" Minestrone. Nice man—hard to believe he's a mobster."

Marsh nodded at that. It made Nick wonder about the reality level among the boys from Annapolis. They obviously had never lived on the street.

"They just had to admit," the commodore continued, "that despite my bizarre notion, no force could more effectively patrol our vulnerable piers and ships than tough, alert longshoremen! Why, even waterfront prostitutes and their pimps could be a counterintelligence corps if properly organized! When we approached the Mafia, however, they turned us down. Didn't trust us to honor our end of a deal. That's when Joe "Socks" got the idea of the Church! You know, to act as a go-between."

Marsh's head bobbed back and forth in agreement.

"So now we're up to date. Your part is simple. You will make the deal with the Mob. After that, you can go back to your priestly duties. That clear, Father?"

"Commodore, what if I want to stick around? Help out a little here and there?" Nick was thinking about Joey Stumpo.

"Not possible," Hahn said. "This is a military operation, Father. Nothing spiritual here for you. No, we'll handle it. And we've got our work cut out for us! No time to waste. No offense meant, of course."

"The key to all this"—Captain Marsh spoke up for the first time—"will, we hope, be the Mafia. But we will be the ones who will stop the sabotage. Not those criminals. All we need to know is just what the heck is happening! Their job is simple surveillance!"

Nick was frowning. The Mafia was wily and ruthless. Yet the navy seemed to be completely trusting. Didn't they have any idea with whom they were dealing?

Marsh looked nervously at Hahn. Clearing his throat, he said: "Uh, Father, there's just one more thing. We'd like you to go to this meeting with someone who's been doing this on a day-to-day basis. Someone . . . experienced."

"Archbishop Spellman never mentioned anyone else," Nick objected.

"It's something *we* want." Marsh jumped up, clasping his hands in front of him. "Our top spy. Worked undercover on the docks. Knows what's happening."

Nick started to protest, but Hahn pressed a buzzer on his desk and immediately the door behind him shot open. To his utter surprise, Nick turned and found he was facing the copper-haired woman who had rescued him from the *Normandie.* She was wearing a white cotton uniform with a cocky white-and-black hat perched on her gathered-up hair.

"Lieutenant Rafaella Massaro," Hahn introduced her. "Our secret operative on the docks. I believe you two have met."

"We have," Rafaella said, shaking Nick's hand in a perfunctory way that said this was all business and let's get on with it.

He had rehearsed thanking her for saving his life and he was pleased he now had an opportunity. Before she had been a mysterious stranger, someone he could but hope to meet again. Now he stood before her. Still, her no-nonsense personality made him hesitate. Perhaps there was a better time for such talk.

"You're navy?" Nick tried to think of something to say, really seeing for the first time her lime-green eyes, which seemed to brim with anger, her high cheekbones, accentuated by dark red hair pulled up off her neck. She was even more beautiful than when he had first seen her.

"I'm in a branch of the service called SPARS, part of

the Coast Guard," Rafaella said with a trace of bitterness. "Women fighting this war are second-class citizens."

"Lieutenant Massaro is on loan from the Coast Guard, Father." The commodore praised her quickly. "Perfect for the job. Speaks Italian fluently, trained in the OSS commando school up in Washington, D.C. Lieutenant Massaro can be trusted in any situation, even that requiring the use of explosives. And as we've found out on the docks, no one suspects a woman!"

"Thanks for the speech, Commodore." Rafaella smiled evenly. "But if I weren't a woman, I wonder if you would have patronized me."

Hahn and Marsh both shuffled uneasily.

Rafaella swung her piercing green eyes to Nick. "You oughta know what you're getting into," she told him. "This is no picnic. It's a crazy plan. The navy working with the Mafia. Lambs with lions. We'll probably get eaten alive. Every pier is owned and operated by the Family. And they got more deals going than you got hairs on your head. They're always looking for angles, and the navy is straight arrow."

"And what is it the Mob wants, Lieutenant?"

"That's what we're going to find out this morning, isn't it, Father?"

Was her toughness just an act? What would she be like when she let her hair down? No woman could be that cool . . . that hard edged. Or could she? Nick had never met anyone even close to Lieutenant Rafaella Massaro. And he disliked that because he could not be indifferent toward her, as he usually could with women.

The blaring toots of a car horn brought him back, and he realized he had been staring into her green eyes. She returned his gaze, unblinking.

"I think," Hahn said, peering out his window to the street below, "that must be Mr. Minestrone."

"Just give me a minute to change," Rafaella said. "I want to go to this meeting in street clothes. I'll meet you below." She exited.

Nick turned to Hahn. "Commodore, what do I have the authority to offer the Mob for their cooperation?"

"Anything short of Fort Knox," Hahn said. "President Roosevelt himself has given this top priority."

13

BRAUTENMEIER SAT ACROSS Church Street on the bus bench with Stot watching navy headquarters. They had seen Remington walk toward the building on the opposite side of the street. Brautenmeier had planned to kill him, but the light had changed at the last moment. And he didn't want to cross against the red. That was against the law. So he had told Stot, who was only seventeen, to be patient and they had waited. The priest would emerge soon.

It had been no problem identifying this priest in his clerical uniform. That was all Fritz had warned them about. Wait, he had said, until you see he is a priest. No priest, get out! Get away! Something would be wrong. But there he had been. And Fritz had said if they saw him, shoot him close, in the head. Make sure. But then the light had turned. Fritz would probably have jaywalked! But Brautenmeier, considering what Adolf Hitler would have done, knew the Fuhrer would have obeyed the light. He was a law-abiding man.

And so Brautenmeier sat there on the bench, hands in the pockets of his long herringbone coat, hat pulled low, heart beating wildly, intently watching the front of 90 Church Street, where he had seen the priest enter. Stot, on his left, had not spoken a word. Good old silent, skinny Stot. They had worked together many times before, like glove and hand on the docks, Brautenmeier making the decisions, Stot, the glove, flexing with him.

He saw the light change to green, and then Stot poked him and he peered down to see a black Packard pull up in front of the address and stop. Suspiciously Brautenmeier got up and Stot followed. If that car was for the priest, they could not allow him to get away. Brautenmeier quickly crossed on the green with Stot.

Nick took the elevator, not wanting to strain his legs. He arrived at the bottom foyer and stood waiting for Lieutenant Massaro (as he'd decided to think of her) when a giant man with a face as wide as a porthole came up to him and said: "The car is outside."

"Who are you?" Nick asked.

"Willy Tigante. Minestrone says it's okay." The giant, voice thickly Italian accented, as big as a tackle and wrapped in a huge black overcoat, pulled his hat down over his monstrously bulging eyes.

Through the revolving doors of the building, Nick saw the black Packard parked at the curb. This was straight out of the movies.

"Okay, Mr. Tigante," Nick said. "I'm waiting for somebody. She'll just be a minute."

This seemed to throw the giant into total consternation. Now that something had happened which required a new thought, Tigante seemed paralyzed. His great mouth worked furiously, but he said nothing. Instead, he turned toward the doors. It was clear he did not know what to do. He spun back and said: "You're supposed to be alone!"

At that moment, Rafaella stepped from the elevator she had taken down. She wore a soft gray business suit, its sternness offset by a ruffled white blouse. Her transformation was startling. Red hair tumbling down to her shoulders, she walked toward him in black high heels.

He closed his eyes, swore softly to himself and turned to Tigante. "We're ready now."

Still the giant stood there. He looked at Rafaella and scratched his head. "A minute," he said. "You wait."

"There's the car," Rafaella said to him, "so what are we waiting for?" And before the giant could grab her, she brushed past and was already inside the revolving doors. Nick turned to go after her, but Tigante grabbed his shoulder.

"No, wait, you can't! Not until I check!" Tigante shouted. Several secretaries hurrying past, coffee cups in their hands, turned, noticing the commotion. "I give all-clear sign!"

Nick felt a sharp jolt in his stomach. Somehow, he felt sure, Rafaella was in danger. He tore out of the big man's grasp and raced toward the door.

When Stot, inching closer to the entrance, saw Rafaella emerge from the revolving door of 90 Church Street, it startled him. Nearby, Brautenmeier, seeing it was only a woman, relaxed his grip on the Luger inside his coat pocket and blew out his breath in disgust. But in almost that same instant, the priest appeared. Both men, taken off guard, quickly drew their pistols and raced forward to apply the absolutely certain bullet.

Nick, unaware of the men running toward him from the street corner, grabbed Rafaella and said: "Something's wrong. Get back inside!"

"What?!" she demanded, standing her ground and not allowing herself to be pulled anywhere.

And then Nick saw the two men in overcoats. The only thing he could think of doing was to push Rafaella down. He felt ridiculous as he watched the men pound

63

toward him, pistols aimed, coats flapping in the winter wind, eyes glued to where he lay atop the wriggling lieutenant. He was very aware of her body pinned beneath him, breasts, stomach, hard pudendum.

Rafaella was pushing against him, trying to get something out of her purse.

Suddenly both back doors on the Packard sprang open, and out leaped two Mafiosi, wearing Walt Disney Donald Duck masks. They brought up .45 caliber machine guns. Stot took the first blast in the knees, then the slugs worked their way up his chest, stopping his forward motion entirely and throwing him back against the brick building. Brautenmeier, ham-fisted and heavy, fell backwards on the sidewalk, skidded and landed several feet out in the crosswalk. Pedestrians ducked and ran. But it was all over in less than five seconds.

Satisfied, the two masked gunmen jumped back inside the Packard and it sped away. Nick realized the Packard had only been the scouting party.

Shakily he rose as Rafaella, gun now in hand, stood, aiming professionally at the corpses, anticipating any movement.

A gray Cadillac limousine suddenly pulled to the curb. The door opened. At that, Willy Tigante emerged through the revolving doors, looked quickly at the dead men. Then, taking both their arms, he forcefully guided Nick and Rafaella into the Cadillac. Slamming the door, Tigante got into the front by the driver. The limo sped off.

In the rear, Nick and Rafaella found themselves beside a short, chubby, expensively-coiffed Italian, about fifty years old. Every part of his body seemed polished and attended to. He did not say a word, but watched as the car expertly shot out into traffic, turned left first on Canal Street, then sped into the Holland Tunnel.

"Good thing we sent that decoy car in first," he said to Tigante, who nodded.

"What about the bodies?" Rafaella asked to Nick's amazement as they drove under the artificial lights of the tunnel beneath the Hudson.

"Navy's responsibility," the man said. "Those two were probably saboteurs. You can take credit for them. Ought to make your people happy since you've done nothing about it 'til now!"

Rafaella stiffened, a motion which the perceptive eyes of the little man did not miss. "I figured the navy would try and send somebody. But not a woman. And one so pretty. My hat's off to Uncle Sugar. He does have some class, I see."

"Are you Minestrone?" Nick asked.

"No," Rafaella answered for the man, that light in her green eyes glowing brightly as she stared unflinchingly. "This is Frank Costello, Prime Minister of the Underworld. Looks like we hit paydirt . . . or some kind of dirt anyway."

Costello bowed slightly. "And can you guess where you are going, pretty lady? I don't know your name, I'm sorry."

"Lieutenant Rafaella Massaro," she snapped. "And just suppose *you* tell us where we're going and stop playing these fucking games!"

The curse word turned him off. No well-born Italian woman swore. Only whores. Costello turned to Nick Remington on his right.

"I am a good Catholic, Father. I'll do anything for my church. I suppose you would too. But I did a little checking. You're no more a priest than I am."

Rafaella spun to Nick in surprise. But Nick ignored her reaction.

"But," Costello continued, "we all have our patriotic duty to perform for our country in time of war and the fact there are additional rewards is icing on the cake, right? Now 'Operation Underworld' can be a terrific success. You saw how we handled saboteurs back there. We can be very, very effective."

"Was that a little show on my account?" Nick asked pointedly.

"You mean did we set it up?" Costello smiled. "Very perceptive, *Mr.* Remington. But I have to tell you, we had nothing to do with it. In fact, it would have been senseless. What if you and your . . . lieutenant here had been killed? Very bad."

The car suddenly exited the long tunnel and they were in New Jersey. Heavy industrial smokestacks belched black soot. Steel plants. Foundries. America was going all out, trying to catch up.

The Hudson River was beside them and Nick caught sight of a freighter, heavily loaded, heading out to sea. As he looked, he saw that that vessel was steaming along at the head of a long line of other ships, all similarly loaded, riding in a single file toward the open sea.

"What gives?" Nick asked Rafaella.

"The convoy wasn't scheduled to depart until tomorrow," Rafaella remarked, seeing them too. "But at Commodore Hahn's request, Admiral Colditz changed the sailing to a day earlier. We hope our German friends will be caught offguard."

"Hahn is a fool," Costello said.

"It's a good plan!" Rafaella spat angrily.

"Sure," Costello shrugged. "No offense." He crossed his pampered hands on his chest.

14

WHEN FRITZ FLECKENSTEIN, parked up the street on Church, had watched Stot and Brautenmeier die on the sidewalk, his first impulse was to order his other two comrades to leap from the car with him and start shooting. But he had held himself in check. The time was not right. Besides, Stot and Brautenmeier had died heroes on the battlefield.

Johann the baker had been shaken. The other *Bund* member, Lorelei Hoffman, pushed up from the back seat. "Why aren't we following them, *Herr* Fleckenstein?! They are getting away!" The black Packard had sped from the curb and was nearly out of sight now.

"Do you still see the priest and the woman on the sidewalk?" Fritz spoke cunningly. "Have you ever hunted, *Fraulein* Hoffman?"

"*Nein,*" she said. Barely eighteen, she had only recently come over from Germany, her passage arranged by Nazi Intelligence. Her family had already immigrated a year before to the US and Lorelei in joining them had the perfect cover. Exuberant, dedicated, she had risen quickly to being a highly trusted saboteur. Fleckenstein had also found her spirited in bed. But Lorelei had a bad habit. Playfully she liked to kiss him and spit his semen in his mouth after he came. Surprised the hell out of him first time she did it. But he'd got even by holding it long enough to spit it back inside her cunt. Fritz Fleckenstein always got even. Still he wondered if it might make her pregnant.

"When you are hunting, the first thing you see are always the does and fawns. The buck sends them out to see if there is any danger. Only after none of them is attacked or shot does he appear. And look, *Fraulein!*" The gray Cadillac limousine magically appeared and a huge man hustled the priest and woman into the car.

In a moment, Fleckenstein started his Chevrolet and pulled out into traffic, following his prey.

He kept pace with the Cadillac, made the left turn on Canal Street, then headed toward the Holland Tunnel. The Cadillac already possessed the token necessary to enter but Fritz had to stop and buy one. That put them a little behind. But Fritz caught up easily. He knew the Mob did not suspect they were being followed now that Brautenmeier and Stot had been killed.

As they exited the tunnel, Johann remarked on the number of ships that were sailing down the Hudson.

Fleckenstein, whistling a little German tune he had learned as a boy, said, "All our little wires are broadcasting. Right, Lorelei?"

"Ja," the young woman said with a smile.

They followed the Cadillac past factories and steel plants, which changed to pasture filled with Guernsey milk cows and dairy barns. Finally, in the foothills, which were brown and spotted with firs, they saw the Cadillac turn off onto a dirt road. Fritz did not stop but passed the road, and they could see it led to a small farmhouse. In front of the two-story white farmhouse and hay barn there were several other cars parked.

Fleckenstein made a U-turn on the highway and parked just opposite the farmhouse road. This stretch seemed quiet. So they loaded their machine pistols and bazooka.

"I want to identify who is inside." Fleckenstein got out of the car. He inserted an eighteen-shot clip into his handgun. "Wait here. If I am not back when they come out, you know what to do."

"*Heil,* Hitler!" Hoffman saluted. She was holding the bazooka.

15

THE FARMHOUSE WAS for sale. Nick noticed the red-and-white sign when they alighted. The gray Cadillac had stopped near a light green government van with a prison decal on the door and another black Cadillac limo parked nearby.

Ushered in by two prison guards, both wearing yellow insignia patches of Great Meadows Penitentiary, Nick saw that the front room was unfurnished and that only a long folding table stood in the center, with half a dozen chairs. Five men were standing, waiting. Costello crossed the room immediately and kissed the hand of a short, swarthy man who stood in the corner. He was dressed in prison grays. The room was darkened, but Nick had seen photos of Lucky Luciano many times. Luciano smiled and whispered something in Costello's ear, his hands flashing expressively, while his jet black eyes studied Nick and Rafaella in total, cold concentration. The right eye, drooping from a beating administered by police when he was a child, stared balefully.

Costello turned and said: "Lucky, I want you to meet Father Nicholas Remington. He is the official representative of our Holy Mother Church."

To Nick's surprise, the gangster fell to one bended knee and, taking his hand, kissed it. "Tell me what you need, Father," Luciano said. "And you got it!" Then he rose with dignity in his baggy, mouse-gray prison uniform and smiled. But still the eyes did not.

"This is Lieutenant Rafaella Massaro," Costello presented her. "She will act as observer for the United States Navy."

"Massaro?" Luciano asked, frowning and taking her hand. "Well, well! Massaro."

Rafaella tugged her hand out of his, went to the corner Luciano had vacated and sat on a folding chair, an unreadable expression on her face. Nick felt something had happened between Rafaella and Luciano when he spoke the name "Massaro." Had the name somehow seemed familiar to the gangster?

"Abraham Moses Polakoff, Meyer Lansky," Costello finished the introductions. "Mr. Luciano's personal lawyer and Mr. Lansky, his business partner."

Nick felt Lansky's limp, three-finger handshake. The infamous Meyer Lansky. He was beginning to feel like Daniel Webster confronting the devil's own hand-picked jury.

Luciano now sat down at the table and lit a cigarette. Nick pulled up a chair and sat opposite him, while Polakoff, Costello and Lansky dragged chairs to a nearby wall and leaned back in them. Luciano took a deep drag, turned to the man standing at the door. "Thanks, Warden. We don't need you." The warden, a sixtyish, balding man, bowed as he went out, closing the door.

"My old warden from Dannemora," Luciano explained. "Came down to make sure I'm comfortable at my new home."

"You moved to Great Meadows?" Nick remembered the arm patches on the guards.

"Closer to our operation." Luciano tapped a Lucky Strike Green in the ashtray on the table. "Navy got it for me. Didn't they tell you?"

"I'm not in their Intelligence," Nick said. "I only came here to act as a bridge."

"Sure, sure, Father." Luciano grinned. "So let's talk. I think we can do business. You don't seem like those navy guys who got a stick up their asses." He watched for Nick's reaction. But Remington's expression remained unchanged. Rafaella, however, shifted in the corner.

Costello cleared his throat. Nick saw he was eyeing the far corner of the room. He turned and noticed an extraordinarily beautiful woman in a tight, low-cut green dress with a perfect body standing in the open doorway of another room. To his dismay, Nick saw that her face was not pretty. To camouflage its crassness, her makeup was thick, lips shiny with bright red lipstick, cheeks heavily rouged, eyes with too much mascara. It was as though the body of a movie star had stopped at the neck.

"Ruthie already knows from Joe 'Socks,' " Luciano said to Costello. "She don't know nothin', right, Ruthie? Look at her in that dress, Frank! Ain't that better than those damn men's suits she always wore when she came to see me?" He laughed and blew Ruthie a kiss. "What can it hurt, Frankie? The fix is in, right?"

The hairs on Nick's neck stood up. It was a funny thing to say. What fix?! Maybe that was just Mafia talk for the "deal." But it was the same tingle he had got from Costello when he seemed to know more about the ships sailing down the Hudson to the sea. He shot a quick glance at Lieutenant Massaro, but her face was impassive.

"I'll make this quick and simple, Father," Luciano said. "I know I got all the cards and I intend to play 'em. Your navy boys—no offense, Lieutenant—can't cut the mustard on the docks. And the Feebs can do no better. 'Cause that mackerel Hoover's got no power there! Why? 'Cause I control the docks. And you got big trouble down there, know what I mean? Now I'm as patriotic as the next guy, but you can see I'm not livin' in the manner I'm accustomed. So for helpin' you stop the sabotage, I want ten million bucks and I get set free." Luciano lit another cigarette to show he was finished.

"You can forget about the ten million," Nick said, pushing his chair back and crossing his legs, an act meant to show that *he* was dealing and not Luciano. "I could probably get the U.S. to authorize it, but I won't. Ten million is a lot of arms and food for our boys who write home to mom and dad. So let's forget about that one. I mean, after all, I know you don't really need that money . . . and we are all patriotic, right?"

Luciano's mouth curled into a smirk. It was common knowledge the Sicilian had never bothered to become an American citizen.

"I could walk outta here right now," Luciano threatened so softly Nick's impulse was to lean forward to hear. But he kept stretched back, looking arrogant, his right toe bobbing comfortably as if he were enjoying a morning's kibbitzing at the park. Out of the corner of his eye, however, he noticed Rafaella stiffen and sit up.

"Go ahead. Walk." Nick shrugged. "But it wouldn't be smart for Charlie Lucky. And more than lucky, you have always been smart, right, Don Salvatore Lucania? Your freedom is worth more than ten million and we both know it."

Luciano studied this big man he was facing, his right eye squinting through its hooded gaze. "You're bluffin'."

Nick attacked again suddenly. But his voice droned on as if he were now bored with all this. "You will only be set free *after* the work on the docks is totally completed."

"That could take years!"

"Up to you."

"Yeah—and the navy! I gotta pin my hopes of freedom on those creeps?! No way!"

"Very well," Nick said, rising. "I'll tell my superiors I tried, but could not cut the deal."

Luciano cursed. But Nick saw the gangster was smiling. "I'll never know if you were bluffin' or what. Sit, sit. You're right, what's ten million? I got a hundred times that stashed away!"

Nick made a show of reluctantly lowering himself to his chair once again. But he said nothing, only waited.

"How you gonna guarantee the fact that Lucky gets out of prison?" Meyer Lansky suddenly asked. "I mean, Governor Dewey puts him away for fifty years, he hates Lucky's guts! There's no way he's gonna agree to let him go after he worked so hard at convicting him!"

"Yeah, Father," Luciano said. "That *infamia* framed me. Bribed my own whores to say those lies 'bout me! He'd do anything to keep me inside!"

"President Roosevelt wants 'Operation Underworld,'" Nick said evenly. "Dewey might not like it. But the security of the United States is more important than his political future. And the Catholic Church will guarantee what we agree on today. I imagine that's why you wanted to have the Church involved in the first place."

"Take the deal, Lucky!" Costello pleaded suddenly. "Only you and our Holy Church can save America!"

Luciano nodded solemnly as though he were deeply touched. He reached across the table and shook Nick's hand. "We're gonna do business, Father! And everybody's gonna be happy. You mark Lucky Luciano's words. Those fuckin' Nazis!"

Luciano got up, jubilant. "Abe, you heard everything, right? I mean, you're a witness. We got a deal?"

"It's legal, Mr. Luciano," Polakoff said, opening his briefcase. "I'll just make a few notes."

The small back window shattered, and before anyone could react a grenade rolled inside. It stopped directly beneath the folding table.

Lansky ran for the front door. Costello merely stood there as if the grenade was an intrusion on his privacy. Only Luciano, reflexes like a panther, leaped for it. But it skittered across the hardwood floor and landed beside Nick. He seized it and in one motion flung the grenade through the large front window, shattering the glass. It bounced against an oak tree outside, ricocheted off it and exploded.

16

Fritz Fleckenstein had gone crazy. He had identified all those inside through a small side window, then listened carefully to Luciano's deal making. But when the gangster referred to the *Bund* as "fuckin' Nazis," Fritz pulled the pin on a fragmentary grenade and hurled it through the window. Then he ran to the front of the house to ambush any survivors who tried to exit.

As Fritz came around the corner, he was surprised to see his grenade bounce out among the trees. He fell to the ground just as two uniformed prison guards took the blast and fell dead on the gravel front driveway.

The driver of the black Cadillac, who had been lounging against a fender when the grenade exploded, ducked down defensively. Fritz circled the front bumper and shot him in the back.

Almost immediately, both doors on the gray Cadillac sprang open and Fritz saw the driver withdraw a .38 and run toward the house. He was followed by a brute who held a gun that seemed toy-sized in his hand. Fritz shot the driver once in the side as he passed, then swung his nine-millimeter machine pistol onto the big one and pulled the trigger three times. The driver had gone down. But the behemoth didn't seem to feel a thing! He just stopped and looked around, trying to figure out where the slugs had come from. Then, spotting Fleckenstein crouched beside the black Cadillac, he flicked off two shots. The slugs hit the car.

Fritz dove, counted one thousand, two thousand as he had been trained in 1936 at the Weimar Camp in Bavaria, rolled out onto the frozen ground, came up off his right shoulder and shot the giant, who was now running at him. This time the effect was apparent. The left side of the big man's head ripped open. The mammoth stumbled, though there was nothing to trip on, and crashed into the side of the Cadillac's front door.

Checking his ammo, Fritz saw he had nine shots left. Time to change position. He'd been taught that too in the terrorist camp of Brownshirts at the Weimar. Shoot, move. Hit and run.

Fritz ran past the gray Cadillac, down the road a few feet and threw himself into the drainage ditch. To his satisfaction, he saw Hoffman and Johann now sprint from his Chevy on the highway and take up positions too. Fuck this Luciano and the Catholic Church. And fuck the navy and any other enemy who tried to cross his *Abwehr!* Who did they think they were dealing with? Amateurs?! The Mob was no match for his well-trained saboteurs! Every one of his men had spent time training in attack camps, taught in detail how to fight like terrorists.

Suddenly the front door to the farmhouse burst open and as Fritz tensed expectantly, Luciano and the warden scrambled toward the green van. He fired twice but missed because of trees. Then Costello, Lansky and the gaudily dressed woman he had seen before ran to the black Cadillac. Fritz checked down the road. His people were ready. He'd get clean shots as they passed. And then Johann and Lorelei would finish them! In a moment, the priest and the navy woman jumped into the gray Cadillac.

But as Fritz turned back to the farmhouse, he saw to his surprise that the cars were heading in the opposite direction, entering fields of short wheat stubble. They were trying to make the highway and avoid his trap.

Quickly he sprinted toward his own parked Chevy. Johann and Lorelei saw the escaping autos and ran toward the car.

The van, with Luciano driving, bumped across the harvested field, raced through a corner of still-standing corn stalks, then smashed apart a three-strand barbed wire fence.

"You're not planning to escape, are you, Lucky?" The warden clutched white-knuckled to the dashboard.

The van careened onto the highway, overshooting the far lane. Lucky swung the wheel, and the vehicle fishtailed expertly back onto the asphalt. In the rear-view mirror Lucky could see Lansky behind him, emerging from the field in a cloud of dust.

"Warden," Lucky said, lighting up with his free hand, "why the hell would I run when I'm gonna get outta this legal?!" He floored the van toward Great Meadows Penitentiary.

17

NICK AND RAFAELLA had been given third position in the break from the farmhouse. Now as he bumped across the field and saw the Chevy closing diagonally in from the highway, he knew why Luciano had wanted it that way. They were the most expendable. The deal had been cut. Polakoff was a witness. Nick and Rafaella's usefulness was finished.

Two slugs suddenly shattered the Cadillac limo's left rear window. Nick swung the big car hard to the right in the field, nearly turning it over. The heavy machine sloughed through the dirt, sideways. He gunned it and aimed its nose at a point in the barbed wire fence that would put them behind the closing Chevy.

They roared up on the highway and came in less than twenty feet behind the Chevy's bumper. As the Chevy overshot them, Nick turned in the opposite direction up the highway. The two cars had passed so close that Nick could see a woman in the back seat raise a bazooka. Fritz and the other man in the front both had turned and fired.

Rafaella had her feet braced against the glove compartment, wedging herself tightly into her seat. "They're turning to follow us!" she said, whipping around to the rear window.

Nick pressed the accelerator further to the floor. The

speedometer read ninety miles an hour. He spun and saw the Chevy was gaining. What kind of madman was after them?! As he saw the needle shoot over one hundred, Nick began to feel clammy.

The Chevy roared up on their rear end, then whipped wildly into the next lane. They were each doing a hundred and ten, the fence posts whipping past.

"Can't you drive steady?" Rafaella screamed. Nick looked over to see her aim a navy-issue .45 at the car beside them!

"Who is it? Nazis?" Nick tried to concentrate on the road flying up at him.

"I know who the bastard is," Rafaella muttered as she knelt backwards on the seat, gun braced. "Stop weaving! I can't get a clean shot."

"If I let them come up, they'll shoot *us.*" Nick sped ahead in the big limo again.

In the Chevy Johann was pointing a pistol with a stock mount at them as Fritz attempted to match the Cadillac's speed. Nick's side window suddenly shattered. Instinctively he ducked. The Cadillac edged off the highway and struck the soft shoulder.

The Chevy dropped back to keep from getting tangled up in the wreckage. But Nick did not touch the brakes. He fought the long limo inch by inch off the soft dirt shoulder. With the big car fishtailing and bouncing, he managed to get two wheels on the highway. Then he made a quick, deliberate correction to the left. The Cadillac responded, regaining the macadam. Nick floored it.

"Nice," Rafaella complimented, sighting at arms' length on the .45. "Where'd you learn that?!"

"Driver's Ed—when I was sixteen. It was theory until now," he remarked drily.

When the Chevy nosed up again, Rafaella shot through the side window, hitting the young man. The impact drove him against the driver.

Immediately Fritz hit his brakes. Looking angrier than ever, he threw the corpse off him, raised his own pistol and fired. The shots struck the Cadillac's hood, piercing the radiator. A sudden gush of steam shot up, blinding Nick. He swerved wildly, trying to see through the hot vapor as it poured across the windshield.

"Jump!" he screamed at Rafaella. She turned, saw the steam and the blanked-out windshield. Stubbornly she whipped back, sighted on the Chevy again. But Nick leaned over, jerked open Rafaella's door. As Rafaella fired, the last thing she saw before being pushed from the speeding car was the woman in the back seat aiming the bazooka.

In a terrible roar, the Cadillac fireballed. Its body separated from frame and tires, hurtling high into the air. The doors blew out and one of them struck the Chevrolet's front tire. The tire disintegrated and sent the car into the left-side ditch.

The Cadillac's frame, rolling on flaming tires, continued down the highway and struck the cab of an oncoming semi diesel loaded with chickens. It did little damage to the big rig, but the blow sent the grisly remains of the limo careening off the highway, through a newly erected cyclone fence, down into an orchard of Delicious apple trees, missing every one of them as it eerily picked its way down a narrow lane, only to plunge over the bank of an irrigation pond and sizzle out in the water.

Fritz Fleckenstein, shaken but unhurt save for bruises and a cut over his eye, had seen the course the Cadillac had taken. Now, climbing out of his wrecked Chevy, he walked up from the ditch. Taking several steps down the highway, he peered along the opposite side of the road to make sure the priest and the woman had not escaped. There was no sign of them. He walked back a couple hundred feet and was pleased to find a cliff edge by the highway that fell far below to the

Hudson River. It was well over two hundred feet to the water. In the distance he could see the sprawling, white Great Meadows Penitentiary, new home of Lucky Luciano.

"For you, you fuckin' immoral guinea," he spat. "You'll regret the day you challenged Germany!"

He turned then and ran back to his Chevy and found Lorelei, stunned but unhurt, wandering around, trying to get her bearings. The car was finished. He'd leave it. Didn't matter who found it since it was registered under an alias anyway. The *Bund* would buy him another. War costs. Quickly he grabbed the girl, picked up the bazooka, and pulled her toward the stopped semi.

"Hey, buddy," the truck driver, a tattooed hillbilly, drawled solicitously as he crawled down from the semi. "Just what the hell happened! I saw a copper back up the road—maybe I oughta go get him."

Fritz, ignoring him, opened the passenger side of the semi and helped Lorelei up into the cab. He noticed with tenderness the tear in her left silk stocking and had the sudden impulse to kiss the hurt place. He would have to buy her a new pair and put them on her himself.

"What in the name of God you think you're doin'?" the truck driver swore in amazement as he now watched Fleckenstein walking quickly to the driver's side and getting into the cab also.

Fleckenstein slammed the door. When he started the rig, the motor rattled loudly. The chickens were squawking behind him so he really didn't hear the truck driver until he mounted the running board and stuck his head up at the window. Not bothering to roll it down, Fritz shot him. Then he ground the gears and started off. The diesel would do until he spotted a car to steal further down the road.

18

It was like a dream. Joey Stumpo and he were seminarians and they were swimming in the big, Olympic-size pool that stood up on top of the hill, guarded by a sign that said: "Keep Out, Seminarians Only!" The sign was supposed to protect them from the Mexican gardener's daughters, those plump *muchachas* who liked to giggle about who was the handsomest seminarian. Jerry Kleig had run off with one of them and Nick had heard they had had no less than nine children, all happy Catholics. But suddenly the warm seminary pool was cold! He fought to open his eyes!

The water was cold and dark green. Nick realized he had opened his eyes. In a panic, he swam upward—up toward the light—and then he struck something hard. Fighting to surface, he saw it was a tree that had snagged him.

He pulled himself up onto the half-submerged tree that was wedged against the river bank. Now he knew where he was—remembered the long fall. Though the river was wide, the current was strong here. Clutching desperately for holds, he managed to knee-walk the tree's trunk to shore.

Collapsing facedown on the steep bank, Nick began to cough. In a great gasp, he bent his face close to the mud and puked out river water and bile. Had he nearly died once again? Weakened, he struggled up. Rafaella. Gazing out onto the swiftly flowing green river, he saw no sign of her. Downstream, along the wintry banks, elms, sycamores and oaks spread their naked, bare branches high into the sky. She was gone without a trace.

Standing unsteadily, he saw his breath was showing steam. He was shivering. He had to find shelter, warmth. Nick began to clamber up the steep, soft earth bank, slipping on its slimy wetness, his shoes, already soggy, now gathering mud in size-fifteen clumps. At the top of the bank, he came upon a small country road. Checking the dim, wintry sun above, he turned south, toward New York.

Less than a hundred yards away, he saw a figure sitting wearily beneath a tree, trembling, head bent over knees. Despite her haggard appearance, Rafaella had made it. His first impulse was to run forward and embrace her. But he stifled that, walked up, knelt beside her.

She looked up, showing neither surprise nor pleasure at his survival. "You knew the river was there when you pushed me out?"

He started to tell the truth, but something, some male instinct, forbade it. She looked so vulnerable. What she needed now was strength. "I know every mile of the Hudson around here. My old seminary's down near West Point."

Rafaella, hair plastered across her forehead, eyes streaked with lines of mascara, grinned at him. It was the first time he had seen her smile, and it made her face light up. "Bullshit," she said. "But thanks anyway."

Insanely he blushed.

She stood, rearranged her soggy wool clothing,

wrung out her skirt, then threw back her shoulders, all business. The smile was gone.

"Gotta get back to New York," she announced. "You really know these parts?"

"Used to hike all over here."

"Any idea where a phone is? I'm frozen."

"Down the road. Three towns to choose from along the river."

"Good, I'll call headquarters," she decided and began walking. "They'll send a car."

"That's not what I had in mind." She paused and turned to see him stopped in the middle of the two-lane road.

"What exactly did you have in mind, Father?"

"Nick will do."

"Okay . . . Nick." She tried it distastefully. "Now what did you have in mind?"

"I'm taking a train home."

"A train?!"

"A freight train," he said. "They slow down for the towns ahead. Quite a few of them move through here."

"I was sent along to protect you . . . Nick." Rafaella faced him. "My job is to see you get safely back, okay?"

"And after that?" He tried not to focus on her emerald-green eyes.

"After that," she said, "our business is finished."

"Yours, maybe." And he started walking down the road.

She caught up to him. "What are you talking about, Father?"

"Nick."

"Okay. Nick! What are you doing?!"

"Maybe we can get some dry clothes up ahead. I'm cold, aren't you?"

"Why are you doing this?!" She hiked up her skirt so

her legs could move faster to keep up with him. "You're going to take a freight train when we can perfectly well ride back to headquarters in a comfortable car?!"

"Correct," he said. "Because I'm dead."

The little towns of Highland, Milton and Marlboro lay along the banks of the Hudson. Bypassing Highland, Nick chose Milton because the tracks skirted that town. The train would slow down and there would be less chance of someone seeing him hop it.

Rafaella, bewildered, unable to get anything more from him, entered the Milton Hardware Store and bought jeans, blue chambray work shirts and denim jackets, staring down the proprietor and his questions about her damp appearance until he gave up, punched the ancient Bally register and accepted the soggy bills in payment.

Outside, Nick stood shivering in the trees behind the store. He had already stripped off his Roman collar and black clerical coat. It would not do to scandalize any innocents with his appearance. Besides, he did not need the ministrations of some Good Samaritan at the moment.

When Rafaella appeared, he accepted his bundle, wrapped in brown butchers' paper. She led him deeper into the trees, close again to the river. She said it was a good spot and tore off the string to her package.

"But where'll we change?" he asked. He did not see this being a really good spot in this open place, populated by tall, thin trees. Anyone down at the river could look up and see them.

"Just turn your back," Rafaella said, already stripping off her woolen jacket and skirt.

Nick averted his eyes, hesitantly pulled off his black trousers, removed his wet underwear and tugged on the jeans, replacing his black clerical silk socks with good, dry cotton ones. When he was tucking in his cotton shirt, he gave in and chanced a peek over his shoulder. Rafaella was just buttoning her blue jeans. Her slim, naked back, undried, glistened in the shadowy sunlight beneath the trees. Long and willowy, she stood, spine twisting sensuously as she climbed into the shirt. He felt a movement in his bowels, a tightening he had never felt before. Realizing it was pure lust, he forced himself to turn away. But the beautiful image of her, the shock of realizing that Rafaella wore no bra, would haunt him long after today.

Clumsily he tightened his belt, pulling on the denim jacket she had bought for him. In a moment, she moved in front of him, throwing long arms through the armholes of her own jacket.

"Ready?"

"Sure," he said, avoiding her eyes.

"What's the matter? You feeling the after effects of that fall? Got a concussion?"

"I'm fine . . . it's just . . ." He tried to think. "I owe you for these clothes and I don't have the money."

"Compliments of the navy," she said, kicking leaves over her wet clothing. "Now let's go catch your damn train!" But as she walked away, he could not forget the sight of her. He caught up to her and tried not to be mesmerized by the movements of her tight little rear in those jeans as she led the way back to town.

19

THEY WAITED NEARLY two hours on the outskirts of Milton, having just missed a freight that was lumbering beyond them when they had first gained the tracks. It was dusk when Nick chose a flatcar on an approaching slow train and levered easily up so he was sitting on the side staring down at her as she ran. He held out his hand, but she ignored it. He allowed himself to gaze at her wonderful, burnished hair, whipping wildly in the ponytail she had tied, high, pert breasts bouncing freely. She took a headlong dive at the car, caught hold. But her strength failed. It took him a moment to realize she was in trouble. Reaching down, he grabbed her belt and pulled her up. As they came together, he held her, not wanting to move, his senses now recalling that intimate moment pressed together on the side-walk, the two gunmen running at them in their flapping overcoats.

"Thanks," she murmured over the clicking wheels. The wind was rippling his thick black hair and the clothes had changed him. She moved a little way off. As they passed a junkyard, some kids threw rocks at them and they had to duck.

"Couple hours ago we were ducking bullets!" He began to laugh. It surprised her. Somehow she had never pictured him ever laughing.

THE SINS OF WAR

The train was picking up speed now, the wind chilly as it raced over them. He buttoned up his jacket.

She stood, motioning to the sheltered bulkhead at the front part of the car. Wobbling to it, she sat out of the wind, legs drawn up, huddled in her jacket.

He scooted in beside her. Again she drew away, even though they were not close enough to touch.

"I never thanked you for saving my life," he said.

"We're even." She shrugged and pulled her legs in tighter. In the twilight, he saw her hands strain against one another.

"Why did that gangster Costello say you weren't a priest?" she asked after the train had click-clacked along for a couple of miles.

"I'm defrocked."

"So you're really not a priest?"

"Technically. But in real life, I'm a welder." He smiled at his joke.

"What happened?" She seemed very intent, her voice sympathetic.

Turning, he saw the hardness in her face was gone, replaced by soft sincerity. And to his surprise, he found himself telling her about his travels across the country, speaking in a hundred pulpits to raise money for the beleaguered Holy Father in the Vatican. How, finally, he had pulled in more than seven million dollars and was about to be named bishop, but a cardinal framed him. When he finished, she sat there, seeming to mull it all over. It was dark now and he could not see her face.

"I have had my share of bad luck with the Church," she said after a long pause. "In Sicily, I was Catholic like all the rest there. My father and both my brothers were killed because of vendettas in my little village of Mazzarino." She picked up a scrap of lumber, broken off from a loading crate, and hurled it violently into the black night flying past them.

"In our town of Mazzarino, there was a monastery of

Capuchin-Franciscan friars, corrupted by the Mafia. The priests used the sacred confessional to hear sins of penitents, then reported what they had heard to the Dons. Anyone accused by the priests of speaking against the Mafia was killed. It was common practice. The monks would also blackmail villagers and extort money and goods. Bands of them roamed the country-side, robbing travelers and peasants.

"The Franciscans' monastery became the scene of orgies and pornography. Women were brought to the monastery at night, dressed in Franciscan habits to disguise their identities." She broke off, shrugged in a fatalistic Mediterranean way he had not seen before. "I shouldn't have told anyone about my money. Not even my girlfriend Maria. One night, three monks came into my bedroom. I was taken from our house to their monastery. There, I was fucked by all of them. Finally in the morning, I broke down and told them where I had hid the money. It was what they wanted. They were bored with such a young, skinny girl when they had their pick of ripe village women. When they got the money, they let me go. My father was furious when he learned what had happened. I did not tell him. One of my brothers heard it as a joke in the *taverna*. Together, my father and brothers decided to journey to Rome and expose what was happening in Mazzarino to the Holy Father. My father somehow managed to be admitted into the Vatican during a general audience. Then, he whispered it to Pope Pius XII himself! Sadly, the pope only replied, 'I find your story incredible!'

"So my father, Angelo, and my two brothers, Canna-da and Fredo, went back to Mazzarino. Four days after they returned, a band of masked men dragged the three of them out into our little vineyard and shot them."

Nick did not know what to say. The bad monks were only an aberration, he could tell her that. But what thing spoken from his mind could touch such a hurt in her body and heart? So he sat quietly beside her, staring off into the now dark night sky, unable to offer any solace but his company.

"So you came to America after all," he said lamely.

"I came. With some help."

"From whom?"

"None of your business!" she said quickly. He was shaken at the vehemence of her reply. Something made him think of the way Luciano had reacted to her name.

"Salvatore Lucania seemed to know you."

"Never met him before." She turned on him. "The Mafia are corrupters! Never trust anything you hear them say! And Lucky Luciano is the king of them! A scourge! The devil himself!"

"We've made a deal." Nick wanted to see where this led. "They'll live up to it, won't they?"

"Oh, sure! Long as it's something they need! They're not doing this for patriotic reasons, believe me! And I got a feeling there's a lot more behind this whole deal than we know!"

There it was—his own odd feelings in the last few hours mirrored. Costello's comments about Commodore Hahn being a fool. Luciano's cavalier attitude toward Ruthie, his girlfriend. "The fix is in," he'd said. Whatever was going on might not be in his own imagination. But if this was true, if the Mafia had used the Nazis for their own ends, then even the Catholic Church had been duped.

"But even if I'm right," Rafaella went on figuring, "all this doesn't change anything. We've got a war to win. And the key to that is stopping the *Bund*. So we need the Mafia!"

"Maybe. But it won't hurt to do a little snooping around."

"You can't get involved! Your job is finished!"

"I have to," Nick said grimly. "I owe it to a friend. The Reverend Joseph Giovanni Stumpo."

Suddenly, off to their left, the horizon burst into brilliant flashes. They rose, facing the eruptions in the darkness.

"My God!" Rafaella cried, realizing. "The convoy!"

Now the thumping sounds, like muffled claps of thunder, reached their ears. The flashes continued. Each meant hundreds, perhaps thousands, of men dying.

"It's a massacre. The U-boats are torpedoing everything. You bastard, Fleckenstein!" Rafaella was livid.

"That guy driving the car?" Nick asked, remembering Rafaella's expression at seeing him.

"Nobody gave him a second thought. Loudmouth creep! All the time we thought it was specially trained types like those who landed on Long Island off that German submarine. But it was right under our noses! The *Bund!*"

"The sonsabitches!" Nick cursed bitterly as new deadly fireworks exploded at sea.

"I didn't think priests said such things," Rafaella teased him half-heartedly.

"Being a priest . . . or bishop . . . has to wait." Nick was focused on the red flames that leapt before his face.

She spun and impulsively kissed him on the cheek. The emotion of being near death and surviving, unburdening herself unexpectedly to him, overwhelmed by the images of death in the dark . . . all these things she would tell herself later when she tried to explain to herself why she kissed him.

"Forgive me, Father," she whispered.

Nick felt something awaken inside. A subtle stirring of unwanted vulnerability. It scared him and so he moved away and pretended nothing had happened.

She turned away too and stared back at the sea.

They stood there for a long while watching the

continuing fiery blasts, feeling the concussioning thumps on their bodies from the deadly fireworks.

They did not speak even as the train arrived in the New Jersey terminal trainyards. And without so much as looking at one another, the two leaped off the flatcar and went their separate ways. Yet when they were apart, each silhouetted in an overhead light, as one, they turned.

He found himself waving. The strange kiss, its heat lingering not physically but as an inner reminder of an absence now felt. She, however, did not wave in reply but spun and hurried away in that marching military style of hers.

20

IN THE NIGHT RAIN, Commodore Hahn gathered his men at the James J. Walker Park. The park was a convenient reconnoitering point for the navy and had served as headquarters during the night. As his men now mustered with half a dozen city policemen for the planned raid, Hahn stood outside the tent he had had erected, holding his Sherlock Holmes pipe, which had gone out in the damp. Joe "Socks" Minestrone, the mobster, was with him, as was Captain Marsh and Lieutenant Rafaella Massaro.

"Good thing we got our own Intelligence," Hahn said to Minestrone. "Two days, you've brought us nothing on the docks. What'd we make a deal with Luciano for?"

Joe "Socks" rubbed the meager stubble on his olive skin, badly pocked from a teenage bout of acne. He hated these military guys. They made him feel low caste, a man without respect. And in the Mafia, everyone, even button soldiers, wanted respect.

"Commodore," Minestrone said, "your men tapped Fleckenstein's phone. So you know 'bout the meeting. And you got all the names of the *Bund* from us. Anyone who was the least suspicious, we gave you that. All of 'em that work on the docks. And we been

94

watchin'! What more can we do? You should be happy. You're just about to clean 'em all out! What does it matter how you're gonna get 'em?!"

Hahn was fidgeting, trying to relight his pipe. Marsh struck a fresh match and held it over the bowl for the commodore, cupping it against the rain. Rafaella huddled further inside her regulation black rain slicker and waited.

"Too bad about Father Remington," the commodore sighed to Rafaella. "A great loss. But he did his part."

"He died a hero!" Marsh exclaimed reverently.

Rafaella tried not to smile. What would both of these eager-beaver brass boys say if they knew Nick was alive? Or rather, *Father* Nick. She must remember that. But she had lied for him, deliberately misled her superiors. Distressed, she squinted through the misty rain and tried to visualize the old Baptist church up the block.

"What are we waiting for, sir?" Rafaella asked, seeing Hahn also stare up the darkened street. "It's after three."

"You're absolutely sure about the *Bund,* Lieutenant? I know you saw that Fritz Fleckenstein. But we were so *sure* it was not the *Bund!*"

"I saw Fleckenstein in the car, Commodore. He tried to kill me! What do you think they're doing in that hall now, sir? Having a picnic?" Rafaella was furious. No one believed a woman.

"Our men verified the presence of one hundred and fifty-two individuals." Marsh corroborated her sentiments quickly. "The *Bund* is very definitely inside their meeting hall, Commodore."

"All right"—the commodore puffed hurriedly on his now steaming pipe as the rain splashed off his helmet— "surround the hall. And remember, no unnecessary shooting, unless they start it."

At that, Rafaella sloshed off across the grass. The sky above was still black. They would not be seen approaching the hall. She waved to her contingent of seven men composed of Coast Guard and navy shore police and made sure Marsh was doing the same. If they were successful tonight, the navy would, in one swoop, gather in the entire group of saboteurs. The war, at least on the docks, would be over.

Quickly the booted men in their dark blues unshouldered their assault rifles and moved down Clarkson Street toward the wood-frame building. The lights were glowing brightly through the stained-glass windows of the *Bund* hall, previously a Baptist church.

Rafaella led her squad to the rear and secured the back entrance. Inside, she could hear Fritz Fleckenstein, his voice rising to near-falsetto, surging with hatred. There was applause. She saw Marsh's group of twenty men crouch at the front doors of the hall. The place was secure. How ironic it would be if, after all the effort to make the deal with the Mafia, their assistance had never been needed. The *Bund* had tipped their hand at the little farmhouse outside Kingston. Fleckenstein's mistake had been to let her live. And that, thanks to a priest . . . or almost a priest. The image of Nick Remington, standing with her on the platform of the railroad car, moving through the night, suddenly warmed her. Where was he now? Perhaps already on the docks, finding Joey Stumpo's killer. All week, despite the long hours needed in tapping Fleckenstein's telephone to record his conversations, she had thought of Nick.

She withdrew her .45, being careful to hold it under the slicker to keep it dry, and waited for the sign to attack. Commodore Hahn had taken up position across the street and had his arm raised. She made herself focus on the gesture, squeezing out the memory of Nick.

She hadn't overlooked the irony that she had kissed a priest. Should have hated the sight of him. All those sweaty monks, putting their hands everywhere, climbing all over her. All through that night, she had shut her mind off from her body, staring levelly back at her rapists until they were unnerved by her silently indifferent eyes. Eyes they finally covered with a blindfold.

After that night, she had gone home, taken a bath, washed everywhere, draining and filling the stone tub until every last place they had touched her was clean. Then, totally rid of them, she had drained the tub one last time, and with it, all memory of their stupidity. She promised she would not let it affect her. She would not even think about it.

And yet, on coming to America, she found herself jittery around men, avoided dates. Perhaps that was one of the reasons she had joined the SPARS, an all-woman organization. Because it was safe. And now, being a lieutenant, she was even safer.

She pulled the hood back off her navy southwester, wanting the rain to strike her face to make her focus on the task at hand. How many times had she been scared to death while working undercover on the docks? That old tingling sensation was returning now.

Suddenly she heard a garbled cry. She turned to see it had come from the commodore. His first attempt at a command had died in his throat. Now he screamed: "Attack, attack!" and brought his arm down as if he were starting a race.

Automatically Rafaella was up, legs pumping, her .45 emerging from her raincoat. Side by side with her men, she pounded up the wooden steps that led to the back exit. The two on point, as planned, both big men, threw their shoulders against the Baptist church's rear doors. Without stopping their momentum in the least, the doors flew inward.

At nearly the same moment, Marsh and his Navy Shore Patrol, at the front entrance, sent those portals crashing down.

Frightened men and women inside raised their arms in surrender. The *Bund* was finished.

21

HE HAD SPENT THE evening with *Fraulein* Hoffman, having told his wife that he had late business in the city and that he would probably not return home to Brooklyn that night. His Lulu had sounded suspicious but he had had no time for that. They were at war, and if his cow of a wife could not fathom that (even though she refused to participate with him in his *Bund*), then it was her fault. And wartime brought forth urgent passions. New, furious needs. Fraulein Hoffman was one of them.

Fleckenstein turned over in the tangled sheets, saw the bedside clock read 12:50. There was time before he had to dress. The meeting he had called at the hall on Clarkson Street was important. Despite that priest and the navy woman being taken out, there was the Mafia. And Fritz knew he had to warn his entire membership to watch themselves on the docks, be extra cautious in their work. Because now everyone they worked with would be watching for saboteurs. But he had waited until the weekend. Weekends attracted less attention.

He lay there, tasting his own sperm. Hoffman had pulled her little trick again. Sucked him off, then surprised him with a mouthful. Why did she do that? Though he liked women, he never could totally figure them out. So he had gone down on her and just as she had starting coming, he had spit the sperm he held in his mouth into her. It had been good revenge.

Fritz almost laughed out loud. But he did not want to awaken the girl. For two days now, he had been cheerful, a condition not usually found in Fritz Fleckenstein. He knew the enemy, and the enemy did not know him.

Information in war was as important as ordnance. Oh, they might suspect. But until they *knew,* absolutely *knew* about the *Bund,* only then could the enemy proceed. The Mafia was a bunch of bungling criminals. He had already proven that with the battle at the farmhouse. And without the Mafia, the navy was nothing. He envisioned more congratulatory telegrams, perhaps even the coveted Iron Cross, from his Fuhrer. Blessed with these wonderful dreams, Fritz drifted back to sleep.

As per his instructions, he was awakened by Lorelei at 2:00 A.M. Dressing quickly, he brushed his teeth and gargled, then led the girl down to her car, an old Ford. It would be another week before his Chevy could be replaced. Packard was making airplane engines for the war; Ford, bombers; GM had also retooled. There would not be a new car on the road until the war was over. So he had to wait . . . even for a used one.

They drove from Hoffman's apartment on the West Side, near Eightieth, using the modern highway that ran above the docks. New ships had come in during the week and were being outfitted and loaded with cargo. As the ships, illuminated by dock lights, passed in the dark, Fritz counted one hundred and thirty. The *Bund* would start utilizing a new sabotage tomorrow. Fritz felt powerful. He reached over, tugged Lorelei's cotton dress up above her thighs and felt her shiver as he touched her.

100

THE SINS OF WAR

At the hall, Fritz told Lorelei first to drive around the block, then park in the rear of the old Baptist church. He always did that as a precaution; that way, if he noticed anything suspicious, he simply hung out the American flag on the front of the building and none of the *Bund* came in. But tonight, it was safe. Even the winos in James Walker Park seemed asleep. The lights in the park, due to wartime, were out but, like all the streets surrounding the hall, it too seemed deserted.

At precisely 3:00 A.M., the doors to the hall were opened. The *Bund* assembled inside solemnly, each taking the partner's hand next to them, united in courage.

When the song was finished and tears were wiped away, Fritz spoke from the stage: "We must be extra careful. Do not trust anyone. Even if they are your friends. The docks will be crawling with snoopers who work for the Mafia. They will look over your shoulders. Make sure you work only with your *Bund* members." He gripped the sides of the podium, his voice rising now as he encouraged his followers.

"About our newly identified enemies"—he began to shout—"I will only tell you this! In the next few days, they will be given something to take their minds off us! In fact, something will occur that will change their minds forever about interfering with the *Bund!*"

The crowd began to applaud and then began to stamp their feet. Fritz knew Adolf Hitler waited for that. He had read in *Mein Kampf* it was a visceral reaction to be trusted above anything. He glanced down to Fraulein Hoffman in the front row and tried to tell her with a quick wink that he wanted her again tonight. But as Fritz gloried in the mounting applause and shoes stomping on the floor, he happened to look down at the podium. Sudden terror surged through him.

101

A tiny 3 × 5 card was taped to the podium's reading board. It said: "YOU ARE ALL IN GRAVE DANGER! THE NAVY IS OUTSIDE!"

It was not signed. But he knew it must have come from the woman on the phone who had warned him about the Church and the Mafia.

Trying not to show the increasing panic he felt, Fritz raised his arms to quiet the group. He glanced at the two doors at the entrance. Why hadn't he posted guards outside? Had he been too overconfident? There was not a moment to lose! Desperately he tried to picture the other exits. There was only the back door. The windows, stained-glass and sealed, were high. Too high to jump through. Some of the *Bund* were puzzled, clearing their throats. Coughing. The smiles slipped away. Restless shuffling could be heard, work shoes against the rough-grained, unvarnished floor.

Fritz knew he could not save them. They did not know it yet, but they were lost. His friends. His recruitments. Tears sprang into his eyes. But clearly he saw what he had to do. In war, you forgot your casualties and moved on.

"I want you all to do something for me," he said, his voice wavering with the emotion he felt but which he held in iron control. "Something right now! I want to test your loyalty!"

A few frowns began to creep across faces.

"Quickly now, the test! When I call your names, I want you to stand!"

"Fechner! Heim! Kieser! Norvis! Krause! Dresden! Selden! Hulbert! Voss! Grumish!" He called off twenty-six names. The best, most powerful, dedicated and cunning. The members began to realize that all its *Offiziers* were now standing.

"Sofort! Sofort!" Fritz began to shout, crumbling the 3 × 5 card in his stubby fist. *"Schnell! Gerade aus!"*

And he dashed from the podium, grabbing Lorelei and leaving an astounded congregation to see the chosen group flee toward the kitchen at the corner of the hall and then witness the front doors of the church splintered open as they were surrounded by armed militia.

22

BURSTING THROUGH THE back doors, Rafaella rushed with her squad through the small connecting coatroom into the main hall. Her eyes pounced on the podium, expecting to find a surprised Fritz Fleckenstein. Instead the small stage was empty. Quickly she mounted it. A quick survey of the crowd told her Fleckenstein was not among them!

"Did anybody get out the front door?" Rafaella shouted to Marsh over the babbling and crying.

"We got everybody!" he screamed back at her.

"Not the leader!" She leaped off the stage and ran to the kitchen door, two of her faithful Shore Patrol doggedly pushing through the milling *Bund* to follow her.

At the door, she paused, swung out of the way and let one of the navy kick it in. Covering the room, she leaped through and found the lights. The room was empty, save for an antiquated stove, wooden counters and a couple of sinks. There was nowhere to hide. Where had they gone? This was the only other room in the hall.

A strange crack in the black-and-white tiled floor caught her eye. She knelt and saw that the crack formed a square trap door.

Without speaking a word, she motioned to the Shore

Patrol, pointing her gun at it. They understood immediately. The biggest navy man ran his hand around its edges. In the light of the naked bulbs overhead, no latch was visible. But his fingers suddenly curled around an inset ring.

Rafaella silently raised one finger, two. On three, the sailor yanked up the door. But no shots resounded from below.

Stepping back to the wall on which the kitchen switch was located, Rafaella threw a sister switch on the same plate. She had guessed correctly. The light blinked on down in the cellar. Still no movement from below. Was the *Bund* planning to ambush them?

A voice made Rafaella and the others spin, guns pointed. Marsh entered the kitchen, his face pale and bloodless. He stammered quickly: "We've counted . . . we're short! We were sure one hundred fifty-two entered this hall! Now . . . now there's only one twenty-four! Twenty-eight are missing!"

"Twenty-eight!" one of the Shore Patrol muttered, looking back at the trap hole and the visible wooden stairs that led down into the cellar. "No room down there for that many!" He got on his knees and almost belligerently stuck his head down into the basement.

For a split second, everyone in the tiny kitchen expected a shot to ring out and the man's head explode into a hundred pieces. Instead he yanked himself out and sat down, banging his rifle butt against the floor. "Oh, shit, shit," he said over and over.

A mass suicide? Fleckenstein dead with others, pistols in mouths?

Rafaella stepped down. Bending, she saw the dank, small cellar with its ancient brick walls. In the dim light, as she descended, she noticed that the brick foundation directly beneath the outside wall of the hall had been smashed. The hole gave out into the neighboring building's basement. It too was empty.

Holstering her .45, she turned to see Commodore Hahn come down the stairs, Marsh at his side.

"Where are they?" the commodore asked, amazed. "My God! How did they get through that wall? It's old, but it still looks strong! They must have had hammers or something!"

"I doubt that," Rafaella said. "They probably threw themselves at it until it collapsed."

The sudden image of a trapped, fanatical *Bund,* those specially chosen by Fleckenstein, frantically clawing and hurtling their bodies at the wall, was mind-boggling. Like trapped tigers, they had used their pent-up hatred to escape.

"He took the cream of the crop." Rafaella started up the wooden steps to the kitchen. She paused just before exiting. "They'll go underground now. Whole new ball game, Commodore."

The commodore stood there a moment, the impact of Rafaella's words sinking in. A guerilla war on the docks. They had allowed the most vicious of the *Bund* to escape. Now the very best would prowl and destroy. The war on the East Coast would escalate!

Drawing himself up, the commodore turned to Marsh, who had been waiting silently, expectantly. "Get me the names of all those who escaped our net tonight! Addresses, places of employment, anything you can. And make sure all the rest of the *Bund* is locked up permanently. I don't care what legal society screams about their inalienable rights. We're holding them out of harm's way!"

"I'm sure we can arrange for the entire lot to be sent to a POW camp. There's several in New Jersey."

The commodore, lost in thought, nodded absently and put a hand on the rickety railing to go up the stairs.

"Sir, this has been a great success all in all, wouldn't you say?" Marsh tried to cheer him.

The commodore swung on his junior, eyes hooded in

the naked light. "Captain," he growled, "we've just let mad dogs loose in New York City. We're gonna be very fucking lucky if those same streets don't run red with blood. It'll be the first guerilla warfare in America. Any target they want. Civilian or military. How I don't know, but we bungled it bad, Captain! So forget kissing my ass. Get your own in gear!" And he swung up the stairs, shouting: "Minestrone!? Somebody get me 'Socks' Minestrone! I wanna talk to his superiors! Now!"

23

AFTER LEAVING RAFAELLA in the trainyards, Nick took a taxi across the bridge to 120th and Broadway and told the driver to stop in front of Angelo's Mortuary. The driver, crossing himself, refused the tip. It was only after he was driving away that Nick understood. If the driver had known why he was really coming here, he would have kicked himself.

Nick found Angelo Bonaparte Eccheveria, part Italian, part French and superpatriotic Basque, in his embalming room. The caretaker greeted his old friend "NEE-KO-LAS!" with a warm hug. He had two bodies he was working on but said they were in no hurry and, removing his elbow-high rubber gloves, tugged Nick to a table on which a hot plate warmed a pot of coffee. The room stank of formaldehyde.

"You, you go away, Nee-ko-*las*," Angelo Bonaparte scolded, pouring coffee in chipped and stained mugs. "I never see you. You used to come have dinner every Sunday afternoon, then *pfffft* you are gone!"

"I'm not a priest anymore," Nick said, taking a cup.

"What does that matter?!" Angelo suddenly bellowed. "My father he herd sheep! And as little boy, in the Pyrenees, I see my father plug those sheep—you know, stick their bony legs in his boots and wap, wap, fug them! He don't know I am there! Did I care? No!

108

Not me, Bonaparte. I know I would not be herdman! But I still love my father!" And with that he downed his coffee in one passionate gulp. Somehow the entire six years of absence had been explained and that was the end of it. Refilling his cup and adding to Nick's, Angelo said, "So, Nee-ko-*las!* What do I do for you?"

Nick told him about Joey, and the old man shook his head and commented, "You should have brought him here, I would have done good job for free." He went on listening, hearing about the Nazis on the docks and how Nicholas had to work undercover now.

Understanding immediately because of his own freedom-fighting days as a Basque in Spain, Angelo jumped up and ran into his back room and proudly pulled out a professional makeup kit from beneath a large sink. Opening it, he said, "You need total change so nobody could recognize you. I understand! And I am master! I fix bodies so mothers love them again!"

Sitting Nick in front of a cracked mirror, he flicked on bright theatrical lights. Walking around him, carefully considering, weighing, judging angles, he squinted in total concentration.

"Just something simple . . ." Nick surveyed the supply of mortician's paints and wigs laid out on the dressing table before the lighted mirror. Did Angelo prop up his corpses here to make them up?

"Shhhh!" Angelo cried. "SHHHH!" He closed his eyes as if testing his vision, then popped them open, totally delighted! "Don't worry, not to worry!" He whispered heavily, "No one will ever know you, Nee-ko-*las!*"

"One more thing," Nick said nervously, eyeing the strange glint that Angelo now had in his eyes. "I know you do a little something on the side. I'll need that too."

"Sure, sure, I make extra pennies. I do photos for you. Don't worry! Not to worry!" Angelo, an artist consumed with his work, was pouring a bottle of hydrogen peroxide directly onto Nick's dark hair, massaging it in with his fingers.

Hours later, Angelo called his wife, Bernadette, down to his shop and introduced Mr. Robert Munroe, who wore a white shirt and tie, a dark blue suit and polished black shoes. ("Nobody needs these no more," Angelo had said.) The man, though tall and handsome, was unusual looking with his orangish-red hair and fiery orange eyebrows and eyelashes, partially hidden behind thick, black-framed glasses.

"You know this Munroe fellow?" Angelo asked Bernadette in Basque.

She stared at the man, then turned on her husband and told him in Basque he was crazy for interrupting the cooking of their supper, which was ox-tail soup, his favorite, and which was now burning. Cursing him, she fled back up the stairs.

"You pass, Nee-ko-*las!*" Angelo said, handing him an expertly faked passport with two of the new photos inside. And when Nick tried to pay, Angelo fell to his knees and kissed his hand. *"Mi padre!"* the little undertaker begged, "bless me. Then go and do what you can for our country!"

24

HE FELT FUNNY walking down Broadway. Why the hell did Angelo make him so obvious? He could have been brown-haired, gray, blond. But flaming orange? He decided the undertaker had done it so if everyone looked at the color, they wouldn't pay any attention to his features. Despite the stares, Nick threw back his shoulders.

At Ninety-fourth, he took a subway to the dock area near his apartment. He didn't really want to go back there, but he didn't have enough money on him to rent a room elsewhere. Besides, his toiletries were there and he wanted a shower and a place to sleep. He only prayed Judy wouldn't be around. Then he remembered his disguise. Would it really work? But before he found out, there was an important call he had to make first.

Since there was only a pay telephone in his building, he cut across Eighth, turned left on Fourteenth Street until he could see piers 57 and 56. A block from the Hudson, he stopped at an oddly triangular, pie-shaped wedge of a building, sitting like an island out in the traffic of Miller Highway. The rumor was it had been built by a rich eccentric. But nobody knew for sure. Cars shot past on both sides, but as he pulled the door open and stepped inside the thick, bunkerlike walls of "The Minnow," all noise ceased. It was the nicest thing about this place and the reason why Nick had always loved this bar. Step in here and the world was gone.

Nick and Joey's custom had been to stop at "The Minnow" after work every day. The long, narrow bar, with the dusty mooseheads and motheaten brown bear behind it, had seemed like home to him. Now, as he walked along the already crowded bar, filled with workers whose days had finished, he saw himself in the mirror, a stranger.

Marty Sherwood, bull-necked, with his usual towel wrapped around his ample waist, was behind the bar. "What'll it be?" he asked when he saw Nick, who was the only one in there wearing a suit. Nick wondered if he was putting him on, so he just stared at him.

"Somethin' wrong, fella?" Marty demanded.

"No." Nick realized the disguise was working perfectly. He *was* dead. It felt very lonely. "Beer."

Marty set up a draft and Nick said: "Hey, friend of yours said I could use the phone. Put it on his account."

"Oh?" the big bartender asked. "And just who might that be?"

"Nick Remington."

"You know Nick?" Marty asked, wiping the counter, keeping his eyes lowered. Several other longshoremen were interested too.

Nick took a sip of the beer, found his hand was shaking and lowered the mug quickly back to the bar.

"And who might you be?"

"Munroe . . . Robert." Nick thought of the passport. He pulled it out and showed it to Marty. "I'm just in New York on business, little short of cash. Rem said it'd be okay."

"Better be okay," Marty said, handing the passport back. "It ain't, you're in the wrong neighborhood to get far."

Good old loyal Marty! Probably kick his ass and stomp him into the ground.

"Thanks." Nick found he was actually sweating.

"Phone's in the back. It's local, right?"

"Yeah, sure," Nick said and hurriedly pushed back from the bar. But as he left, he heard somebody say: "Hey, I heard that guy Remington bought it."

"Yo, he got outta that *Normandie*." Nick kept walking toward the back office and entered, closing the door.

"Somebody said he got killed in a car crash over in Jersey."

"Who told you that?" Marty demanded.

"Heard it by a navy guy," the docker said. "Seems that guy Remington was really a priest. Can you beat that?"

"Tend the bar, will ya?" Marty reached one of his beefy arms beneath the glasses and brought out a sawed-off baseball bat. "I'll be a minute."

The phone had been answered by the prison operator almost immediately. But when he had requested to speak to Lucky Luciano, he was kept waiting. The talk he had heard at the bar made him uneasy. What the hell was keeping Luciano? Where did they have to go to fetch him? Quickly he glanced over his shoulder at the closed door of Marty's office. Crates of beer, whiskey and gin were stacked all around his desk. How often had he made calls here, paid Marty when he had the money later?

"Yeah?" the familiar raspy voice suddenly demanded in the phone.

"Nick Remington."

There was a pause and then Luciano laughed softly. "I knew you wasn't dead. What can I do for you, Father?"

"I need a job. On the docks."

"What gives?"

"Never mind. And the name is Robert Munroe."

"Okay," Luciano said. "I don't know what you're

113

doin', but it must have somethin' to do with our friends. Play pretty rough, don't they?" He paused and then all in one breath said before he hung up: "See 'Big Al' Mattechek. He's got the *Liberty*. You know the one they're fixin' up to replace the *Normandie?*"

The door behind him swung open and Marty Sherwood's huge frame filled it. He slapped the baseball bat in the palm of his hand. "Just who the hell are you?" he asked.

"Nick Remington," Nick said, hanging up the receiver.

"The hell you say."

"It's me, Marty. Honest."

Sherwood flicked on the light. He stepped forward, wide-eyed, studying the tall man's face, bat held ready. Then suddenly he shook his head. "Some of my men out there think you're dead. What gives?"

"I've got to find out who set fire to the *Normandie* and killed Joey Stumpo."

"You coulda told me."

"Sorry. What I'm going to do nobody can know about. Or I really will be dead."

"You a priest, Nicky?" the big bartender wondered.

"Was. Joey too."

"Holy shit. All this time. And me tellin' all those dirty jokes and all those women in here . . ." He thought half a second. "Hey, you're all right."

"Thanks, Marty. You're all right yourself."

"You coulda told *me,*" Sherwood said, sounding suddenly hurt. "What are friends for?"

"So keep it to yourself, Marty?"

"I'll tell everybody out there you was a good friend of Nick's," Sherwood said. "You better go out the back way."

"Yeah, and when this is all over, I owe you a drink." Nick winked and went out into the alley.

Marty laid the bat on the desk and sat in the chair.

THE SINS OF WAR

He opened the desk drawer and took an unopened bottle of gin out and poured himself a glass full to the top. Being a reformed alcoholic, Marty never drank. But now he upended the glass until it was empty. "Fuckin' war! That was for you, Father Joey," he said. Then he screwed the top back on the bottle.

25

In the quiet old upstate town of New Paltz, Stony Morgan heaved himself out of bed. It was 5:30 A.M., time to rise and shine. He sat there for a moment, feeling the cold sweat climb all over him. God, he had to quit drinking! How much was it last night? He couldn't remember. His fuckin' liver was probably yellow. He hated the thought of it. He stood shakily and was about to call for Myrna to make him some coffee when he remembered his wife had left him nearly a year ago. Took the four kids too. Ah, what the hell. That's life. You win some, you lose some.

Pulling on his regulation olive-green trousers, which he had flipped on the floor last night, Stony grabbed his shirt with the decal of Daisy Maintenance Company on its front, sniffed an armpit and decided it would do for another day. Now the coffee. And oh, shit. It had taken him fifteen minutes to get dressed. 5:45. He'd have to drive like a maniac to make the eighteen miles. Otherwise that fuckin' warden'd call his boss and he'd be fired for sure this time.

He stumbled to the kitchen, filled the coffeepot with tap water, found a spoon, ladled six teaspoons of Folger's on top of yesterday's grounds and set it on the fire. Now brush your teeth, Stony. Suck in your gut. Shave. Look human. Jesus, he felt terrible. He remembered now he had drunk submarines at Willy's last night. Jesus! You didn't drink submarines at age forty-seven, Stony, and get up for work the next morning. Whatta meathead!

He padded toward the bathroom, realized his feet were cold, so he headed back to the bedroom, caught sight of himself in the mirror. Stony did not like to look in a full-length anymore. It was awful to see the truth. He straightened up, tried to suck in his gut but couldn't. Giving up, he took his shoes and lumbered off to the bathroom.

Just as he had lathered his face, there was a knock on the back door. At this hour? And who the hell was at the *back* door?! Cursing, he threw the razor down and stomped across the tiny wood-frame house, shaking its floor. When he swung open the door, there was no one there. He slammed it shut. The clock over the kitchen sink said he had ten minutes to get to work. As he hurriedly returned to finish shaving, someone knocked again.

With his famous temper flaring, the one that had caused him so much grief in his life, the one that had provoked him to beat his wife and kids and made Stony hate himself, he yanked open the door, his face strawberry red, eyes bloodshot, ready to kill.

But someone outside the door was more ready. Big hands shot to Stony's throat and lifted him cleanly off the floor. Holding him high, strangling him, the killer walked through the kitchen, past the now boiling coffeepot, Stony's feet kicking ineffectually in mid-air, his eyes bulging out like a bottom fish brought up from its depth.

Krause choked the anger out of Stony. When the maintenance man moved no more, the assassin tossed the body into the bathtub and stripped him.

26

COMMODORE HAHN TOLD "Socks" Minestrone after the raid that he wanted an immediate meeting with Frank Costello. But Minestrone knew there was no way it could happen. Costello never took any meetings until ten. So the commodore was forced to cool his heels the remainder of the night. Finally Minestrone told him to show up at the Waldorf Astoria Hotel. That was Costello's place of business, and even the cops tailing him knew better than to intrude on the classy, old-world ambience of the famous hotel. Everyone who worked inside—the barbers, the bellboys, hotel clerks, house dicks, even the maids—were on Costello's pay-roll. Each morning at ten he would have his nails manicured and his hair trimmed, and all the while grant requests or hear out Tammany politicians seeking deals. Usually the Waldorf "gang," as the cops had tagged them—Joe Adonis, Little Augi Pisano, Meyer Lansky, "Socks" Minestrone and Costello's partner, Dandy Phil Kastel—could also be seen there, reporting to "Uncle Frank" on business. A "man of respect" holding court.

Hahn and Marsh, stiff in their navy uniforms, waited impatiently outside in the lobby corridor that led to the barbershop. There was a long line of supplicants ahead of them equally eager to see Costello. In a minute or two, Minestrone returned, looking sheepish.

"It'll be a couple more minutes." He shrugged helplessly.

Hahn was tired from last night's raid and edgy about the worst of the *Bund* escaping. "You go right back in there and tell Costello we've got a deal! And I want to see him now!"

Some of the men in line turned and eyed the loud-mouthed navy man. It was in bad taste.

"I can't do that," Minestrone pleaded in a whisper. "Frank's talkin' with somebody."

Hahn suddenly shot to attention. "This is an emergency! And I will take care of this myself!" He launched himself forward past the long line, heading for the closed glass doors of the barbershop. Marsh, feeding off the commodore's fury, fell in, close behind.

When the barbershop doors burst open, Costello was speaking to a prominent Wall Street banker. Both men were startled. The banker nervously backed away. Costello's bodyguards drew their weapons.

"Don't! For God's sake!" Marsh cried, throwing his hands in the air. But Commodore Hahn, spotting Costello and dismissing the weapons aimed at him, strode directly to the red-leather barber chair and announced: "Mr. Costello, I believe we have a deal, do we not?"

Costello nodded almost imperceptibly and the body-guards put away their pistols. The Wall Street banker mumbled something about there "being a better time" and left.

"I'm sorry, Mr. Costello. He wouldn't listen," Mine-strone apologized, appearing now at the door.

Costello smiled and asked the barber for the mirror. He accepted it, appraised his haircut. "Good, Richie, looks good." He got out of the chair, then sat on a

119

nearby plastic-covered bench, patted it and said to the commodore: "Tell me what you want, Commodore."

Hahn brought himself up and, clearing his throat, sat beside the mobster. He looked around, wondering if he could speak. The barbers were chatting between themselves. Minestrone was with the guards.

"You raided the *Bund?*" Costello suggested. "But some got away."

"You know?"

"Twenty-seven missing. No, make that twenty-eight, with Fleckenstein."

"It couldn't be worse," Hahn said, sitting up ramrod straight. "We thought if everything went well last night that . . ."

"You wouldn't need us?" Costello finished. By the officer's slightly crimson expression, he knew he was right. "Well, nothing has changed, Commodore. Our word is our bond. Now how can we help you?"

"If I'm right," Hahn said, his eyes narrowing, "they'll go for the next convoy with a vengeance. That's where we'll wait for 'em. But we need your help more than ever."

"I'll have our dock workers alerted. They'll report anything even slightly suspicious to you at your 90 Church Street headquarters, all right?"

"I want to meet with your dock foremen myself," the commodore said. "I don't want any slip-ups. We can't afford them. This convoy is big—very big. Besides, we can't lose our new ship, *Liberty,* which is replacing the *Normandie!*"

"Of course," Costello agreed. "I'll tell the Vapido brothers and 'Big Al' Mattechek on the West Side docks to expect you. Mr. Minestrone, please take care of that, will you? Arrange it all for the commodore." Costello stood and put out his hand. "I don't think we have been formally introduced, Commodore. I am Frank Costello."

Hahn stared at the hand. "I am forced to do business with you for the sake of my country. I don't think this has to go further."

Costello smiled, apparently amused, and lowered his hand. But inside he was seething.

"Commodore?" Costello stopped Hahn just as he was exiting the glass doors. "A word of advice . . . from one who knows the streets. Men like Fleckenstein"—Costello was grinning—"will strike back hard. If I were you, I personally would be very, very careful."

"I'll keep that in mind, Mr. Costello. No one ever said terrorists played by the Geneva conventions!" As Marsh held the door open, the commodore stalked angrily out.

Normally Costello would finish the morning's business. But now he took down his gray fedora from the hat rack and went toward the front door. Minestrone raced up to him and said: "I'm very sorry, Mr. Costello."

"Never mind. See to it all, will you, Joseph?"

"Sure, sure."

One of Costello's bodyguards shouted: "You want me t'tell those goombahs in the corridor to git outta here, Mr. Costello?"

"Yes, Mike," Frank said. "Tell the *gentlemen* if they would, please, come back tomorrow. I'm going for a walk."

"You want us to walk with you?" the other bodyguard asked. Sometimes Costello liked to walk the streets of New York like any ordinary businessman, which is what he wanted to be.

"I'm just going back to the apartment for lunch," Frank said. "I have a little headache and I need some fresh air."

The bodyguards nodded and Mike went out to tell the corridor filled with waiting supplicants that the day's business was concluded. In his expensively tailored gray suit, white shirt and black silk tie, Frank Costello left the Waldorf, turned right and headed uptown toward his apartment between Seventy-first and Seventy-second streets. There, he knew, "Bobbie," his wife of twenty-eight years, would fix his usual chicken salad sandwich.

Despite his calm appearance, Frank was furious at the rejection from Commodore Hahn. He passed St. Bartholomew's Church, caught a green light and walked up Fiftieth past the New York Archdiocese Chancery, then past the rectory behind St. Patrick's Cathedral. Briefly he wondered if Archbishop Spellman was home and what he would do if he would simply pop in on him now.

Impulsively he turned toward Fifth Avenue, then turned on it and strode up the front steps of the cathedral. Stepping to the top, he viewed the massive, gleaming doors he had given to St. Pat's. It made him feel better. The Catholic Church had reciprocated and come to his aid on the Luciano deal. In Costello's mind, that made perfect sense. A payback. They had respected his gift. Lost in thought, he gazed at the beautiful doors. Stories were cast in burnished bronze from the Bible—Eve handing Adam the apple . . . Cain killing Abel . . . Moses receiving the Ten Commandments. Stories he chose himself. He still had respect. The doors proved it.

"Frank Costello?" a thickly-accented voice inquired from behind him.

Feeling good and relaxed, Frank turned with a smile to face the muzzle of a German Luger. He tried to duck.

"From the *Bund!*" the bald man in the heavy overcoat shouted.

The bullet pierced Frank's head, and a gush of blood spurted onto the cathedral steps. As Frank fell, he felt foolish. With all his advice on precaution, he had been so easily taken.

27

Otto Krause had driven Stony's maintenance truck carefully through the streets of New Paltz, passing Irma's Diner. There was always one Nazi sympathizer, it seemed, in whatever place the *Bund* required help. Someone like Irma Halle. Irma had eagerly filled *Herr* Fleckenstein in on Mr. Stony P. Morgan, a close personal friend. She was a loyal *Kamerad*.

The drive to the prison had taken exactly twenty-two minutes. As he pulled up the long gravel driveway, the stark-white prison appeared like some squatting stone toad. He rolled to a stop at the first guard's gate, hearing the crunch of the tires of the Daisy Maintenance truck on the sharp gravel.

"You're late . . . oh, thought you were Stony." The guard scowled.

"Stony's sick. The company wants me to cover for him today," Krause said.

"I'll *bet* he's not feeling well," the guard said and motioned him through.

Otto Krause drove slowly through the gate into the prison.

28

JOE "SOCKS" KNEW Uncle Frank had been pissed at the commodore. But a deal was a deal. It was up to him to arrange what Hahn wanted. He hurried out the main entrance of the Waldorf and into his waiting car. He noticed Costello was standing at the corner of Fiftieth and Park, waiting for the light. So he was going uptown just like he said. Walking off his bile. Maybe that's why Costello liked to walk so much.

"Where we goin', boss?" Lou Asserello asked as he pulled away from the curb. He was wearing his favorite green plaid suit and red tie; Lou thought it made him look like a country gentleman. Yeah, a Harlem country gentleman, "Socks" always told him.

"West Side first. I gotta see somebody."

"Sure, sure. That *capo* Frank Costello. He pissed or somethin'? Walked right by me like there was a dark cloud or somethin' hangin' over his head."

"Don't you worry your ugly face about it! You work for me and that's all you need to know. And turn that radio down 'cause I don't like those sisters' singin'."

"Sure, sure, boss." Asserello acted properly mortified. "I didn't mean nothin'."

"Go to Pier Seventy-one, just below Bellevue. Take Third down, it's faster."

"Sure, sure, boss. Anythin' you say." Asserello

nodded cheerfully and made the turn at Forty-eighth. At Third, he turned right again. But, as he did, a bus ran the red light and crashed into them.

"Jesus!" Asserello hung onto the wheel and pulled over to the curb. "Fuckin' buses!"

"Shit!" Minestrone cursed, brushing the tiny shards of glass off his suit. "Anybody got any idea how fuckin' hard it is to score a clean car nowadays?"

The bus had not been traveling very fast. The driver now stepped out of the strangely empty vehicle and shook his head apologetically. The right front fender of the bus was crumpled; the damage to Minestrone's car, considerable.

"Get the asshole's name," Minestrone said as the buck-toothed, long-faced, smiling driver approached the car. He was carrying a satchel. "We'll sue the whole fuckin' New York Transit!"

Asserello tried his door, but it would not open. "Hey, it's bent shut!" He pushed hard against it.

Pedestrians began to gather, curious. The horse-faced driver suddenly withdrew a grenade. He pulled the pin and heaved it through the broken front windshield of the car and ran.

"What the fuck?!" Asserello managed. The car ripped wide open, spewing fire to the Hotel Middletowne's striped entrance awning.

29

At 90 Church Street, Commodore Hahn and Captain Marsh, having changed into civilian clothing, were waiting to hear from the Mafia's dock foremen. By eleven-thirty, when the calls had not come in, Hahn angrily rapped his pipe out into one of the crystal ashtrays and grabbed his overcoat. "Something's wrong!" he snapped at Marsh, who was perusing *Jane's Fighting Ships,* studying the details of a destroyer he hoped one day to command. "Stay here in case they call. I'm going down to the docks to see what I can find out."

He took the elevator down and went quickly through the revolving doors and out onto the sidewalk. His staff car was parked where Marsh had left it when they had arrived back from the Waldorf Astoria. As he began walking toward it, he remembered the captain always left the keys under the seat.

Behind the commodore a truck loaded with carpeting suddenly veered off from the street. Its tires rumbled over the curb and onto the sidewalk. The driver, instead of braking, floored it. That sound made the commodore turn just as the truck hit him.

The impact of the heavy vehicle's fender crushed his left hip. The commodore struggled up. In pain, he looked up, expecting the truck driver to leap out and help him. But the truck was now backing up, its tires burning rubber! Hahn desperately rolled away as the truck missed him by inches. Spotting the nearby Church Street Stationery Supply store, the commodore staggered into its refuge.

Inside the proprietor looked up just as the commodore hobbled quickly past and a truck rammed its rear through his store's front window.

Glass flew across the room, striking a blond customer. The commodore threw himself down on the floor. The truck lurched forward, then reversed and rammed into the store again. "Somebody call the police!" the proprietor screamed.

The commodore spotted the back exit. He limped painfully for it. The truck was revving up again, rolling forward for another attack on the store.

Throwing the back door open, Hahn set off the emergency burglar alarm in the store but found himself in a shadowed alley that led back to Church Street.

The sunlit street lay ahead. People were running by the alley toward the truck around the corner. His hip hurt like hell. But he felt proud. He had been in battle. Real battle. It was satisfying. His wound throbbed as he ran.

Suddenly a short, dark-haired woman sprang from another doorway in the alley. He had spotted her too late. The commodore tried to twist around, but his hip would not let him. *Fraulein* Hoffman's razor blade struck unimpeded at his throat.

Marsh, alerted by the strange screeching sounds on the street, went to the window and saw the commodore get up from the sidewalk after being run over. Sprinting from the offices of Hahn and Marsh, he took the stairs three at a time.

As he gained the sidewalk, he saw the driver of the truck escape from the loaded vehicle and race out into traffic, barely dodging a taxi.

Marsh peered into the battered stationery store and saw the proprietor crouched over a blond woman who was bleeding from her bare arms and face.

"Commodore Hahn?" he screamed, entering.

The shopkeeper, dabbing ineffectually at the woman's wounds and nearing a state of shock himself, could only gesture to the rear door.

Marsh surged through the store and out into the alley. He saw the prostrate form lying near Church Street. With a burst of speed, he arrived at the commodore, who was lying facedown. "Sir, are you . . ."

But the head was hanging only by skin at the back of his neck. The remaining words gagged inside Marsh. He slammed backward against the brick wall of the alley and lost his stomach.

30

Every day after lunch, Charlie Lucky took a steam bath. Since there was no proper facility inside the prison, he had "persuaded" the warden to empty out the showers on the third level and turn on all the hot water taps. The big room got hot and steamy. Lucky would enter and sit there, thinking up new deals, "emptying out," he told the warden, "all the poison through my pores."

He had just finished his morning exercise in the courtyard surrounded by the forty-foot concrete walls. As he walked around the asphalt, prisoners approached him for favors. Whatever they needed—alcohol, drugs, a judgment on some wrong, a communication outside the walls—he did it for them. For free. Until later, when he would need a favor. Luciano was the king. And like the ancient Mafiosi in Sicily, lord of his castle. The feudal system had been brought to Great Meadows Penitentiary by Don Salvatore Lucania.

Lunch was served in his cell on white linen. Today was trout amandine, scalloped potatoes, fresh peas and a bottle of French blanc de blancs. Dessert turned out to be a lemon-chocolate mousse. All prepared by the prison chef. Amazing what talents money brought forth in a man.

When he had finished and lit a Lucky Strike Green to

celebrate the repast, he lay down on the double bed that had been brought specially into the extra-large cell because of his "back pains." A doctor's certificate had attested to that.

When Lucky finished his cigarette, he stamped out the butt in an ordinary tin-can ashtray, rolled over and went to sleep. His bodyguard, Bruno Casselli, serving a term for selling heroin, would arrive in a half-hour and awaken him for his steam bath.

Otto Krause was dizzy. The muriatic acid he was using on the showers had rushed up his nose. No one had told him about not sniffing the stuff. It felt like he had burned the insides of his nostrils. What lousy work slopping down these scumpots. No wonder the man he'd strangled liked to drink! Wearing thick rubber gloves, hands and arms sweating, he squatted down, reaching into toilets, urinals, showers, swabbing them out with a huge bristle brush.

He'd finished the second floor, so he stood up and tried to get some air. Someone shuffled in toward a urinal and undid the drawstring on his prison grays.

"Hey, acidman," he called out with a smirk. "Where's Stony?"

Otto sighed. In this country there was always someone below you. And above.

As he exited the shower room and walked past the cells, his spirits revived. Now it would all be worth it! At a signal to the guard that he was ready, Otto Krause was led through locked wire doors and up the stairwell toward the third-floor showers.

On the third floor, the guard handed him over to a new desk.

"Where's Stony?" that guard asked.

"Sick." Otto kept his head down and moved forward into the corridor.

"Well, hurry it up in there," the guard called after him. "Stony tell you 'bout Mr. Luciano?"

"Sure, I know. Just be a minute." Otto waved and, pushing open the door, disappeared in a rolling cloud of steam.

Bruno Casselli led Lucky Luciano, bundled in his white silk robe, past the cells on the third floor. The men at the bars stared silently in respect or murmured hushed greetings. Some said *"A sante,* boss!," knowing where he was going. Luciano responded by nodding his head. It was hot up here on the third floor. The heat of the day gathered and made it muggy. That's why Lucky lived on the bottom level.

One of the guards who patrolled the third level in that section of the prison now unlocked the door that led into the shower corridor. Normally it was locked until shower days, which were Saturdays and Wednesdays.

"We got a acidman in there, Mr. Luciano," the guard apologized. "Sorry. The regular didn't show. This one's a little slow."

"I'll get him, boss." Bruno turned up the corridor.

While Lucky casually lit another cigarette and bantered with the guard about the horses at Jamaica Race Track, giving him a tip on a two-year-old named Bolero U, Bruno entered the shower room. After a bit, he emerged, sweating, and said: "No one in there, Mr. Lucky."

"He's supposed to come back and report to me." The guard looked miffed.

"New guy. Probably don't know the ropes." Lucky winked. "Maybe he went to the next section."

"Maybe," the guard said. "I'll call ahead, check just to make sure. You go in and enjoy yourself, Mr. Luciano. I got everything already goin' for you."

Like a giant, muscular bat, Otto Krause braced

132

himself in the corner above the door. Steam stung his eyes but his strong arms and hands pressed into the walls, supporting him easily. His feet rested on the molding of the doorframe. In his teeth, he held the icepick.

The door opened and Luciano entered in a swirl of hot mist, crossing the open area between both rows of shower heads.

He took off his robe. With a towel around his waist, he sat on the wooden chair that the guard had readied for him. The heat felt wonderful. The splashing of the water from the socket heads striking the tiled floor around the drains made a soothing, forestlike sound. Waterfalls. He closed his eyes and breathed in the hot, moist air. He was outside the prison, in the Turkish baths on Forty-second Street. Free. He wore diamond rings again on his hands, saw himself walking into Club 21 . . . to his table . . . the maître d' complimenting him on his $1,200 suit, his snazzy black- and white-topped shoes.

A noise made him open his eyes. Something in the corner?

He stiffened reflexively and peered through the gray columns of steam but could not see as far as the door. His mind receded, body in control now. He waited. What was he sensing?

He had to wipe his eyes. The water was gathering on his lids, making them heavy. Nothing. It had to be nothing. Bruno was right outside. And this was a fuckin' prison. The safest place in the world, right? And everybody loved him here, right? He was Charlie Lucky! The most powerful man in America . . . maybe the world! And they knew it!

Forcing himself to relax, he grinned. Paranoia, kid. Too much worry. Relax, relax. As he closed his eyes, somebody suddenly grabbed him from behind. Strong as a steel cable, an arm clamped against his windpipe.

133

He tried to stand, but the arm held him down on the chair. Fingers clawing at the arm, eyes wide open, Lucky tried to get a view of his assailant! But already he knew. The "acidman." An assassin. Even as he struggled, his mind clicked over his enemies. Meyer Lansky? Vito Genovese? If so, Bruno Casselli, his bodyguard, was involved. And he was standing right outside the door, keeping watch until the "acidman" was finished. Even if he cried out, no help would come.

Feeling himself overpowered, Luciano gagged dramatically, then slumped forward, willing every muscle to go limp. The assassin, unconvinced, tightened his hold, continuing to strangle him.

Wait, Lucky told himself. Wait. The pressure was building in his ears. His lungs were ready to explode.

Sensing no life, the assailant loosened his grip momentarily on Luciano's throat and brought up the long icepick. It was exactly what Lucky had waited for, and now he made his move.

With all his strength, Luciano shoved back with his legs. Long ago, he had learned on the streets that if a guy's bigger, go with him. Use his size to hurt him. The movement caught the assassin totally offguard. He had been exerting a great amount of strength in pulling his victim's neck back. As the chair tipped over, the assassin fell down heavily on the slippery floor.

Lucky scrambled away on all fours, trying desperately to get his swollen throat to open, his mind working. Where to hide? He knew he could not go out the door. Bruno was there. That fuckin' Lansky! This hit had to be that smart Jew's doing!

Quickly he rolled through streams of hot shower water, scalding himself badly, then came up behind its blasts. He stood directly beneath one of the shower nozzles and willed the searing pain to go away. Somehow he had lost his towel and the fuckin' boiling water had burned his goddamn nuts. He made himself concentrate and focus through the rushing water. There was nowhere else to hide. Prisons never had stalls or anything. It was just one big room!

A face suddenly materialized inches from him! Lucky saw the icepick thrust upwards toward his heart. In that same millisecond, Luciano aimed the shower nozzle's hot blast into the assassin's eyes. With a muffled cry, the assailant lurched backwards, icepick dropping from sight.

Keeping his bare back firmly against the tiled wall, Luciano scooted away. The assassin was tracking him, coming at him now along the wall beneath the shower heads! He had discovered his trick!

Quickly Luciano crouched down in the corner, defenseless. The figure came forward, right arm outstretched, jabbing the icepick ahead cautiously.

Lucky's hand brushed against something. What? Then he almost laughed! He had lived up to his name again!

Otto Krause stood over him. This mobster was cowering, probably half-dead, after being strangled. It was all over.

Krause wiped his face of the stinging hot water. He planted his size-eighteen shoes in the boiling water that was draining around his feet. Remembering he had been told by Herr Fleckenstein to announce a message before he killed Luciano, he bent low to the huddled, pitiful form of the naked mobster and said: "From the *Bund!*"

At that, Luciano looked up in surprise.

Krause grinned at the effect the mention of the *Bund* had. It was good. It had caused fear even in this one. He rammed the icepick toward Luciano's hairy chest. But something splashed in his face. That foolish criminal had thrown a can of water. It made him want to laugh, yet he could not breathe. The foul fumes were making him gasp and his eyes were searing. He began to shriek at the terrible pain. His mouth and tongue and mucous membranes were smoking.

Luciano watched as the assassin, flesh burning, eyes dissolving, screamed in agony.

Bruno came running in. He saw the writhing form on the floor, legs kicking maniacally, arms beating the terrazzo, hands tearing at the scorched flesh.

"Mr. Luciano?" Bruno cried. "Mr. Lucky?"

He knew it was safe. It had not been a hit. Fuckin' Nazis. So they wanted a fuckin' war? Well, now they had one. It was personal now.

The prison guard, alerted by Bruno's shouts, pushed through the door, gun drawn.

"The acidman!" the guard cried. "Shit, how did he get in here?! Who is he?" He kicked the unconscious assassin in frustration.

"A Nazi," Luciano said. He realized he was still holding the empty can of muriatic acid. Getting his freedom was going to be a lot tougher than he had expected.

31

AT DAWN, NICK was awakened by a knock on his apartment door. He could hear a heavy rain outside and wondered if he had imagined it. But the knock came again, soft but insistent. He was sleeping in only a T-shirt. Groggily he staggered from his bed and was about to open the door when he remembered it might be Judy—or worse, Fritz Fleckenstein! Was the *Bund* checking to see if he had really died?

"Who is it?" He couldn't think of anything else.

"Me," a familiar voice said. He opened the door and there stood a soaked Rafaella Massaro in a blue pea coat and a pair of khaki overalls, the type she had had on when she rescued him.

"We raided the *Bund* yesterday morning," she said.

Even though the room was darkened he remembered he was partly naked. He returned to the bed, pulled the covers over himself. "You got them?" he whispered excitedly.

"Fleckenstein and twenty-seven of his best got away." She came in and closed the door.

"My God!"

"Yeah, somehow the *Bund* knew about the raid."

"Just like they knew about our meeting on the farm! Both times the *Bund* was tipped off!"

"Question is—who's doing it?" She was silent a

moment. "Maybe there's a leak in the Mafia's organization."

"Or in yours."

She caught her shin on the desk. "Ouch, shit!" She rubbed it. "Mind if I turn on a light?"

"The desk, there, to your left."

She fumbled over to it, flicked it on and gasped when she saw him. "Sweet Jesus, you look like a fire engine!"

"The disguise works. I've already tested it."

He saw her staring at him. She *was* beautiful, even in this light.

"Uh, how'd you find me?" he asked, fighting to break his reverie.

"Easy. You live here. And since you're dead, you've got no reason to hide somewhere else. That is, until you don't pay your rent." She shook her head incredulously at his orange hair. "You're right. Nobody'll ever recognize you."

"I got a job on the docks this morning and nobody knew a thing."

She sat wearily at his little desk. "I've been on the docks all day. When I reported in, I found . . . terrible things."

"What's happened?" he whispered, watching her now rub her eyes. She seemed exhausted.

"Commodore Hahn is dead, killed in the late afternoon."

"What?" He couldn't imagine anything more violent than hot ashes from his pipe landing in the commodore's lap.

"Joe 'Socks' Minestrone got hit too. The *Bund* blew him up with his driver, Lou Asserello. One of them shot Frank Costello but miraculously, he'll live. Bullet stayed beneath the skin, came out the back of his head. An attempt was also made on Lucky Luciano up at Great Meadows. Our 'Operation Underworld' is a shambles."

138

"What about you?" Nick was suddenly worried. "And Captain Marsh? They'll try for both of you next!"

"Marsh has brought in the FBI and is surrounded by bodyguards. Reason Fleckenstein didn't go after me and never will is—I'm dead too, remember?"

"You're sure he didn't see you at the raid?"

"Positive. Or else I'd be decapitated like Hahn."

"So Fleckenstein must think he's on top again."

"That's what we want him to believe . . . for the time being." She leaned forward and wriggled out of her pea coat.

"But what are you going to do? Someone, sooner or later, will spot you on the docks."

"I've given it some thought," Rafaella said. "I need to get close to Fleckenstein, maybe even get admitted into his *Bund*. So let's get married. They'll never recognize a married couple."

Nick felt his heart leap absurdly at her suggestion. What *was* he REALLY feeling toward her? He had the hormones of a damned teenager! What did she appeal to? The adolescence he never had in the seminary?

"I'll do a little disguise too. Fleckenstein's men will never remotely suspect," she continued.

"What about Captain Marsh?"

"After getting over the shock that you're alive, he liked the idea. He's changed, Nick. He's really taking charge. He plans to use his Mafia contacts to spy on any *Bund* activities. But his real hope is that we can penetrate the Nazi organization and gain their trust. Operate on the inside. What do you say?"

"Mrs. Robert Munroe."

"Huh?"

"Munroe. My new alias."

"Oh, good. Then it's a deal?" She reached out and he shook her hand. Then she shut off the light. He could hear her undressing, the soft brushing of material as she dropped her overalls to the floor. "God, I'm soaked through and through. Mind if I sleep here? I think we'll be safe tonight."

"Sure. But there's another room just down the hall. It's got a bed. My friend Joey left it neat and clean."

"Uh-uh. Too spooky."

He could see her slender naked figure outlined in the light of the streetlamps outside as she undressed. "I'll get some blankets," he said quickly and, without turning on the light, went to the closet and pulled a pillow and two blankets down. When he backed out, he found he was facing her.

"I'll sleep on the floor," he told her.

"Don't worry about me." She took the blankets. "I'll be just fine on the floor." She lay down, wrapping herself into a cocoon. He stepped over her and got into bed again.

She was inches below him, the soft scent of her wet hair like fresh wet grass, a delicate aroma like jacaranda rising from her. He felt himself grow hard.

He heard Rafaella sit up. "Forgot how a floor feels," she murmured.

"Let me sleep down there," Nick said eagerly. Pain would take his mind off the situation. "I don't mind!" As he stood, his hand brushed against her breast.

"Don't," she suddenly cried.

"Sorry," Nick apologized, backing off.

Rafaella rose and slipped quickly into bed, rolling into a tight ball in the blankets. She lay there, ashamed she had been so startled, but she had not seen him so near and his touch had surprised her.

Yet, feeling him against her had crystallized everything. It made her realize she wanted to be touched, to be healed. To erase the past that she had told herself was so tightly under control. All lies. This was really why she had kissed him on the train. Why she had wanted to come to his apartment tonight. What a fool, she thought bitterly. It was priests who had raped her! Of all the queer desires to have!

Nick lay very still on the floor. He had wanted to hold her. Had she guessed it?

He heard a sharp intake of breath, followed by a low moan. And he knew Rafaella was smothering sobs.

He felt like a coward as he lay there. For in his heart, he knew she wanted him too.

II

PURGATORIO

*Give us this day the daily manna
without which, in this rough desert, he
backward goes, who toils most to go on.*
—The Divine Comedy
Purgatorio, canto I, 1.13

32

By Washington's birthday, February 22, 1942, the *Bund* had been reported along the East Coast at Poughkeepsie, Kingston, Long Island, Newark, Boston and as far south as Charleston. Americans, having read the headlines and heard the news over the radio about the bungled raid, were seeing Nazis everywhere. American Germans, overheard speaking their native tongue, were accused of being *Bund*. Strudel-eaters were viewed with suspicion—and several frankfurt concessions in New York City were wrecked by roaming gangs of juvenile delinquents. *Bund* hysteria sprouted like overnight mushrooms across the states of the Eastern seaboard. In addition to "Keep 'em rollin', Keep 'em flyin'," "Loose lips sink ships," "Buy bonds 'til it hurts," people now added "Stop the *Bund!*"

The intensity of the war effort had made everyone crazy. Two thousand, four hundred and three men lost in Pearl Harbor and ninety-six percent of all Americans savagely working to avenge them. Traffic fines were payable either in dollars or in car bumpers. Women's silk stockings were donated to the war effort to make shell slings on ships and women painted their legs tan with watercolor and thought nothing of the sacrifice.

Everybody dutifully used their "A" tickets to buy their three gallons of gas a week; everybody went to see *Casablanca* or *Road to Morocco* or *The Magnificent Ambersons* and cheerfully put up with all the shortages of sugar and coffee and nearly everything else. They told Jack Benny jokes they had heard on the radio and sang the line from the song "Get Me Some Money," purred by a sultry blond named Peggy Lee, and danced the jitterbug. Now that the enemy was among them, now that the *Bund* had been identified, the feeling of danger was even closer.

Families along the Eastern coastline gathered on beaches at night and counted how many convoy ships leaving from the many ports blew up. Some evenings, the pack of German U-boats, waiting less than a hundred miles off Maine, Massachusetts, New York, Delaware, Georgia and the Carolinas got a half-dozen. Other nights it was twenty or more. Police herded the watchers away. But they returned.

The *Bund* was cursed in articles as a monster. It was rumored to have thousands in its organization, all somehow tipping off the wolf pack of U-boats offshore. Ships, departing harbors up and down the coast, continued to be torpedoed and by March, the count was nearing four hundred. Sub-hunters and U.S. warships were unable to stop the slaughter.

Captains of freighters who had survived these nightly attacks complained of being easy targets, outlined in the night skies against the backdrop of city lights. So the navy ordered further dim-outs. Windows, street-lamps, car headlights were painted black. Marquee signs on Broadway were ordered turned off. Restaurants, hotels and nightclubs up and down the coast shut down neon advertising outside their establishments. The East Coast sank into a grayish haze, visible, the navy hoped, only a few miles offshore.

But the people who continued to stand on the beaches in the freezing night air still saw convoys blown up. And in New York, as the next convoy was being readied, the frantic search continued for the *Bund* and their secret way of alerting the German U-boats.

33

March 3, 1942
Washington, D.C.

ON MARCH 3, Governor Tom Dewey had been kept waiting in the White House for twenty-seven minutes. Dark-haired, handsome, impatient, his rise from private lawyer to district attorney of New York City to governor had been smooth, almost ordained. His future, he felt, lay in the Oval Office, occupied at this moment by a crippled, ailing man. It was just a matter of time. And since Tom Dewey was a man in a hurry, he had hoped he'd get his shot in 1944. Now this damn war had put a kink in his plans. Presidents didn't change in the midst of a crisis. Besides, how could you attack a president in a campaign? Nervously he stroked his fine, pencil-thin black moustache, cut per his instructions to look like Clark Gable's.

He checked his gold Cartier wristwatch again and was about to make another remark to the appointment secretary who sat reading behind his large desk when the door to the president's office opened and out stepped the roosterlike Senator Harry Truman.

"Tom," Harry said, shaking his hand. "President's all tied up. C'mon, let's talk."

"I came to see Roosevelt," Dewey said pointedly. He hated this know-nothing former tax assessor from Missouri . . . or was it Indiana? A bureaucrat currently filling the powerful position of chairman of the Senate's special committee to investigate waste in the National Defense Program.

"I know, I know, Tom," Truman apologized, smiling broadly. "This'll just take a second. We can sit here." He gestured to the couch on which Dewey had been sitting.

The man had no graciousness! He would have liked at least a cup of coffee, having made the journey by train down from Albany to the capital, leaving without his usual breakfast of eggs Benedict and his freshly squeezed glass of orange juice.

"Tom," Senator Truman said, perching next to him on the divan whose bronze label on the wall proclaimed it was once Dolly Madison's and that he had been forced to study for twenty-seven-and-a-half minutes. "You've heard about 'Operation Underworld'?"

"I was briefed by the State Department *after* it was organized. 'Bout a month ago." He remembered at the time he was angry FDR had not even bothered to call him.

"Well, the deal needs some help. It isn't working."

"Didn't think it would. You can't trust those mobsters. I oughta know. Put most of 'em away when I was DA!" He had quickened into his machine-gun-fire way of speaking which he used in court and on the hustings.

"The president still believes in 'Operation Underworld,'" Truman said, seeming to ignore Dewey's statement. He sat back and adjusted his bow tie.

Stupid Democrats! "What can I do, Harry?"

"Well, you know I don't like waste or inefficiency. And so the president and I feel we can best proceed with solving our problem of the Nazi U-boats off the coast if the leader of the Mafia *personally* helps run the operation. The navy and we think it's a good idea!"

Despite Dewey's mastery of control of every facial muscle, the corners of his mouth began to quiver. The idea was repulsive. This was an obvious political move on FDR's part to make Dewey look bad.

"You're asking me to set Lucky Luciano free?"

"Only until this next convoy in New York sails. We feel that with Mr. Luciano working directly with his own men, we can best clean up this mess!"

"I refuse!" Dewey found himself standing. "Either way I lose! Why, this is nothing but goddamn politics!"

"This is war, Governor!" Harry shot to his feet, moving close. "And that's an order from your goddamn commander in chief!"

The appointment secretary pretended to study his daily sheet. Two generals on the opposite side of the foyer began to chat loudly.

It was blackmail. They had him either way. He had built his political career on sending Salvatore Lucania to prison for fifty years on charges of prostitution. He was known as the man who cleaned up New York City, made it fit for citizens to walk the streets. Now he was being asked to free Luciano.

"We'll keep it top secret." Truman was smiling. "The papers won't get any of it." He winked and whispered: "So just do your duty for the war, Tom. Oh, and say hello to your lovely missus."

Truman shook hands and jauntily departed, waving hello to the two generals.

A surge of bitter desperation welling up in his throat, Dewey spun and strode for the door. No way could they make him do this for his archenemy! And what else had they agreed to? A pardon for his services? Well, let them just try and make him toe the line on that one too!

"Oh, Governor?" The appointment secretary's voice rang after him as he reached the door.

He turned, black eyes bulging with anger.

"You forgot your hat."

34

THE FBI AGENT took a deep drag off his Camel and asked: *"Verste'hen Sie mich?"*

Lulu Fleckenstein shook her head. She had not slept for more than forty-eight hours. But she pursed her lips tightly as if to keep the words inside from escaping.

"We know you speak English," the same special FBI linguist told her. *"Sprechen Sie Englisch?"*

Lulu shook her head violently. *"Ich bin krank! Ich brauche einen Arzt!"*

The agent turned helplessly to Captain Marsh, who was sitting in the corner of the interrogation room borrowed from the New York Police Department.

"I know, I know," Marsh said in exasperation, "she wants a doctor. She's sick." It had been the same all night and the day before that.

As if to once and for all deliver her message, Lulu rose and vomited on the scarred wooden table.

"Oh, Jesus!" one of the other agents said. "Get her a doctor. Maybe she *is* sick."

"We're all sick. And tired," Marsh said, pulling out a handkerchief from the breast pocket of his captain's uniform. "And her husband is still loose somewhere! Let's clean her up and continue questioning her!"

Lulu was weeping, bent over the table, stringy mucus hanging from her quivering mouth. She wished she *could* tell them where that bastard was. She wished she could leave this country forever! But police everywhere were the same. If she started answering even one of their questions, she would have to tell everything. And the only person her knowledge would implicate would be herself and her children.

"Iche mochte gernessen," she said.

"She wants something to eat." The linguist who had been closest to the splash of upchuck was wiping his suit pants and shoes off with a paper towel.

"She'll eat when she talks," Marsh said grimly, "and not before!"

Lulu begin to wail loudly.

"Tell me this Nazi bitch doesn't understand English." Marsh wiped his hands disgustedly. He had surprised himself at his sudden use of such language. Normally he never stooped to gutter talk. But now he was obsessed. The image of Commodore Hahn's head had not let him alone for a moment.

There was a knock at the soundproof door and a Coast Guard lieutenant stuck in his head. Marsh rose and went outside. He could hear the interrogation continue now, the tones rising in stridency as they questioned Lulu.

The lieutenant handed him a telegram from Admiral Colditz.

"TOP SECRET. Captain M . . . STOP. Eighteen ships out of Charleston sunk off Florida Coast. STOP. Less than 100 miles offshore. STOP. One sub-hunter sunk. STOP. Urgent, repeat Urgent. *Bund* must be rounded up! STOP. Await your reply as to new clues. STOP."

"Tell the admiral we're working on it." Marsh crumpled the telegram and stuffed it into his rumpled uniform pocket.

"He wants specifics," the lieutenant said.

"There are none, Lieutenant!" Marsh shouted.

Then, regaining control of himself, he said in a calmer voice: "Tell the admiral we are concentrating all our efforts on the New York docks and hope to have concrete data about the *Bund* shortly."

"He'll want to know when, sir. He's madder'n a nest of hornets."

"I am awaiting a call now."

The lieutenant saluted, turned smartly on his heel and hurried out of the Fifth Precinct headquarters.

Marsh walked quickly to the front desk. An overweight desk sergeant was doing paperwork.

"For the thousandth time," the desk sergeant said, looking up before Marsh could speak, "no calls. And even though I've got to piss so bad my bladder's bustin' wide open, I ain't left this phone for two seconds!"

"I'll be in interrogation." Marsh slumped. What was taking them so long? Governor Dewey had released Luciano from prison two days ago. And the Mob chief promised the set-up would happen yesterday, he remembered glumly. Was it possible the Mafia had *not* spotted any *Bund* on the docks as they had claimed? Had they merely concocted that story to get Luciano out of prison? It was their only lead. Please, God, let the Mob be right about the *Bund!*

He pushed through the interrogation-room door and was immediately assaulted by the stench. But before he could close the door, the desk sergeant appeared. "Captain Marsh?" he whispered. "Man called, left a message."

"Luciano?"

"No, sir. His name was Mattechek. Said Mr. Lucky already knew. Said tell you: 'It's them. Dock forty-six.'"

The break they hoped for. The *Bund* had been definitely located!

35

THE *LIBERTY* WAS moored at Dock 46. A large transport ship, it was being refitted from its World War I duties. Workmen swarmed over her low-slung superstructure as Mr. Robert Munroe, Quality Supervisor, observed with a careful eye. This ship was no match for the *Normandie,* but she would carry over five hundred troops to battle and she was the largest America had at the moment.

It seemed like a replay. The urgency to get the *Liberty* overseas, the outfitting. Did only certain death wait for her as it had for the *Normandie?*

The quality supervisor, a position created by foreman Mattechek so he could move about with maximum freedom on any vessel at the docks, scanned the plain ship's ancient decks and remembered the classy dining rooms, the empty swimming pools, the 389-seat theater and the whimsical Babar murals in the children's playroom he had helped strip from the *Normandie.* Joey Stumpo? It all seemed a lifetime ago. Only the grief that still surged up inside reminded him the *Normandie* and Joey had been mortally wounded less than a month ago.

From the stern ladder, he saw the two Vapido brothers, both built like bulls with huge, oversized heads, approach. Tony was entirely bald; Albert's thick, curly hair bristled in the cold afternoon breeze.

"Mr. Munroe," Albert said, lighting his usual cigar. "Gonna be trouble in a few minutes at the loadin' winch."

Nick felt his stomach tighten. This was what they had been waiting for.

"We already called it in," Tony growled, rubbing his naked head in the cold. "Pistoli made 'em for sure. Used to work with the little wop you're gonna save." He laughed a short nasal blast at some hidden joke.

"Yeah"—Albert was smirking—"just don't hit this wop too hard, huh?"

The two gangsters moved on, shouting warnings to a hoist operator who was lowering scrap metal down to nearby docks.

Nick walked along the starboard gunwale. He suddenly realized he had never hit anyone before. Did they expect him to punch this Italian? Could he? He flexed his right hand and strode quickly forward toward the set-up at the winch. If this worked . . . then he . . . they . . . were back in business with Fritz Fleckenstein.

At midships, he saw Rafaella pass below on the docks. She wore a large, oversize, button-down cap that covered her hair. Round eyeglasses finished her disguise. For the first time, she was wearing makeup and the effect, instead of being too much as she had predicted, made her only more stunning. Uneasily he paused to call to her, the name "Hazel" half out of his mouth in greeting when suddenly he saw her step behind a pile of stacked hawsers and disappear.

Edging forward to get a better view, Nick saw a balding old man with a fringelike crown of white hair slip in beside Rafaella. The man was familiar. But he couldn't see his face clearly. Rafaella seemed to be listening to what the old man was telling her. They

155

seemed to be speaking in some confidence, trusting they were not being seen by anyone. Rafaella started to turn away but the old man grabbed her corduroy jacket with a pincerlike squeeze and would not let go until Rafaella shook her head in agreement. It was only when he buttoned up his black overcoat and turned to leave that Nick saw it was Abraham Polakoff, Luciano's lawyer.

The glance he had seen between Luciano and Rafaella at the farmhouse sprang into his mind. "Massaro"— the gangster had identified her. He *did* know Rafaella! And despite her denying it on the train from Milton, Nick wondered if she had lied . . . if she had, could he trust her?

What did she have to do with the Mafia? Did Rafaella work for Luciano? Was she his link to the docks, informing him of everything the navy planned? Like that departing convoy that Costello had known about? Was she even responsible for the entire deal concocted between the U.S. Government and Luciano? Maybe that was why she "liked" him!

Rafaella now stepped from the piles of rope. He pulled back, allowing the edge of the gunwale railing to hide his face. He felt cut off from the one person he had believed in!

Suddenly her behavior with him all made sense. He had wondered why Rafaella, a near stranger, had gushed to him about her sordid past with those monks . . . and why she had come to his apartment that night.

An uncontrollable trembling invaded his legs. Weakened, he found a capstan and sat down. It dawned on him in a flash: he was alone in all this.

At the bow of the ship, shouting broke out.

"I saw you touch my tools!" an Italian was screaming at the top of his lungs at a tall blond man.

The blond seemed more afraid of the gathering crowd of longshoremen around him than of the Italian. He tried to walk away from the confrontation but the Italian wrestled him to the deck of the *Liberty*.

Nick pushed through the cheering dock workers. The Italian was on top of the other man, slugging away. The blond seemed unwilling, for some reason, to defend himself. Nick guessed he was more afraid of blowing his cover than of taking a beating.

"Get off!" Nick cried, pulling the Italian up.

The Italian took a swing at him. Nick ducked and surprised himself by reflexively slugging him squarely on the chin.

Yanking the blond up by the arm, Nick whispered close to his ear: "Tell Fritz he has more friends than he knows about! Tell him I have a plan!"

The tall blond man stumbled backwards, picked up his watch cap and hurried away.

Had it worked?

The Italian was getting up, being helped to his feet by a dozen longshoremen. Rafaella appeared, eyes questioning, as she caught Nick's gaze. Trying to hide his feelings, he looked away.

"All right, break it up!" The Vapido brothers had magically appeared. "Get back to work. You think you get paid for loafin'?"

The dockers drifted away, excitedly conversing, pumped up by the fight. The Italian Nick had hit was joking with Tony Vapido. Nick laid a hand on his shoulder.

"Thanks," he said. "Hope it didn't hurt you too much."

"You don't hit *that* hard, Father." Lucky Luciano turned to face him.

Nick froze.

"When the *Bund* tried to knock me off, it got personal. So here I am."

Nick checked Rafaella. But she seemed already to know about it.

"I'm only out 'til the convoy sails," Luciano said. "So let's move it, huh?"

36

THE MUNROES HAD been put up in one of those small government flats that crouched beside East Houston Avenue. Filled with derelicts, winos and poverty-stricken families mostly on welfare, the housing complex's running joke was there were more rats than humans and more cockroaches than kids.

Nick and Rafaella occupied a sixth-floor, two-bedroom apartment containing a bathroom, kitchen with hot plates and a living area. The furniture had seen many occupants and the linoleum on the floor was worn through in black holes. Captain Marsh, in "civvies," had arrived and now sat across from Nick. Rafaella was at the kitchen table, while Luciano lay sprawled on the sofa.

Nick would not look at Rafaella. Though things had been tense between them since that night in his flat, she could not figure out why she was getting a particularly cold shoulder today.

"I'm happy to find you alive, Father," Marsh began. "I was sad to hear we'd lost you."

"Gone but not forgotten?" Nick said without the trace of a smile.

"Father"—Captain Marsh stuttered so violently all looked at him to see if he were having an attack— "I know I've been a stick in the mud. I also know the best are fighting elsewhere while I'm stuck here. And I guess I'm where I should be. Rear-action fumbler. But I'm trying hard. I want to win this battle and I hope someday they'll let me join the best . . . over there." He stuck out his hand. "Can we start again?"

Nick was surprised at Marsh's words. Then he realized he had caused this admission to surface by his anger at Rafaella. He shook Marsh's hand.

"Good! But first I'm afraid I have some bad news for you, Father. I believe with this new, dangerous plan, you should step back. Rafaella and Luciano's men can take it from here."

"I'm in," Nick said. "Luciano and his men should stick to the dock areas. Rafaella and I will pull off the robbery."

Captain Marsh studied Nick for a long moment. Was this the amenable priest who had served as go-between for the Church and Mafia? Who used to take orders so readily? Something had changed him too. There was a toughness, a readiness to fight he had never sensed in him before. But if Marsh "the marshmallow" had turned into a warrior, why not a priest?

"All right. You're in, Father."

"Robert Munroe is my name."

"Mr. Munroe." He paused, shot Rafaella a quick glance. But she looked away. What was happening between them? They seemed to hate each other.

"Admiral Colditz is extremely upset," Marsh began explaining. "Everywhere the story's the same. Ships sail. Ships still get blown up!"

Luciano suddenly sat up. "We got the fuckin' docks sealed tighter'n a lawyer's asshole!" he shouted. "There ain't been one goddamn *Bund* on any docks 'til now! Not one face we don't know! And first time one showed up, we fingered 'em for you!"

"Then they've switched tactics," Marsh suggested.

"No matter what we do, the U-boats know exactly where our convoys will be. And even though we send out decoys filled with rocks, the Nazi submarines bypass them and go straight for the supply vessels. So don't tell me the docks are clean, Mr. Luciano! Somehow, the *Bund* is still operating effectively. Or perhaps you think all the tonnage being sunk is by chance!"

"Not one face!" Luciano repeated, shaking his finger. "My boys been watchin'! No one gets on the docks we don't know! You tell me, Mr. Navy Man, just how the hell they doin' it?!"

"We've swept every ship for radio transmitters, mines, anything," Marsh said. "We've even brought in Geiger counters in case they're using some low-grade form of radioactivity. All for nothing."

"Perhaps the transmitters don't activate until they're at sea," Rafaella suggested. "We suspected they were using them on previous convoys."

"From different beachheads, our technicians have been busy focusing directional radio receivers on the convoy, following them out to sea more than two hundred miles. Even when the torpedoes start hitting them, there are no radio signals. Whatever the *Bund* is doing is brilliant!"

"We'll learn their secret," Nick said suddenly. "And when that happens, we'll break them!"

He spoke with such determination everyone turned and stared at him, surprised at the vehemence of his outburst. Rafaella tried to catch his eye, but Nick sat there, jaw muscles working, staring at the floor. Somehow she felt Nick's anger had been directed at her.

"All right, look," Marsh said. "We have a shot at getting inside the *Bund*. But until then we got another problem! The *Bund* keeps figuring out what's going to happen before it happens. I mean, if we don't find the leak, they'll burn us on this one too!"

Rafaella swung accusingly toward Luciano.

"Don't look at me," he said, propping his feet up on the couch and yawning. "If the leak was in my organization, I'd be dead by now. That big goombah who came after me in the showers was a Nazi and I can prove it!"

"Maybe somebody just hates you," Rafaella said with intensity.

"Yeah. And maybe Italians eat pasta." He yawned again to show how bored he was. "I ain't got the problem, folks. You do."

"If he's right," Marsh said to Nick, who was staring at Rafaella but quickly looked away, "the traitor could be among us."

"Could be at that," Nick said.

Rafaella thoughtfully took off her button-down cap, shook out her red hair and studied him.

"It goes sour this time," Marsh said, "not only is the convoy finished but so's our deal, Lucky. It would be senseless to continue if you're not making any headway."

"That's why I'm outta the pen." Luciano grinned. "Like I always say, you want somethin' done, do it yourself! So don't worry." He pinched something suddenly off the coarse woolen clothing issued to him by the navy. "Anybody bother to get these rags deloused?!"

He stood up suddenly. "I need a shave, haircut and some decent clothes. And maybe a room at the Waldorf so I can rest!" He put his hand on the front doorknob to leave.

"You step out that door," Marsh said evenly, "and you get a one-way ticket back to Great Meadows. Or maybe Dannemora."

"I'm supposed to sleep *here?* You see this joint?! It's crawlin' with shit! And there's niggers on both sides!"

"You wanted to help," Marsh said. "Sit down. I'm not letting anything blow our cover!"

162

Lucky sat, grinned, tapped out a Lucky Green and lit up. He sighed and blew out a long stream of smoke. "The king, back in town!" He ruefully gestured to the battered, shabby furniture and stained walls.

"What are we going to do about the leak, Captain?" Rafaella turned to Marsh.

"If anybody knows, Lulu Fleckenstein does. She's tough, but we'll break her. Until then, go about your business." Marsh checked his watch. He rose to go. "I've got to get back to the Fifth Precinct. Call the number I gave you." He went out.

"Just one big happy family," Luciano mumbled, noticing Rafaella and Nick avoiding each other, when the door had closed. "I had more peace and quiet in the pen." And instantly he turned over and started to snore.

Rafaella got up and went into her bedroom. Nick splayed his fingers on the unpainted and smudged kitchen table, trying to figure out what to do next. Suddenly he heard men's voices come from Rafaella's room. Curious, he got up, went to the door and knocked quietly. When there was no answer, he opened it.

"Rafaella?" he started to ask.

She sat before him, hands bound behind her, on a hard wooden chair.

Shocked into speechlessness, he forced his brain to catch up with his reaction. But instantly the muzzle of a nine-millimeter Luger was shoved under his chin.

"Come in, close the door, please," the blond man whom he had rescued on the docks said.

Nick complied, noting Rafaella's calm expression, hiding her real feelings. How long had the *Bund* been in here? Had they heard everything?

Turning boldly to his accomplice, who was standing behind Rafaella, pistol drawn, the blond man said: "Tie him too!"

As Nick was being trussed, the blond opened the door again and peered out at Luciano's sleeping form.

"It's that dock worker," the blond said, ducking his head back into the bedroom.

Nick breathed a sigh of relief. They had not come in in time to hear their conversation. Otherwise the Nazi would have known who was on the dumpy couch.

"I hit him too hard." Nick smirked for effect. "He didn't feel good so I let him come back and sleep it off."

The blond man squinted once again at Lucky Luciano. Satisfied, he closed the door. He motioned to the window, which was open. The other Nazi grabbed Rafaella's raincoat and threw it around her, then pushed her out onto the icy metal fire escape.

"Is it necessary to tie us?" Nick asked as he stepped awkwardly through the window and started down also.

"Keep your mouth shut, please!" the blond said. "You may be a friend. Then again you may be a spy!"

As Nick fought for his footing on the slippery rungs, he saw Rafaella descending below with the other Nazi. He had nearly fatefully uttered her name as he had entered the bedroom. That single slip could have killed them both. He would have to be careful.

When they had gained the sidewalk below, they were hustled into a waiting blue Ford. Nick settled in the back seat and leaned with spousal affection toward Rafaella.

"You all right, Hazel?" he asked.

"Fine, Robert." She smiled. "Who are these men?"

"Friends we want to help."

"Of course." Rafaella smiled knowingly at the two men in the front seat as the car started away.

But when she saw they both faced forward, she shouldered Nick away and stared out her side window, ignoring him.

* * *

The droopy eye opened first. He listened a few moments more. Then, like a cat, Luciano rolled from the couch.

At the bedroom door, he listened again. Assured they had gone, he swept inside and ran to the window. Far below, he saw the blue Ford pull out into traffic. Whistling for his two men stationed at his command below, he saw the Vapido brothers appear from a doorway. At his signal, they leaped into their own car and followed the Ford.

Lucky closed the window, shutting out the chill. Long ago, he had learned to sleep with one eye open. You did that if you wanted to survive. On the streets or in prison. He had instantly heard the strange sound of the German voices inside Rafaella's bedroom and remained motionless, even when he sensed the Nazi staring at him, pistol in hand.

Reentering the living area, he picked up the phone to dial the number Marsh had given them. But halfway through the process, he hung up.

A thought crossed his mind. It might prove valuable for only him to know where this *Bund* was operating. That way, he could put the Nazis out of business himself and earn his freedom. No more bungles by the navy.

He called another number he had long ago memorized. Time for a little pleasure. It rang three times and then a female voice answered.

"Ruthie?" he asked.

37

THE WAR WAS NOT being kind to Coney Island. Closed down because of the dim-out order, rubbish lay wind-blown against the entry fence. The tunnel of love needed patching. Huge holes in the amusement booths gaped from some youngster's vandalism. The towering roller coaster, once white and gleaming, was peeling and splintering, its rails warped. Even the deserted beach was now eroded, the waves pounding relentlessly day after day.

The blue Ford pulled past the admittance booth, drove toward the baseball pitch and stopped. A sign on the broken-down cyclone fence said: CLOSED FOR THE SEASON.

The blond man pulled Nick and Rafaella from the car and led them toward the fun house. Unseen by them, the Vapido brothers pulled off the highway above the amusement park and watched.

As Nick entered the dilapidated fun house, he saw that the lock had been ripped off its hinges. For the moment, as they stood in its low-ceilinged, darkened interior filled with broken mirrors, it appeared no one was there. Then a figure emerged from behind a corner, short and heavy-shouldered, face shrouded in the murky light.

"Who are you?" the short man demanded.

"I'm Robert Munroe. This is my wife, Hazel." Nick's eyes were adjusting now. He could see the room around them was a maze of twisting corridors, surrounded by mirrors. The one behind the shadowed figure reflected an even shorter, squatter image.

"We're sympathizers," Rafaella said suddenly.

"So I hear. But how do we know you're not spies? Everybody's after us."

Nick tried to make out the face but could not. In the little light from the black-painted ceiling above, only the lips, thick and pouting, showed.

"We've got a plan," Nick offered. "If it works, it'll cripple the docks for months!"

"We already control the docks! With just a few of us, we have *Amerikaners* totally defeated!" The man threw back his head and laughed. Then just as suddenly as it had erupted, the laughter stopped and the short man stepped forward into a pool of light. Nick and Rafaella saw it was Fritz Fleckenstein.

He was standing less than three feet from them and Nick could see every outline of his square face, mouth framed by the infamous handlebar moustache. He saw him pointing the gun at them as they drove alongside at breakneck speed. If their disguises did not work now, they were both dead.

"Wie sagt man sie auf deutsch?" Fleckenstein asked.

"Munroe," Rafaella replied. "We didn't change our name. We're Americans. And I don't speak German well enough, so cut the crap."

Fritz peered intently at her. "Step closer," he said. "I need to see you."

Nick felt Rafaella brush past him as she boldly came into Fleckenstein's light. Nick too stepped forward. They were within a foot of one another. Rafaella's disguise was only the makeup and glasses she wore. For what seemed like a millennium, Fleckenstein squinted at them, eyes examining every detail. Would he remember seeing her that day at the farm? Nick wondered what was the expression emerging on Fleckenstein's face now as he studied him too. Satisfaction at placing them both? A leer of recognition twisting his lips?

"So," Fleckenstein said finally, "we have already checked you out with our internal security and you passed. But why should I bother to listen to some plan? My *Bund* are arriving from the ports up and down the coast. Soon we will concentrate on this convoy. Everything is under control. We don't need any *good* help from you."

"Then you're a fool," Rafaella said. "'Any revolutionary movement that closes its mind to new possibilities is doomed.'"

Fritz smiled. "You quote *Mein Kampf?*"

"We have a plan to steal money that is both military and longshoremen's payroll," Nick said coolly. "It will disrupt operations at their very core."

"Impossible!" Fritz challenged the concept. "The Port Authority's bank has twenty, thirty guards! Not to mention dozens of MPs on duty! You would never pull it off!"

"But if we do?" Rafaella wanted to know.

Fritz smiled and slowly pulled a Luger from a shoulder holster. "If you try and fail . . ." he leaned very close to Nick and Rafaella ". . . do you know what I will do?!"

Suddenly he whirled and began firing. Mirrors splintered and crashed around the room. The darkened room filled with the stench of cordite and swirls of dust as mirror after mirror shattered.

Other *Bund* members began to fire. One shot out their small overhead light, the only source for the room, plunging it into darkness. Nick pulled Rafaella down as fiery streams spurted from gun muzzles. And then, as suddenly as it had began, the gunfire stopped and Nick saw the door swing open briefly, admitting daylight. Fleckenstein had used the cover of his gunfire to move offstage like a magician.

Nick rose. Not trusting any of the walls because of shattered glass, he stretched his long arms up to the low, barely nine-feet-high, ceiling of the fun house.

"Hold on to me," he said to Rafaella and felt her hand find his belt, then self-consciously move upward to his arm.

He began to walk toward where he had seen the door, shoes crunching on dangerous slivers of glass, hands moving, palm over palm, on the ceiling, blindly feeling his way. Rafaella kept close, silently inching her way beside him. When Nick's hands struck a glass wall, he brought his hands carefully down and gingerly guided them around it. He saw dim light entering a crack. Feeling against it inch by inch, he found the door handle. In an instant, they were outside, both of them covered with tiny, shrapnel-like pieces of mirror.

"Quite a guy," Nick said, sighing in relief and noting that the blue Ford had disappeared. Coney Island seemed deserted.

"Bastard!" Rafaella spat. She brought up her hand and tried to brush off some glass. "Ouch!"

They stood there in the stiff wintry breeze off the ocean, waves beating and crashing heavily down on the beach.

Nick suddenly turned from the sight of the turbulent beach. "We've got work to do. Not to mention a long walk home."

"There's always the train." Rafaella said.

But he strode off briskly, pieces of deadly glitter flying off his hair and shoulders.

38

THE VAPIDO BROTHERS knocked at Apartment 617 and waited outside in the gusting wintry air that was blowing through the smashed windows in the housing corridor.

"Hang beef in here," Tony complained, slapping at his bald head.

"C'mon, c'mon!" Albert knocked again.

The door sprang open and Ruthie stuck out her head. She was wearing a wraparound yellow silk robe and had not bothered to tie the front. Her breasts stood up proud and firm, nipples hardening in the blustery wind. Feeling the two men's eyes on her, she covered herself. The Vapido brothers, grinning, entered.

Barefoot, Luciano was sitting at the kitchen table in Nick's bathrobe, drinking whiskey. The robe was mauve and wooly-warm and there was an insignia of the Archdiocese of Boston on its front.

"Well?" he asked when the brothers stood in front of him.

Albert nodded at Ruthie.

"Go ahead. She's okay."

"We tailed 'em down to Coney Island, boss," Tony began his report.

"And then?"

"They left the girl and priest there. Lammed out in a hurry. Shot up the fun house."

"That's right," Albert cut in. "And we didn't stick around to help those two because you told us to find out where the Nazis went!"

"You didn't lose 'em." Luciano poured some more of the amber liquid into his glass. "Tell me you didn't lose 'em."

"No, sir, Mr. Lucky." Albert's full head of curls shook violently. "We kept right with 'em."

"Across the Washington Bridge and into Jersey," Tony said. "Right to a warehouse in the Morris Canal Basin."

"Good work, boys," Luciano said. He reached into Nick's bathrobe and pulled out a couple of thousand-dollar bills and handed them to the longshoremen.

"Thank you, Mr. Luciano!" Tony said. "You are very generous."

"I can afford to be generous, right, Ruthie?" Lucky laughed.

"You got generous all over you, Lucky." Ruthie crossed her legs on the couch, a movement that swung open her dressing gown and revealed not only her slim long legs but a manicured bush. She seemed in no hurry as she pretended to recognize the mishap and reach out to rearrange the garment. She smiled up at the Vapido brothers: "More than you could ever afford, boys. Don't even think about it."

Luciano burst into loud laughter. "This moll's some-thin', ain't she, boys?" he asked. "Look at her!" He got up, came over, sat beside her and kissed her heavily made-up mouth. When he pulled away, he gazed into her eyes. "In the pen I get anythin' I want. But I never get enough of that."

She kissed him playfully. "Whatya gonna do about these Nazis, Lucky?"

171

"They worry you?" he teased her.

"A Nazi's a Nazi."

"Well, when the time's right, maybe me and the boys'll visit 'em. Right, boys?"

"Right, Mr. Luciano!" Tony replied eagerly.

"When you want to do it, Mr. Luciano?" Albert asked.

"Soon," Lucky said. "But first we give that dumb-ass priest and that Massaro dame who thinks she's a man a chance to get those krauts' trust. They'll have their guard down then."

There was a knock and Luciano motioned to the brothers to get the door. Tony swung it open and outside stood an army of painters and fumigators in overalls. A pretty young woman with fabric samples said: "I'm Miss Carpano. Interior decorator here to see Mr. John Smith?"

"Wrong apartment," Tony said. "Ain't nobody here by that name!" He started to slam the door, but Luciano said: "I'm Mr. Smith. Come in."

They paraded in.

"Tony, Albert," Lucky said. "I need a place of my own. Vacate both apartments on the right."

"What if they don't want to leave?" Tony asked.

"Then throw their fuckin' cootie furniture out on the street," Luciano said. "And make it quick. My people here are waitin' to get started!"

172

39

THE NEW YORK Port Authority, in its long, faded green and rust-streaked building, was on Thirtieth Street next to the river. Located between piers 68 and 76, the headquarters for Harbor Commissioners and Port Authority Bank, it collected foreign and domestic taxes and tariffs, and made payroll for eighteen thousand longshoremen.

Its two hundred employees routinely handled ships filled with cattle, cheese, sugar, green coffee, fish, grains, tobacco, fruits and nuts, tea, cocoa, vegetables, alcoholic beverages, fuels, rubber, lumber, wood pulp, textile fibers and wastes, industrial diamonds, asbestos, ores and metal scrap, chemicals, machinery, footwear, furniture and a thousand other necessary myriad items to satisfy millions of Americans.

Now that the war had begun, Admiral Colditz had also taken residence inside the Port Authority, moving his staff into the cramped third floor of the four-story, damp concrete structure. The Port Authority Bank was now forced to handle not only the payroll for long-shoremen and employees connected with the docks, but also payroll for U.S. Navy sailors, both enlisted and officers, Merchant Marine, Coast Guard and SPARS. More than one hundred millions dollars flowed through the bank every week.

A standard detachment of nine Shore Patrol, two NYPD officers and six Coast Guard stood guard out front of the Port Authority Bank and inside its glass doors. To the employees who worked every day in the bank, it was a surprise when Admiral Colditz replaced all those familiar faces with only five navy sailors. No reason was given. Everyone figured it had something to do with Colditz's preference for his own men. Why so few, they could only speculate.

Determined to keep up their appearances as husband and wife even in private so they would not somehow slip up in public, Nick and Rafaella emerged from their separate bedrooms, made coffee, ate breakfast and read the Sunday *New York Times*. They sat stiffly, eating their eggs and sausage, ignoring their tealike coffee (Rafaella did not know how to brew it), trying to get through the weekend without feeling giddy and nervous about the planned bank robbery tomorrow.

Marsh called at one that afternoon and said he had gotten no information out of Lulu and that they would be forced to release her. She would hit the streets sometime Tuesday, the day after the bank robbery. Before he hung up, he confided that he had forbidden Luciano to see them, even though he now lived next door. Marsh did not want to take any chances of them being spotted with Luciano. Fleckenstein would most certainly remember the mobster's face.

"I gotta hand it to that guy Luciano," Marsh added with an unusual chuckle, the first time Nick had recently heard him laugh. "You should see his apartments. And I do mean plural. He knocked out the wall between two of 'em, painted everything red, put in stained-glass windows probably stolen from some church, white satin drapes, fancy furniture, thick rugs. Even has a running fountain as you enter! Open the door, you think you're suddenly on Park Avenue!"

At about two, no longer able to withstand the confines of their cramped apartment, Nick cleared his throat, tossed down the crossword puzzle he had been unsuccessfully attempting to complete and said: "I'm going out."

"Out where?" Rafaella asked, looking up from the bestseller, *Gone with the Wind.*

"For a walk. Anything."

"I'd better go with you then," she sighed.

"You don't have to," he replied sullenly.

"It's not that I want to," she said, getting her coat.

Outside the wintry day was finishing. The naked brick towers of the government houses cast long shadows across Avenue D, the sun already low enough to leave the air chilled. The gray sky promised snow with its scudding low clouds.

They turned left on East Houston Street, crossed East River Drive on the overhead pedestrian pass, then walked along the baseball fields and basketball courts toward the Williamsburg Bridge. As always, Nick was amazed at the scarcity of people. Manhattan, on weekends, emptied out as regularly as low tide. The traffic was thin, and leisurely by New York standards.

Nick could no longer think of a way of approaching Rafaella. He was sure that somehow she was in cahoots with Luciano. How, he could not yet fathom. And now he had to work with her—her betrayal weighing heavily on him all the while. And yet all of that pain had a bright side since there was no choice any longer to feel tempted by Rafaella.

He was more determined now than ever to flee back to the institution of Holy Mother Church. In the last few days, he had found himself itching to solve the mystery of Joey's death simply so he could get on with his life.

They were under the Williamsburg Bridge, on the mall of the East River Park, when suddenly a man approached behind them and said: "Do not say a thing. Follow me."

Attempting not to act surprised, Nick took Rafaella's arm and guided her toward the fireboats anchored at the river's edge. The man, unknown to either of them, gestured for them to remain there and walked away.

"Maybe FBI or OSS Must be important." Rafaella was focused keenly on the river walk, trying to catch a glimpse of who would emerge.

"Just keep walking," a new voice said from behind. Immediately they were both surprised to see Fritz Fleckenstein join them, a frosty smile on his face.

"Three friends," he said, grinning at a couple who was passing, "together for a walk in the park. Isn't this nice?"

Even through her thick camel's-hair coat, Nick could see Rafaella stiffen.

"So when is it?" Fleckenstein kept his smile plastered on. He was wearing a hat slouched over his face and a heavy Irish overcoat.

"Tomorrow," Nick said reluctantly.

"Good, good! I go with you!"

Rafaella pulled up short.

"Keep walking!" Fleckenstein ordered, taking her arm. She started forward again.

"You can't do this," Nick said under his breath. "It'll upset our plans!"

"You wanted my attention, you got it!" Fleckenstein said. "Only I want my *Bund* to take credit for this! Not yourselves! Come, *Kameraden*, don't be selfish!"

Nick had no idea what to do. The robbery, staged for the *Bund,* was set to go. The actors were in place for tomorrow. The money would be taken and given back. No one hurt, since the guns used were to be loaded with blanks.

"I don't see any problem." Nick was suddenly surprised to see Rafaella smiling at Fritz. "We could use a good man!" And to Nick's embarrassment, she leaned into Fritz and added: "And so could I."

Fleckenstein's face broke open as he understood the sexual message. He looked quickly at Nick, then back to Rafaella. "You are pretty!" he said levelly to her, his eyes now twinkling with anticipation. "Even prettier than in the fun house."

"It was dark in there." Rafaella smiled back at him. "I like lots of light, don't you?"

"*Ja!*" Fleckenstein agreed lustily. He shot a quick glance at Nick's increasingly red face. "You and your husband, you are, how do you say, platonic?"

"No interest whatsoever," Rafaella whispered back.

Fleckenstein laughed loudly at that. "We are friends," he said to Nick. "No hard feelings, *Kameraden*, where it counts?"

"Don't worry about me," Nick said, trying to squelch the terrible humiliation Rafaella was causing him. "Our real love is only for Germany!"

Fleckenstein nodded, impressed. They were under the bridge and not a soul was near them. He stopped, took Rafaella's hand and, after glancing quickly around, stared deeply into her eyes. "You are the voice, then?"

Rafaella did not answer.

"You know, the voice on the phone? The one who told me about the raid?"

"That's me."

Fritz leaned in and kissed her heavily on the mouth. To Nick's chagrin, Rafaella kissed him back.

He was forced to look away. What was this goddamn traitorous woman making him feel now?! Jealousy? Rage? He realized at that moment he could easily have killed Fleckenstein with his bare hands.

When they finally pulled apart, Fritz said to her: "I

177

know where you live. I'll be there at dawn tomorrow so we can see one another in the light!"

And kissing her hand with great passion, he walked away, down the path beneath the bridge to the river's edge. There he leaped aboard a pleasure craft that suddenly appeared from somewhere. Nick noticed it had no markings on it as it pulled out into the river.

"So," Rafaella said as she started to walk, "that's how the *Bund* has been warned! Some woman's been doing it!"

"Don't change the subject!" Nick caught up to her. "What in the hell did you mean by kissing that Nazi?!"

"Why, Father! You're cursing again!" Rafaella said, stopping suddenly to face him.

"You made me feel awful!" Nick regretted his words almost before they were out. It sounded childish. But that was how he felt!

"Your feelings don't matter!" Rafaella lost her bantering tone.

They walked along together silently, Nick glaring at her. She had stopped him cold. But he refused to let it go.

"What about tomorrow?!" he demanded. "What did you mean when you said you'd see him at dawn . . . in the light?"

"It means," Rafaella said, walking faster, "I am going to put blanks in his gun so we don't have a slaughter at the bank! And if that means seducing the bastard, then so be it!"

Realizing what she planned to do, Nick found himself watching her receding back as she crossed East River Drive back to their apartment. It was clear Rafaella was continuing her betrayal—how else would this make sense?

40

THE STOLEN, 47-FOOT pleasure craft cruised down the East River, crossing beneath the Manhattan and Brooklyn bridges, then rounded the tip of Manhattan at Battery Park. Grumish motored it in slow circles for several minutes to check if they were being followed, then drove across the Hudson into New Jersey at the Morris Canal Basin.

Morris Canal was studded with oddly shaped shipping houses made of corrugated tin, asbestos, drywall and scraps of anything that could serve as a makeshift shelter. These docks were loading stations for heavy industry, and company signs hung on the dilapidated sides of the shacks.

The boat passed deeper into Morris Canal, made a right turn into a waterway that resembled the snaking pipe beneath a sink, cut its engines and floated silently to a wharf that had rotted and sunk.

Grumish and his two crewmen stepped off and tied her up. Then Fritz Fleckenstein popped his head out from the cabin, pulled the hat down over his eyes, strode quickly along the length of the boat and jumped off.

As the tin doors were rolled back on the old warehouse, Fritz stepped quickly inside. Throwing off his hat and coat, he looked around. The warehouse, which seemed insignificant from the outside, now revealed itself to be more than seventy-five feet long by thirty feet wide. Its cement floor, though old and cracked, was swept clean. Piles of German armament, including limpet mines, incendiary bombs, radios, rations, ammo and bale upon bale of copper wire, stood piled neatly along its rusting walls. Near the copper wire were rubber swim fins, oxygen bottles and face masks.

Satisfied it was all shipshape, Fritz went to the potbellied stove and warmed his hands.

"Did you succeed?" the blond man, who was called Grumish, now asked. They had not spoken on the boat.

"*Ja,* I go tomorrow to rob the bank!"

"And us?" Voss, who was tall and thin, asked eagerly.

The rest of the *Bund* who had gathered from ports up and down the coast now congregated at the iron stove. All of them had arrived except for Hulbert and Farrell, whose car had broken down and who were stranded in Norfolk.

"I do this alone," Fritz told them. "They have a plan."

"And if they do get the money"—Lorelei Hoffman appeared—"what will it do that we are not already accomplishing?"

"Without money, the longshoremen will strike, *mein Schatz!* It will cripple all ports!"

Several men clapped their leader on the shoulder. But Lorelei, now seated on a gunnysack of old wheat, stared fixedly at Fritz. He noticed and smiled. "What is it that makes you so glum?"

"There is someone waiting to see you," she said, inhaling deeply from her cigarette.

"Who?" Lorelei was acting peculiar.

"A woman," Voss said. "She is under guard in your office."

"She knew about our warehouse!" Lorelei smashed

180

out her cigarette. "How did she know that, *Herr* Fleckenstein?"

Fritz understood that Lorelei was jealous. Stupid woman! What was important was this person. How had she found out?!

Pushing his way roughly through his men, Fleckenstein marched to the little office in the corner of the warehouse. Its walls were only thin plywood, thrown together to keep out prying eyes of longshoremen, to give the foreman some privacy.

Bashing the door open with his fist, Fleckenstein charged inside.

"You!" He recognized her. "How did you find this place?"

"It doesn't matter," she said. "What matters is they know you're here!"

"Who is 'they'?" he demanded.

"The Mafia! Who do you think I mean by 'they'?"

"I don't believe you!" He swept forward and gripped her arms hard, digging in his thumbs.

"You're a fool." The woman showed no pain. "And if you want to keep me as a friend, you'll act like a gentleman!"

"Liar!" Fleckenstein could not control himself. He slapped her face. "You are not the voice! I have already met her!"

"Whoever that was," the woman said, a trickle of blood seeping from her torn lip, "was the liar. I called you at your home to warn you about the meeting taking place with Luciano. I pasted that three-by-five card up in the old Baptist church. Want to know what the card said?"

He backed off as though struck by an invisible hand. "I have been betrayed!" He clenched his huge fists and shook like he was having a seizure. "I will kill her! Kill both of them!"

She dug in her handbag, brought out a handkerchief

and held it to her lip. "I don't give a shit about you or your *Bund.*" She withdrew a Camel from her handbag and lit up. "In fact, I hate you fuckin' Nazis."

"Then why?"

She laughed sourly, took another drag. "I'd rather tell my troubles to a rat."

The woman started toward the door. "Oh, Luciano's planning on raiding you tonight."

"And the robbery?" Fritz fought to keep his anger from flaring up over that news. He had to find out all this woman knew.

"Robbery?"

"The one they are planning! The Munroes!"

"I don't know anything about that."

"But you know them?"

She opened the door, started to say something, but went out.

When she was gone, Fritz maniacally began to kick the desk. When he realized his *Bund* was watching him through the open door he kicked it one last time. "That bitch!" he screamed.

"What about that woman?" Lorelei demanded to know. "Are you just going to let her leave?"

"Of course! She is our friend! It's that Munroe cunt! She lied to me! She told me she was the voice!"

"That woman then who was just here has been helping us?" Grumish asked.

Fritz nodded, his small eyes narrowing. "So tomorrow *is* a trap!"

"Yes!"

"Then you must not go!" Lorelei came into the room and took Fritz's arm.

"Oh I will!" Fritz grinned. "But there will be a different ending than these Munroes, whoever they are, expect! And we will have a surprise for Mr. Luciano too!"

41

Midnight was the time chosen by Lucky Luciano, so Frank Costello, head bandaged, eyes swollen from his shooting trauma, met the Vapido brothers, a half-dozen button soldiers and forty handpicked longshoremen at Pavonia Avenue on the New Jersey docks. The men were armed with baseball bats and axe handles. They were not told whom they were attacking.

"We're ready." Tony Vapido bent into Costello's lighted Cadillac.

"We wait," Uncle Frank said. He looked wan and old in the interior overhead light of the car.

In a little bit, another Cadillac pulled up and Lucky Luciano got out. He was dressed in a white silk muffler and heavy black overcoat against the chilly night. Lighting up a cigarette, he waved away Costello. The businessman did not need to be seen there tonight. Besides, this was his show. Costello's Cadillac roared away.

Luciano turned as Ruthie climbed out of the car, bundled in her heavy fox fur, naked legs revealing she wore little beneath the coat. Albert Vapido approached with his brother.

"You shouldn't be here either, boss," Albert complained.

"I gotta see this!" Luciano said.

183

"But if the navy gets word . . ."

"Who's gonna know? 'Sides, we clean up these rats, I'm a national hero. Icing on the cake, boys. Time for us to kick ass, right?"

"You heard the man!" Tony Vapido told his brother. "Let's do it!"

The truckloads of longshoremen were driven down Warren Street, then onto York. Turning finally on Van Vorst, they cruised slowly, lights out, to the water's edge, where the men noisily bailed out of the trucks and charged the lighted derelict warehouse. Swinging open its unlocked doors, they found only naked light bulbs burning in their long rows above the vacant cement floor.

"What the fuck?!" Tony Vapido screamed.

"Maybe this is the wrong place!" one of the longshoremen suggested.

"Shut up, mouth!" Albert commanded. "We followed 'em here! Somethin' funny's goin' on!"

"Hey, wait a minute!" Tony pointed to the far end of the building. "There's *somethin'* down here!"

The group of men started cautiously forward.

"Maybe it's a time bomb!" somebody said.

The men dropped back, unwilling to risk their lives. The Vapido brothers went forward, finally standing over the large mound, then stooping down to peer at it closely.

Luciano's car, at his orders, drove through the open front entrance doors of the warehouse and rolled inside along the cement. He stepped out, furious.

"Ain't nobody here, Mr. Luciano," a longshoreman announced.

"I can see that, stupid!" he exploded. "What's that down there?" He was looking at the Vapido brothers shining their flashlights on the floor.

"We don't know, sir," a small man said. "Maybe a bomb or somethin'!"

"It's nothin'!" Tony suddenly yelled, seeing Luciano.

"It belongs to 'em?" Luciano demanded.

"Uh, yeah." Tony and Albert exchanged glances.

"Well, bring it here!" Luciano turned to the long-shoremen in their watch caps and rough clothes. "Maybe a clue to where the bastards went!"

"Who are the bastards, Mr. Lucky?" the small man asked.

"Nazis."

"We thought so," a big, hairy-looking gorilla muttered. The men were obviously in awe of Luciano and stayed a respectful distance from him.

"Yeah, I got a personal score to settle," Luciano was saying.

"We heard," the little man who was becoming a spokesman for them said. "We were sorry 'bout that."

"What the hell you doin'?!" Luciano screamed at the brothers when he noticed they were not coming. "Get your asses down here! I ain't got all night!"

The brothers seemed to confer, then Tony shrugged, pulled off his greasy pea coat and held it while Albert stacked some of the things left behind by the *Bund* into it.

The men watched tensely as the brothers approached, their eyes showing nothing.

"What?! What!" Luciano cried impatiently when the Vapidos stood in front of him and made no effort to open the coat. "I gotta do everything myself?"

"They was tipped, Mr. Luciano," Albert apologized. "We followed 'em here. I swear it!"

"What's in the coat?!"

"They *was* here," Tony offered also. "Take our word for it, boss!"

"I gotta bunch of fuckin' idiots workin' for me!" Luciano said. "When I say do somethin', you jump!" And he grabbed the coat from Albert and flipped it open. A small amount of steam rose up and it was a

185

moment before Lucky Luciano realized he was staring at clumps of fresh human feces.

"Animals!" He threw the coat down, outraged. "I swear on my mother's grave, they're dead!"

He got in the Cadillac. The driver did a quick U-turn in the warehouse and sped out.

42

GRUMISH DROVE HIS Studebaker with its changed license plates into the parking lot behind Dr. Schillinger's offices. He had to search for a spot to park. This was the busy time for the doctor, 2:00 A.M. until dawn. He alighted and went up the three flights of rickety wooden stairs in the back and knocked five times, one for each letter of Hitler's first name. Lorelei opened the door.

"He's downstairs with the doctor," she said. Latching the third-floor door, she led Grumish through a maze of medical equipment stockpiled there. Most of it was broken and old. Somebody had said the doctor kept it around to depreciate every year for the IRS. It was a good joke. The money the doctor saved on taxes went to support the Fatherland's activities here in America. Though not a member of the *Bund,* Dr. Schillinger was a staunch anti-Semite and believed the world would be far better off if the creeping threat of power-hungry Jews was dealt with once and for all. His favorite topic was a "final solution."

The second floor contained operating rooms. Since abortions were illegal and highly controversial in 1942, a good abortionist was hard to find. Dr. Schillinger was a skilled surgeon who had turned his talents to this much-in-demand wartime service. He had never lost a patient, never caused so much as one case of internal hemorrhaging or infection. By day, he was chief of surgery at a posh midtown Manhattan hospital.

Through a small glass window in the door, Grumish saw Dr. Schillinger, a slight, balding man with the gentle mien of a grandfather. He was working on an unconscious young woman, her legs held up and apart in stirrups, and listening to Fritz Fleckenstein, who had donned a surgical gown and mask. In operating room #21 the American *Führer* gesticulated as he spoke, telling the doctor his views on when precisely the United States would surrender.

Lorelei was standing beside Grumish, looking in through the window.

"Do we go in?"

"No, the doctor only allowed Fleckenstein in." She was staring intently, her eyes mesmerized. "Did you move the stuff?"

"All of it," Grumish said. "The men are waiting at another warehouse."

"Did the Mob come?" She seemed far away, the questions coming automatically.

"*Ja!* They found our little going-away present too." He chuckled at the memory of seeing Luciano's reaction. From where he and two of the *Bund* were hiding in the shadows of a fallen-down dock, they had had to hold in their laughter.

Suddenly the way Lorelei stiffened made him swing back to the window.

The doctor was now totally absorbed in conversation about Jews with *Herr* Fleckenstein, all the while holding up a twelve-week foetus that looked like a fully formed small infant.

"Sometimes," Lorelei said, her voice haunted, "the doctor told me if it is too big he has to cut off the head, arms and legs to get it out of the mother's uterus."

Dr. Schillinger tossed the foetus like a rubber doll into a large steel pan. To Grumish's surprise the foetus began to cry. Its gagging filled the room. He had sent hundreds of men to their death at the bottom of the ocean, yet the way the baby was wailing now made him turn away from the window.

The foetus in the stainless steel pan lay choking until it expired.

Forcing himself to look, Grumish saw that Dr. Schillinger and Fleckenstein had not broken stride in their conversation. Schillinger was making a point, waving a suction device in his hand.

"The nurse will come shortly," Lorelei whispered suddenly. "And take it to the furnace."

She pushed away and lit a cigarette.

"Don't let it get to you." Grumish tried to make a joke. "I hear we're giving the Jews the furnace treatment too."

"You wouldn't joke like that if you were pregnant." Lorelei took a deep drag and blew it toward the floor. Grumish turned and stared at her in amazement.

Fleckenstein pushed out then, ripping off his paper gown and face mask. "Ah," he said, seeing Grumish, "everything go okay?"

"Perfect." Grumish could not hide his astonishment at Lorelei's statement.

"And the Munroes, were they there?"

"No."

"Doesn't change a thing." Fleckenstein, absorbed in thought, took Lorelei's cigarette and puffed on it before giving it back.

"But what if the robbery is a trap just for you?" Grumish was worried.

"They're not interested in capturing just one man. They want all of us, remember?" Fritz turned back to the glass window. Inside, the doctor was just finishing up. "Now that we are again on the run, Dr. Schillinger has graciously allowed us to stay on his third floor. Such a loyal *Kamerad!*"

"He's a butcher!" Lorelei ground out her cigarette beneath her boot and strode away.

"What's wrong with her?" Fleckenstein asked Grumish.

Grumish shrugged evasively. "I'll go get the men." He went up the stairs toward the third floor.

Fleckenstein swung to the operating room as the doctor stepped out. "You must not toy with these Munroes." Schillinger referred back to what Fleckenstein had told him. "Do not take chances, *Herr* Fleckenstein. Kill them now!"

"*After* the robbery," Fritz promised, "when I have the money. In the meantime, I will play along with their little charade."

43

RAFAELLA LAY IN HER twin bed, tossing and twisting in the sheets. She had lived a long time without any desire to be with a man. It had been more than ten years since she had been raped in Sicily. Now all of a sudden she could not get this priest who slept less than twenty feet from her out of her mind. She hated him, and hated herself for being so adolescent.

Why had she told him everything on that train, gushing like some infantile teenager instead of a career officer, which she was? Why had she gone to his apartment? And what did she expect when he turned her down? God, it was all a mess. The robbery tomorrow morning had to be perfect, right down to the last detail in Captain Marsh's plan. And now what if that Nazi idiot showed up in a few hours?

For the thousandth time, she rolled over, trying to find a comfortable place for her hips and shoulders. The pillow felt like a rock against her face. She wanted to cry. She could feel that welling-up pressure in her throat like a balloon filling, ready to burst.

Suddenly she heard the window on the fire escape being pried open.

Quickly she faced it and was surprised to see the false dawn already showing its grayish-blue light. Outside, dimly silhouetted, was a stubby, muscular figure stooping through the window. Her gun lay a few feet away on the chair. It would do her no good. The real weapon was beneath the sheets. How ironic! It would all be just a strategic move to insure the safety of those in the bank.

"I watched you before entering." He spoke now. He was above her.

She stared up at him, naked shoulders against bleached white sheets and navy wool blankets. Strangely she found herself hoping he would not recognize the blankets. No one had foreseen that her cover would have to include her bedroom!

"You didn't think I would come?" He was grinning at her immobility.

"I knew you would," she forced herself to say huskily. Her feet and hands had become cold.

He turned and closed the window. When he faced her again, he leaned down and kissed her. Then he peeled off his coat.

As he undressed, she watched him place his nine-millimeter Luger in its holster on the floor near the bed. She was glad for the dim morning light as he crawled in beside her. It kept him from seeing her quivering chin.

He arranged himself beside her, face inches away. "We haven't got too much time. We'll have to hurry."

"I . . . know."

"Hey, maybe this wasn't such a good idea." He got angry, hearing rejection in her voice.

"No! I'm just sleepy. You . . . surprised me." She wrapped her arms around his thick, hairy waist. "It's not every morning a woman gets a man to crawl through her window, you know."

And she kissed him.

But as she did, the fat, sweating face of a monk breathed on her.

"You're naked," he said, smiling. "You *were* expecting me." He ran his hand down her tight, flat stomach and stopped on her triangle. She shivered in disgust at herself.

"Easy, easy." He misunderstood. "There's not *that* much hurry!" And lowering his massive head, he began to kiss her breasts.

44

Nick lay awake in his bedroom. He had told himself Fleckenstein would not go through with his threatened tête-à-tête. It was just a bluff. Even if the Nazi showed up, would *she* go through with it?

He awoke at one and sat up, having dreamed it was morning. But the window in his bedroom, which looked out on Rafaella's and his landing on the fire escape, was black, except for the streetlights below.

He lay back and realized he was sweating. Why was he even worrying about her? Hadn't she betrayed him? And her country?

For the rest of the night, he lay there, listening to the occasional traffic passing.

He turned to find light streaming into his room. Wide awake, he stared at the offending window. Then he heard voices next door. Fleckenstein was there.

That slimy Nazi! Well, what did it matter? Two of a kind! Let them go at it! It didn't bother him!

He rolled over and clamped the pillow over his head. That was better. He couldn't hear a thing. But he suddenly remembered Rafaella in his old apartment, her shoulders shaking violently in sobs.

"Goddamn!" It was a word he had never used.

Leaping from his bed, Nick slammed his feet down on the cold floor. The air in the room made goosebumps rise beneath his cotton pajamas, but he began to pace back and forth.

Glancing around the room quickly for a weapon, he found nothing. Just his toiletries. What was he going to do? Beat Fleckenstein to a pulp with his hairbrush?

He opened the top drawer of his bureau and took out the .38 Captain Marsh had given him. It held blanks while Fleckenstein had a real gun. And what if all this ruined the robbery set-up?

"What am I doing?!" he muttered, as he rushed out of his room.

45

Lucky Luciano RETURNED to the housing development early in the morning despite Ruthie's insistence at dropping in at Club 21 for a drink. Luciano had said it could ruin everything if the navy found out he'd been around town. So they had come home, made love and gone to sleep.

Being the trained light sleeper he was, Luciano heard footsteps on the sixth-floor metal fire ladder that angled past his two apartments. Curious and more cautious than ever after the Nazis' uncanny escape from the warehouse, he eased from his white silk sheets and, pulling on his royal-purple robe, pushed the drapes back and peered out the window. At first he saw nothing. Then a figure passed his bedroom. To his surprise, Lucky Luciano realized it was Fritz Fleckenstein!

Since he vaguely knew about the planned robbery on the Port Authority Bank, the presence of Fleckenstein was extremely disturbing. What the hell was this Nazi doing up here? And just hours after having eluded his own dragnet.

"Your ass is mine!" Luciano whispered. He went to the closet and withdrew the .38 snub-nosed pistol the Vapido brothers had illegally supplied him with. Opening the window carefully so as not to awaken Ruthie, he stepped out onto the fire escape and padded quickly forward along its icy metal surface. But the Nazi had disappeared.

He saw Rafaella's open window. Then, suddenly, it was slammed shut. Lucky quickly pressed back against the dirty bricks of the tenement. Why wasn't she shouting or something? What the hell was going on here?

He eased to the window. Rafaella looked like she was smiling while the Nazi undressed! Shit, maybe this navy bitch was a traitor. Or was this part of her act? As he watched, Fleckenstein got into bed with her. Cocking the .38 police special, Luciano threw up the window and stepped inside.

Fleckenstein, naked and completely surprised, leaped from the bed for his Luger.

"Do it and you're history," Luciano said in the half-darkness.

"Who is this guy?" Fleckenstein growled at Rafaella, who was sitting up, the sheet held tightly to her breasts.

"I don't know . . . a thief?"

Something about the expression on her face made Luciano feel uncertain.

"He's not a thief," Fleckenstein surmised. "He's wearing a goddamn robe! Who the hell are you anyway?"

"Get out of here, you, whoever you are!" Rafaella shouted.

"You heard the lady!"

"I'm not going anywhere, you prick!" Luciano shouted. But Rafaella frantically shaking her head behind the Nazi's back forced him to reconsider. Just what the fuck had he stumbled into?

"Don't I know you?" Fleckenstein suddenly started toward Luciano.

More than anything at that single moment in his life, Charlie Lucky wanted to put a hole right through that fucking handlebar moustache! As Fleckenstein advanced, he thought about it! His trigger finger danced on the slender, curved strip of metal. But, undone by a nagging feeling that he had blundered into something he knew nothing about, he backed away. If he was screwing something up, his release from prison would be in jeopardy.

"Just go, please go!" Rafaella was desperate as she sat up in bed and Fleckenstein continued to advance on a retreating Luciano.

Suddenly the bedroom door was kicked violently open. Nick stepped into the room, gun in hand. "You!" He pointed the weapon at the naked Fritz Fleckenstein.

"Not him!" Rafaella pleaded. She pointed at Luciano.

Nick, surprised to see the mobster in the room, stood for a second, stunned. Then he brought up his pistol and fired.

It amazed Lucky that Nick had done such a thing. Recoiling but feeling no pain, Lucky knew he had missed. Bringing up his own gun, the mobster aimed it at Nick, but Rafaella, kneeling up on the bed, waved frantically toward the floor. Nick shot three more times.

Lucky Luciano clutched his chest and went down.

"I've got two others in here for you." Nick swung on Fleckenstein, who had started for his own pistol. "Pick it up and I'll shoot you like a dog . . . you adulterer!"

Fritz froze.

Nick crossed the room quickly and picked up the Luger from the chair. "I'll give you this when you need it." He scooped up Fleckenstein's clothes and threw them at him. "Get dressed! Outside!"

Fleckenstein was trying to get a closer look at the

man on the floor, but his face was turned away from him.

Nick jammed his gun hard against the Nazi's naked ribs. "Time to get moving!" he told him.

"You cunt!" Fleckenstein spat at Rafaella. And he strode out.

Nick mumbled angrily at Rafaella as he closed the door behind him.

Despite the morning cold, Rafaella felt warm all over. She leaped from the bed and began to dress quickly.

"Turn your head," Rafaella commanded when she saw Luciano grinning up at her. "You could have blown everything!"

He sighed and said nothing, glad that his goof had not done any serious damage.

Outside in the living room, Fleckenstein was nearly dressed. He thought his part in this charade—for that was what it was—had gone very well. These Munroes were amateurs. But something about the way they moved tickled his memory, though they didn't exactly look like anyone he'd ever known. But he was almost sure the man "shot" in there had been the gangster Lucky Luciano. In the dim light he could not be certain. Anyway, the whole playacting had been for his benefit—that he *was* sure of!

Allowing that fool Munroe to take his gun had been a heavy price to keep his role going. When his Luger was returned, Fritz was sure it would be loaded with blanks.

Fritz tied his shoes and knotted his tie. The door to Rafaella's bedroom opened and he caught a glimpse of the vacant floor. The "body" had already disappeared. He smiled to himself, pulling on a heavy overcoat.

Robert Munroe also emerged. His door had been left open so he could watch Fritz Fleckenstein. He was dressed in a fresh business suit and seemed nervous.

"Ready?" he asked her.

"Let's do it!" she said.

"Here's your weapon back," Munroe told Flecken-stein. "Watch how you use it."

"Don't worry about me," Fleckenstein said. And without bothering to examine his Luger, which was still inside its leather holster, he put it on.

46

NATTIE WALSH EMERGED from her apartment on West Seventeenth and Seventh, hair pomaded straight back off her high forehead, held in place by a black hair net. She walked primly down to Fourteenth and Eighth Avenue and caught the IND line at precisely 7:45. Riding it uptown toward her destination of the Port Authority Bank, Nattie caught a glimpse of herself in the darkened subway's windows. Small, tight, birdlike, she looked afraid. Nattie hated that in herself. She looked away just as a black man sat down beside her. She rearranged her coat so it touched no part of him.

Automatically her nervous hands strayed to the black leather bag that sat in her lap. Nattie always carried her .25-caliber gut shooter. It made her feel safe. Right now, she envisioned the black man trying to rape her. She jumped up while he was ripping her dress off her tiny breasts, fished for her weapon, pulled it out and shot him point-blank in the stomach. Right where the gun salesman had told her to. He was the one who had called it a gut shooter!

The black man was staring at her in a peculiar way. Smiling. Nattie realized she had been reliving her nightmare again and looked away. A small amount of perspiration had risen on her moustached upper lip. She cleared her mind to calm herself. This black man was no danger. No danger, she repeated as the wheels beneath the subway clacked on.

Oh, sure it was illegal to carry a gun in New York. But weighing the consequences, she'd rather do a thousand years in a safe prison than have one of these criminal types who populated this town abuse her. Growing up around Greenwich and lower Manhattan as a child, Nattie had never worried—you used to be able to walk the streets. Now, with the influx of all these Puerto Ricans, Southern blacks, greasy Italians and loud-mouthed Irish, it had all changed.

Rapists, all of them! They said it with their eyes. When you walked by, they hooted or whistled and said things like "Hot tuna!," "How 'bout a hair sandwich, sister?" or "Catch that piece of tail!" Nattie had memorized them all. A woman received no respect. Well, she would have respect. Plenty of it. And you could bet every last nickel you owned, Natty Walsh would use her handgun if anybody tried a thing.

As she got off the subway at Thirty-fourth at Penn Station, Nattie walked quickly along her everyday route toward the Hudson, her no-nonsense flats tapping out a hurried dance as she whizzed by other pedestrians. Once, as she turned off Thirty-fourth toward the lower streets, she saw a man, about twenty, smile at her. Her hand automatically tightened around her purse so she could feel the outline of the .25. It gave her the courage to stare back at any sexual deviant!

Arriving at the Port Authority Bank on Thirtieth, Nattie swept through the front glass doors that looked out onto the bustling West Side Expressway. Five navy guards, the new ones who had arrived the day before yesterday, waved her through. It was obvious they knew who the head teller was. When they had first arrived, they had insisted on searching her handbag. Nattie had raised an awful fuss, summoning her superior, Vice-President Orion Beals, to pass her through.

That had taught these navy boys a lesson! No one fooled with Nattie Walsh!

Setting her bagged lunch, which she always brought, in the women employees' bathroom, Nattie checked to see if her hair was tight against her head, her blue-and-white polka-dotted dress presentable around her angular body. It would not do to arouse any man to lust. Satisfied at her appearance, she left the tiny bathroom and went past the vice-president's office. Mr. Beals was inside, talking with his secretary.

"Morning, Miss Walsh," he intoned as she passed.

"Good morning, Mr. Beals!" Nattie glowed at the compliment of being recognized. He was such a nice man. About her age. The image of him naked sprang into her mind. It made her momentarily confused. What a terrible thought. Where had that come from?

She walked fast across the foyer of the bank, signaled to Mrs. Kimberly, teller #3, to admit her. The buzzer sounded and the latch gate opened. Nattie strode to her position at teller #1, worked the combination on her box from memory and withdrew the drawer key.

Inserting the key, she opened the lock and pulled out her long drawer, which was empty.

The officer manager, Mr. Crowthers, wheeled up the money cart. There were stacks of hundreds, fifties, twenties, tens and fives. "Monday is payday for sailors, as you know, Miss Walsh. Please double-check my count." He handed her banded stacks of bills.

Nattie silently counted. Anything short would be deducted from her paycheck. "I have received two hundred fifty-seven thousand dollars," she announced when she finished.

"Correct," Crowthers said. "Sign for it, Miss Walsh."

She did.

Crowthers pushed on to teller #2, a young man freshly out of Columbia. An asthmatic, he had failed in his join-up efforts and was miserable he could not fight for his country. Nattie liked him. He seemed kind and was soft-spoken. And she imagined no terrible images, the kind she always had with Vice-President Beals. It was comforting to have teller #2 so near.

Nattie moved her handbag from her teller's seat to a shelf just beneath her drawer. She climbed onto the high teller's stool, scooted to the position at which she always sat and placed the stool's four legs squarely in the worn holes on the cement floor. Folding her hands, Nattie waited patiently for the other tellers to finish their counting.

When Mr. Crowthers wheeled the empty money cart back into the massive Swiss-built safe, Nattie automatically checked the clock on the wall behind her. It was 7:58 A.M. Banking hours used to begin at 10:00 A.M. But a war was on and payroll had to be met. Outside the glass doors, she could see the ship captains, both civilian and military, already lined up, ready to carry cash to the men serving on their vessels.

It made Nattie proud. She brought her knee up and pressed it against the gun she could feel outlined in her purse on the shelf. The bell rang, signaling the bank was open for business. The navy guards unlocked the front doors. The other guards, already in their positions, stood spread along the walls of the bank as the captains entered and queued up in front of previously designated tellers.

"Here we go," the young man said to Nattie, and he winked.

But Nattie was already focused on her first customer, a burly merchant marine. "Ship number and code, please," she demanded, taking his passport and registration certificate.

47

EACH GUARD HAD BEEN shown photos and knew what Nick and Rafaella looked like; Captain Marsh had also apprised them about Fritz Fleckenstein. If there was any "shooting," the guards were told to fall down and make it look convincing. The tellers had not been let in on the scheme since they were civilians and their expressions would look more real if they did not know. Besides, there was no danger from any of them since they had no weapons.

After leaving the bank with the money, Nick and Rafaella were supposed to run along the wharf above the Hudson toward Pier 68. There, a speedboat would be waiting. Before they jumped into it, Nick was accidentally to drop the bag of money in the water. Captain Marsh would be hidden with his Navy Shore Patrol beneath that pier and retrieve it. The *Bund* would be convinced about the Munroes' loyalty to their cause. The money, needed to meet payroll, would not be lost. It was an effective and ingenious strategy.

The water on the Hudson that morning was still and greasy. Along the docks, blue and red streaks of diesel oil lay in patches among the freshly recruited freighters. Farther out, no wind was up. The Hudson seemed to stretch unflowing toward the Statue of Liberty and the open sea. There had been a red dawn and sailors on the ships awoke uneasy. With the terrible decimation of past convoys, and now the promise of a stormy ocean when they sailed tomorrow, even old salts became moody.

At 8:22, Rafaella, Nick and Fritz Fleckenstein swept through the doors of the bank.

"This is a stick-up!" Rafaella shouted.

Nick covered the five navy guards. They dropped their rifles. Fleckenstein took the left side and was amused to see the guards almost eagerly lay down their arms. Just for the hell of it Fritz "shot" one. The kid overacted and crumpled dramatically onto the terrazzo floor.

"You asshole!" one of the sea captains shouted. Fritz wheeled and pointed his Luger at his face. The captain and others shrank back.

This could get dicey, Fleckenstein realized. Only some of these guys in here were on to the act. He sidled away to a teller's window. Already, the Munroes, at windows #2 and #5, were getting bags of money filled. It was strangely exhilarating to be holding an empty gun. He wheeled and pointed it at an old spinster behind window #1.

"Give me your money!" he demanded.

Nattie Walsh had seen the trio enter, had seen the guards drop their guns, had been astonished at their timidity and the officers in line! Didn't they realize the bank was being robbed? This money was vital to the war effort!

"Fill a bag!" Fleckenstein shouted when he saw Nattie was not moving but only glaring at him. "Or I'll blow a hole through that stupid face of yours!"

This man was a Nazi. She suddenly remembered seeing his photo in the back lunchroom of the bank. Moral duty in the form of bile rose to her throat. She screamed at him: "Never!"

To Fleckenstein's astonishment, he saw a small-caliber pistol appear in the woman's hands.

"Nazi pig!" Nattie screamed. She fired.

The bullet whistled over Fleckenstein's right shoulder, inches below his ear, ricocheted off the floor and whined into the front glass door, shattering it. Sea captains fell to the floor. Guards rolled for cover. Nick and Rafaella swung in astonishment.

Fritz Fleckenstein did what came naturally. He fired back.

The muzzle velocity struck Nattie in the face. Her trigger finger jerked. Another shot went over Fritz's left shoulder and hit Vice-President Orion Beals, who, standing by his office door, had his hands raised. Clutching his groin, he fell to the floor, moaning loudly. The guards seemed undone. None of this was supposed to happen.

Fleckenstein stepped back and continued to fire. Paper wads from the blanks struck Nattie in the chest and arms, stinging her. She continued to fire. The third shot struck teller #2. He fell unconscious off his teller's chair, blood spurting from his wrist. Pieces of that same bullet struck a navy captain in the foot. Nattie emptied the gun. A fourth and fifth bullet found their targets in two of the guards: one hit a rifle and sent splinters from the stock into the man's finger; the other struck a heavy-duty boot and lodged innocuously in the sole.

The sixth and last bullet struck the edge of the marble on Nattie's teller's counter. It disintegrated and the shrapnel flew back into Nattie. Unaware of her bleeding hands, she continued to squeeze her eyes shut and click the empty revolver, spraying imaginary bullets around the bank.

"Jesus!" Rafaella shook her head when the shooting stopped. She got to her feet and ran toward the doors.

"Everybody stay down!" Nick ordered when he saw several officers start to rise from the floor.

"Crazy old broad!" Fleckenstein was shaken too as he gained the front doors. There was moaning everywhere. Behind the counter, Nattie Walsh was still shooting.

They ran along the wharf. Nick was carrying both bags of money. Halfway between the Port Authority and Pier 68, Nick tripped on a rail used by a mobile crane. The bags went sailing into the Hudson.

"Oh, no!" Rafaella looked dismayed.

"Sorry!" Nick said, rising and peering over the side of the quay to the bank's canvas bags that were now floating in the river.

Behind them, sirens started up.

"We've got to go!" Fleckenstein shouted. He didn't seem dismayed at all.

They continued toward their designated spot at which their speedboat would be waiting.

"No! Here!" Fritz motioned them to follow him as the luxury boat that had picked him up the other day appeared. Reluctantly they got down into the stern.

Nick noticed an unmarked outboard spurt toward the floating bags.

Good, he thought. Marsh has got them.

Suddenly, above them, there was the sound of automatic weapon fire. They wheeled to see Fritz Fleckenstein standing atop the cabin with a .45 machine gun in his hands. Two other men on topside began firing from the wheel. Navy men in the outboard threw themselves down as pieces of transom chipped off their boat.

Raising his head cautiously above the padded gunwale, Nick saw Marsh reluctantly order a retreat.

In a moment, one of the men, whom Nick recognized as the blond he had hit on board the *Liberty* and who had taken them to Coney Island, jumped down with a boathook and retrieved the dripping sacks of money. Then the driver gunned their luxury craft and they shot off across the Hudson. The Port Authority and piers were being left far behind.

Fleckenstein climbed down the ladder, his Thompson pointed directly at them.

"Well, I'd say the robbery was a success, wouldn't you?!" he screamed over the roar of the diesels. "Now there's only one thing left to do!"

"And what would that be?" Nick smiled.

"Find out just who you really are! And why this was all an act for my benefit!"

Rafaella reflexively drew her gun.

"Go ahead!" Fleckenstein shouted. "But this one has real bullets!"

"Hey, c'mon!" Nick shouted up. "We should be having a drink to celebrate our victory!"

Fleckenstein looked amazed. "Well, I'll be!" he screamed. He slapped his leg in recognition. "From this angle I can really see your faces! The priest and the lieutenant! You had me fooled with all that makeup. Funny how when you think someone's gone, you don't give 'em a second thought!"

"We're the Munroes!" Rafaella stood defiantly. "And we're on your side!"

"I don't know how you escaped that car crash," Fritz screamed back. "But who you are now is dead!"

48

To Fleckenstein's surprise and chagrin, the total take from the Port Authority Bank was $21,600.

"That stupid bitch!" he said when they had arrived at the back parking lot of Dr. Schillinger's abortion clinic in Brooklyn. "If that old bag didn't have that gun, we'd have been able to stay there and get millions!" He smashed his fist into the side of the blue Ford they were standing beside.

"What do we do with these two?" Grumish asked, holding a gun on Nick and Rafaella in the back seat. Their hands were cuffed in front of them.

"Take the priest to our usual place," Fritz ordered. "For her, I got plans!" He reached roughly inside and dragged Rafaella out.

Nick lunged and grabbed for her. Grumish brought down the butt of his Luger on his head.

"You bastards!" Rafaella, seeing Nick unconscious and his head bleeding, fought loose momentarily from Fleckenstein.

"How sweet. You like priests, huh?" Fleckenstein snarled.

Rafaella swung her manacled fists up and caught Fleckenstein on the chin. Infuriated, he grabbed her and slapped her harshly.

"Herr Fleckenstein, *Herr* Fleckenstein!" Grumish

whispered in warning. Voss, the driver, was also turned in the front seat, concerned. "Someone might see you!"

Fritz grabbed Rafaella by the hair. "I oughta kill you here. But I'm going to see how good you really do fuck!" He dragged her toward the clinic's outside stairs that led to the third floor.

The Ford sped out of the parking lot and joined the traffic on Schermerhorn, passing the skid-row streets of Brooklyn that were filled with growing bands of roving juvenile delinquents, the mentally ill, winos and derelicts. At Clinton Street, Voss turned the car toward their killing ground in distant Long Island. Nick, unconscious, lolled back and forth in the back seat of the automobile.

One by one they took her.

She lay gagged, arms and legs bound to the bedposts, still wearing her long coat, thrown open to reveal the smooth lank of her naked body. Fleckenstein was first. He pumped a long time, concentration broken by her steady eyes which gazed back at him. Suddenly he pulled out, fed up. Grasping his member, he furiously ejaculated on her. She closed her eyes in triumph.

Other *Bund* entered her when Fleckenstein had left.

Spread-eagled, she did not know how many, since she had closed her eyes. She made herself relax and lie there like a piece of dead meat, feeling nothing, aware only of the shaking of the small bed, not hearing the moans and grunts.

Someone made the joke that she was a sperm bank and deposits were being made.

Who was it? Farrell? Keller? Frame? She had heard all those names called out.

This man was hurting her. She tried to roll away. Angrily he slapped her face hard. She struggled against him, ripping away the towel that held her ankle, kneeing him hard in the groin. He roared in protest. Fleckenstein appeared, tore the gag from her mouth.

"We're not finished, Navy!" he grinned and stuck a plastic mask over her face. It smelled sickeningly sweet.

She struggled, kicking her free foot wildly in the air, and could hear the men laughing at her. Then blackness rolled across her open eyes and she felt herself sinking down, and it was the monks howling while they took her again and again.

49

FROM A WINDOW inside a tiny recovery room of the abortion clinic, Lorelei Hoffman had watched Fleckenstein roughly shove Rafaella across the parking lot, then up the wooden stairs toward the third floor. What was he going to do with her? She knew the woman was their enemy. But normally, executions were performed at the burnt-out toy factory on Long Island. This woman was good-looking, even beautiful.

Forcing herself from her bed, Lorelei reached for her robe. Dr. Schillinger at her request had aborted her last night. Pregnant two months, he had said. She had closed her eyes and waited for the foetus to cry but there had been no sound. With his horseshoe-shaped cutting tool, the doctor had silenced it inside her. She vowed never to tell Fleckenstein what she had done. It was her business. But so was this woman he was with now! Forgoing her slippers, she limped painfully out the door of her ascetic room and headed up the corridor to the elevator.

Fleckenstein was not visible when Lorelei opened the door on the third floor. Some of the *Bund* were playing cards to while away the time before the convoy sailed the following night. Their jobs were nearly done, except for one final ship.

"Where is *Herr* Fleckenstein?" she asked Hulbert, who was playing poker.

"I have not seen him." He did not look up.

The other men would not look at her either. Lorelei turned her gaze onto Fleckenstein's makeshift bedroom, a corner partitioned by sheets on clotheslines.

"I would not go back there right now," Hulbert said. "Why don't you join us for some cards, huh?" He scooted his chair over to make room for her at an old examining table, which served as their playing area.

She walked away, weaving through the stacks of doctor's-office furniture: old X-ray machines, dusty baby bassinets, glass-faced storage cabinets, porcelain bedpans, catheters and the *Bund*'s row of stained, sheetless hospital beds. As she approached Fleckenstein's corner, she could hear murmuring.

Unhesitatingly she advanced to the nearest sheet and yanked it back on its runner. Fleckenstein, sitting on the bed, whipped around at the intrusion.

"Get out of here!" He had his hand on the woman's naked thigh. She was wearing only her shoes and knee-length stockings and her long camel coat. The woman appeared drugged and was only semiconscious. But even drugged, she was pushing at him, moaning something unintelligible, distinctly negative.

"Do I mean nothing to you?" Lorelei exploded, sweeping into the partition.

Fleckenstein rose, stunned. He watched Lorelei shrink into a sobbing puddle, shoulders folding in. The woman on the bed moaned and tried to rise, attempting to pull her only garment, the long coat, around her nakedness.

"Hulbert, Keller!" Fleckenstein shouted to his men at the other end of the big room.

The two men appeared at once.

"*Jawohl!* Herr Fleckenstein!" they saluted.

"Take the enemy out of here!" He shot a thumb toward the bed.

"And do what?" Hulbert wanted to know.

Fleckenstein bent solicitously to Lorelei Hoffman, who was gaining control over her weeping. "What do you want done with her?"

"Kill her!" she muttered.

"Of course, my dear Lorelei."

"Put her on a ship. One that will be sunk tomorrow!" Lorelei loved her thought.

"Excellent, my little *schatzy!*" Fleckenstein squared his shoulders ramrod straight. "And will that please you?"

"Very much!"

"We have one ship remaining to be sabotaged?" Keller suggested. "The *Liberty.*"

"Put this trash in its hold. Lock her in tight. Tomorrow she will die at sea."

Hulbert and Keller roughly rolled up Rafaella in the blanket and carried her through the broken medical equipment, then out the exit door.

"I have made a decision," Fleckenstein announced solemnly. "I wish you to bear a male child for me!"

"But you already have three children."

"By that cow Lulu. Two dumb oxen boys and a girl who will grow fat and lazy like her mother." He raised her chin with his index finger. "When I saw you cry a moment ago, I knew I loved you, Lorelei. We will raise pure, intelligent children. Aryan stock! The best in the world!"

"But how?! In this time and war, we . . ."

"Shhhh," Fleckenstein said, lowering his voice, checking that no one was near. "I have already arranged for a submarine to pick me up at Montauk Point tomorrow night. My work here is finished. My face is too well known for me to be effective. So I return to our homeland to fight the war there."

"And the *Bund?*"

"They will carry on," Fleckenstein said evasively, eyeing the groups of card players and sleepers in the big room.

"But without you, they will . . ."

"We all have our destinies," Fleckenstein intoned. "And while there is no room for all of them on the U-boat, there is for you. Will you come with me, my pet? I want you now, Lorelei! I have to have you! I want to be inside you. Tell me you love me, Lorelei, my *Kamerad!*"

"With all my heart and soul!" Lorelei said, opening her arms, smiling and trying to hide her fear of how she was about to be hurt. But she could tell him nothing.

The sounds behind the sheets were unmistakably that of lovemaking. The men around the poker table tried to ignore the cries of pain from the woman and the savage grunts from their leader. But like Hitler, this *Führer Herr* Fleckenstein had the right to choose with whom he wished to mate. The leader's seed was the best. The purest got the pure. That was what they were fighting for, wasn't it?

"I'll see you and raise you a dollar," Mann stated solemnly, even though he was bluffing.

50

THE OLD TOY factory at Mintville on Long Island had closed long ago. Abandoned by its owners because of soil and well contamination caused by the massive use of paint chemicals, the burnt-out concrete structure was off-limits to neighborhood children. The factory itself was an eyesore and dangerous, its polluted wells drilled to draw up water from the aquifer that lay beneath the bedrock, deep and dark and smelly and open to the morning sky. The gossip around Mintville was that it was a favorite "dumping place" for the Mafia and that there were bodies in the factory's wells.

Voss swung the Ford onto the grease-soaked dirt in front of the factory and killed the motor. Salt air from nearby Long Island Sound had eaten away the cyclone fences, leaving only grotesque slashes of rust hanging like cobwebs off poles. Several rotting car bodies lay nearby.

Grumish got hold of Nick, who was still out, and opened the door. "Give me a hand," he said to Voss. "He's big."

They got him under the arms and dragged him across the filthy yard, shoes creating little trenches.

"Put him inside?" Voss asked. "Milty should be gone by now."

Grumish chuckled. A member of the *Bund,* Milty, had been suspected of being an informant to the FBI. It was never proven. But Fleckenstein's order was law. It was now more than a year since Milty had plummeted down the big cistern inside the factory; even his bones should be gone.

Nick was awake. He tried not to move as he was being dragged, tried only to open his eyes. But he could not focus and his head felt like someone was beating on it. The coagulated blood that had dripped down his forehead had sealed one eye partly shut. Desperately he tried to make his mind work. What could he do? These two Nazis were strong and he could barely lift his head.

They entered through doors hanging off their hinges. Nick saw the floor was made of rough-hewn wooden planks. Rotten. Old.

"Careful," Nick heard Grumish say. "These boards are weak!"

In almost the same instant, there was a cracking and Voss said: "Jesus! They're twice as bad as when we were here last time!"

"Put him down," Grumish said. "I want to check out the hole first."

Nick felt himself being dropped. Unable to support himself, he gritted his teeth to keep from crying out as his head banged down convincingly on the floorboards.

He heard them cross the floor. He raised himself very carefully. Trying to concentrate, he watched them gingerly test different boards as they worked their way toward the well in the corner. Several times boards cracked and they stepped back quickly and circled around the dangerously weak areas. Nick memorized every move.

He thought about running. He could get up now and maybe make the car. But he was almost sure he had suffered a concussion. He would not be able to drive . . . nor even walk far. The only way he could escape would be to kill these two.

They were bending over the low-walled well at the far wall, peering down into it.

He made himself stand. Dear God, his legs were weak! Throwing the weight of his torso forward, he forced himself to ease forward. Just another five seconds! Please, God, let the floor beneath his feet be firm! He moved quickly, silently, avoiding the weak boards.

"Can't see the bottom," Voss was saying as he peered down the deep shaft.

"Drop something." Grumish searched at his feet for a piece of board.

Nick froze, seeing the tall man bend for the nearby scrap of wood. But the Nazi did not turn around.

Voss dropped the board into the well and in four seconds, there was a reassuring splash. "Deep," he said just as Nick drove his shoulder into him.

It took Grumish only a moment to realize Voss was falling into the well. He grabbed for him but Voss's legs disappeared over the edge of the low concrete wall. As he drew his Luger, he heard Voss strike the polluted water far below.

The priest was attacking again. It was an easy shot. Grumish raised his pistol to fire. But the priest tripped and fell through an opening in the floor.

"Help me!" Nick begged as he caught himself on the edge of the hole.

Grumish could see the priest hanging onto a board. He was done for. It was all over. He turned back to the cistern. He could hear Voss far below whimper: "My eyes . . . Grumish? I'm burning up!"

"I have to get a rope to get you out," Grumish called down.

"The acid . . . it burns . . . everywhere!" Voss cried.

The priest needed attending first. One shot between the eyes. Then his friend Voss.

Hurrying toward Nick, who was still hanging on, helpless, Grumish cocked the Luger. This would be quick. But on his third step, the floor collapsed beneath him!

In that millisecond, feeling himself drop into clear space, Grumish shot out his hands. Clawing for a hold, he caught onto the edge of the hole he had made but those planks, rotted through, gave way and he slipped down further until he was dangling by a single hand. Forty feet below, twisted pilings and a sloshy dark pool of acid beckoned.

The plan had worked. The German had even allowed his friend to hurry him up. With great effort, Nick pulled himself up, the floorboards creaking as he levered his chest onto the surface, then rolled over.

Carefully picking his way across the floorboards he'd memorized, he arrived back at Grumish. From the well, Voss's voice was barely audible. It sounded like he was drowning.

"For God's sake!" Grumish screamed. "You're a priest! You must help me! Help both of us!"

"How do you sabotage our ships?"

"You set that trap deliberately! You wanted me to walk to you."

"Yes."

Grumish lunged wildly for a better hold. His fingers were slipping.

"Please, Father! I am a Catholic!"

"So is Adolf Hitler. How do you sabotage ships?"

"You're not a priest!" Grumish bellowed as he fell.

Nick looked down to see him impaled on a sharp piling. It protruded through his stomach. With a sickening cry, the Nazi expired.

"Maybe I'm not a priest," he whispered, fighting off the dizziness that was making everything swim suddenly. "But I am an American!" He pushed back from the hole, terrified at falling in.

Lying down in a safe spot, he knew he had to rest, but before he knew it, he was asleep.

51

"Looks like we got here a little late," Lucky Luciano said when Nick opened his eyes. Luciano was bending over him, grinning his shark's smile. He stuck out his hand and helped Nick up.

"What time is it?"

"'Bout five."

"I've been sleeping for six hours!?" Nick rubbed his head, which was only slightly throbbing now.

"Ain't you glad I showed up to rescue you, Father?" Luciano walked with him toward the door.

"It doesn't change anything!" Nick grunted. "For all I know, you and the Nazis are working together!"

"Hey, hey, Father. Those are powerful words!"

"Oh, yeah? Then just what were you doing in Rafaella's bedroom? And don't tell me you didn't know Fleckenstein was going to be there?!"

"Say"—Luciano changed the subject, knowing there was no use explaining—"where *is* that girlfriend of yours? They kill her or somethin'?"

"She's not my girlfriend!" Nick protested loudly. "I'm a priest!"

"Sure, sure," Luciano said. "My eyes must be bad."

Nick strode angrily across the floor, ignoring the cracking sounds, and shot through the open doorway. Luciano grinned and followed.

Nick stopped in the yard. There were at least five carloads of Mafiosi.

"Thought I'd come prepared." Luciano shrugged. "Just in case you were still alive."

"Yeah"—Nick spun on Luciano—"and just how did you know I was here?"

Luciano suddenly seemed nervous. He smiled a little too broadly and said: "The Vapidos was doin' a little, uh, business for me around here. I mean, we use this place sometimes. And they saw that Ford parked there. Well, they never forget a car, right?"

"You're full of little surprises," Nick spat angrily. "Full of angles! That why you got Rafaella working for you? To cover that angle too?!"

"That Lieutenant Massaro and me got nothin' goin'."

"Don't give me that innocent stuff. I'm onto you! I saw her with Polakoff, your messenger boy! I saw the way you reacted to her last name at the farmhouse!"

"Listen," Lucky said, the easygoing smile he wore all the time slipping away now, "Rafaella's uncle Joe Massaro brought her to the states. He was the head of the New York Mob and my boss . . . until someone killed him. I knew she was around here somewhere. I just never met her before!"

"She works for you!"

"She doesn't work for me, you imbecile! Can't you tell anything? She HATES me! I took over from her uncle Joe!"

Nick felt like someone had socked him in the gut. If this was true, Rafaella was no traitor to her country. She had not been working for the Mob. All the things she had told him were true . . . including the parts about the monks of Mazzarino raping her and killing her father and brothers. Even coming to his apartment that night was real. She *had* wanted him.

"I saw her meet with your attorney on the docks," Nick resumed accusingly.

"Look," Luciano said, pointing to the highway and a blue-and-white navy truck that was appearing. "Here comes the captain. I called him when we found you were out here. Why don't you ask him about Polakoff?"

The navy transport swung into the yard, its back covered with a tarpaulin. "Father!" Marsh greeted him as he jumped down from the cab and twenty Shore Patrol began bailing out of the truck.

Nick strode toward him, determined to nail Luciano if he was lying about Rafaella. "Captain," Nick said, without returning the greeting and causing Marsh to frown as he heard the intensity in his question, "what was going on between Lieutenant Massaro and Abraham Polakoff?"

"She . . . was acting on my orders, conveying my agreement not only to allow Lucky here out of prison for the set-up but to let him stay until the convoy sails tonight."

Nick felt like a fool. Rafaella had opened up to him and he had failed her.

"The *Bund*'s got Lieutenant Massaro." Nick forced himself to focus. "We've got to free her!"

"Think you can locate their hiding place?" Marsh was intensely interested.

"I can try. I remember the building. I made a mental note of the cross-streets." Nick tried to picture it. "Schermer . . . Schermerhorn and . . . something."

"That's in Brooklyn!" Luciano fingered the location.

"Then we've got 'em!" Marsh declared.

Nick, ignoring his feelings of weakness, stepped up

onto the running board and pulled himself inside the cab.

Luciano ran to his limo. The cars with the Mafia men inside pulled out past the lumbering navy truck. With Luciano's Cadillac in the lead, the force sped toward Brooklyn.

52

It was nearly sunset when they arrived at Dr. Schillinger's clinic. Nick could see the lighted docks across the river illuminating the convoy. Last-minute loading was taking place for its imminent departure.

The truck pulled up on Schermerhorn and the Shore Patrol, in their neat white spats and gloves, jumped out. Shoulder to shoulder with the mobsters, they ran toward the clinic. The Mafia were brandishing pistols, the navy carbines. At Marsh's signal, Luciano led his men to the rear of the building through the parking lot. Marsh, with Nick at his side, rushed the front door.

The office area, filled mostly with pregnant young women, rang with hysterical screams as the navy tromped past them into operating rooms. Dr. Schillinger, in surgical gown and mask, emerged from one of them enraged. "What is happening?" he demanded. Nick shoved the doctor as he ran up the stairs, knocking him to the floor.

Schillinger rose and ran after them, cursing obscenities, as the navy and Mafia jammed up the stairs too. Together, they searched the second floor, then broke the door down on the third.

The *Bund,* hearing the commotion below, was ready. The first wave of navy coming through the door were cut down in a hail of automatic gunfire. The Mafia, being wilier, popped off two of the Nazi gunmen, then dove through the door. In a brief but fierce gunfight, four *Bund* members were killed.

Searching the third floor and finding it empty, Nick, Marsh and Luciano led the combined forces onto the roof. There they found the rest of the *Bund*. Schillinger's building was not connected to any other, so the *Bund* had been forced to make their last stand there.

The navy lobbed fragmentary grenades and killed three of them that were firing from behind the chimney. Bricks blew down into the parking lot below, denting cars.

When Captain Marsh tossed another grenade at them, the rest of the *Bund* decided they had enough and surrendered. Altogether, counting the dead, Marsh realized they had captured fourteen of the twenty-seven members in the *Bund*. With the two killed by Father Remington at the toy factory, that made sixteen. Eleven were yet missing, including Fritz Fleckenstein and Lorelei Hoffman. Where were they?

The survivors assembled on the roof were questioned immediately. But they refused to speak. One of them spat in Marsh's face. Schillinger, still ranting and threatening to sue everyone who had forcibly entered his establishment, tried to call the police. Marsh had him handcuffed with the rest.

"None of these are going to help us," Marsh told Luciano and Nick.

"I can make 'em talk," Luciano boasted. "Just give me five minutes with 'em."

"Captain Marsh!" a lieutenant called from below. "Radio message, sir!"

Marsh, followed closely by Nick, strode down the building's outside wooden exit stairs to the parking lot.

"It's the Fleckenstein house, sir!" A gawky, skinny young officer in the truck's cab handed the captain the message. "It came in code, sir!"

"What does it say?" Luciano asked, appearing as the captain gazed at the complicated ciphers.

"Pay dirt!" Marsh said under his breath. He turned to Luciano and Nick. "I had the Fleckenstein house watched just in case something like this happened!"

"The *Bund* brought Rafaella there?" Nick asked excitedly.

"I wish." Marsh handed the secretly coded sheet back to the lieutenant. "But we did get the head honcho. For some reason, Fritz showed up to get some things. Seems he was going on a trip! And he was with Lorelei Hoffman! My men have them both under arrest!"

"But that still leaves nine others?" Luciano was lighting up a cigarette, cupping it against the cold wind coming off the East River.

"Fleckenstein will tell us where they and Rafaella are!" Nick ran toward the navy truck.

"How will you make him do that, Father? By blessing him?" Luciano called out after him. His men, who were standing around him now, laughed.

"He's right, you know." Marsh swung up in the cab also as Nick started the engine. "Fleckenstein is one tough sonofabitch. We'll never make him talk either!"

"You want us to go with 'em, boss?" Tony Vapido approached Lucky Luciano as first Nick's and then the other navy truck filled with the prisoners swung out of Dr. Schillinger's parking lot.

"Naw. You boys go down to the docks, keep a watch out for kraut faces."

"How 'bout you, Lucky?" Meyer Lansky stepped forward. Lucky had noticed him earlier. He had been

228

impressed by the way the little Jew had shot one of the *Bund*. Still, a Jew was a Jew. Couldn't trust 'em.

"Don't worry 'bout me," Luciano told Lansky for the benefit of his gang. "Me, I better tag along with that priest, case he ain't up to it."

As his men roared at the implication, Lucky Luciano flipped his butt away and got into his limo.

53

NINE MEMBERS OF the *Bund*—Hulbert, Keller, Fechner, Heim, Myrdahl, Farrell, Frame, Halle and Kieser—as they had done every night for the past week, pulled into the New Jersey Hoboken terminal. Myrdahl, who was driving slowly, watched carefully for cops. Farrell and Hulbert sat up front with him in the Princeton moving van, guns ready in case of any trouble. Once a cop passed in front of them and flipped on his red light, only to pull over a speeding motorist. They continued on to their newly rented warehouse, which replaced the previous one on the Morris Canal Basin.

The truck stopped just as the sun went down over the New Jersey cliffs. It stained the Hudson bright red, then orange and finally purple. For the *Bund*, it was just another day's work. The last, they had been told by Fleckenstein. As of tonight the convoy would be totally rigged. The only difference tonight was Hulbert and Keller were in charge of a package—to be delivered to the *Liberty*.

The woman had been bound with rope and gagged with heavy swirls of electrician's tape. She was naked, even though her coat had been buttoned around her. All afternoon she had lain in the back of the truck, which had been locked and parked in Dr. Schillinger's lot. It did not matter that it was hot or that she had been without water for more than six hours. She was going to die anyway.

Silently the nine members of the *Bund* undressed and pulled on swimming trunks, then rubber fins and oxygen tanks and finally masks, which they spat in and rested on top of their heads. For these nine, it would be a four-thousand-foot swim underwater to Pier 46.

Since they had only nine scuba outfits, the woman would be floated on the surface in a small dinghy. If there was any trouble, they had been ordered to kill her quickly with their underwater knives. It seemed silly to take this woman all the way over to Pier 46. But an order was an order.

When the sun was gone entirely and the lights from Manhattan were the only source of illumination in the sky, the *Bund* dropped into the oily water at the warehouse's edge and started across the Hudson. They kept a keen eye out for the Coast Guard cutter *Dolly Madison,* which patrolled this section of the Hudson. They carried no bombs. No radio transmitters. No limpet mines to be used on the sides of unsuspecting ships. But it was a slow swim because each man was laden with a large coil of thin copper wire.

Hulbert, Keller and Kieser, in addition, pulled the small rowboat in which lay the woman.

54

The Fleckenstein house was shabby and small. Leaning out a side kitchen window, Nick could have touched the tract house next door.

He found it was in a poor Brooklyn neighborhood and the cars parked in the driveways were old Chevys or Fords—not a Lincoln or even a Packard in sight. Kids stood out on the sidewalk and watched the commotion as navy, FBI and Mafia filtered in and out or hung around on the front steps. More than fifteen official cars, including the navy truck, were parked out front.

Lorelei Hoffman was being guarded in the living room while Lulu and the Fleckenstein children, two little boys and a girl, sat together in the only bedroom, the girl holding her mother's hand while she wept unconsolably. It was hard to tell what was causing her to cry the louder, her husband being captured or the fact he had been planning on leaving with another woman. She kept begging the FBI men to spare her husband, yet cursing him in the next breath.

At the kitchen table, Fleckenstein, smoking, could hear his wife. "Tell her to shut up, will somebody?" he suddenly shouted.

"You're not giving orders anymore," Captain Marsh

told him. "Now for the last time, where is Lieutenant Rafaella Massaro?"

"Never heard of her." Arrogantly the Nazi stood up. "I got my rights! You got no evidence on me and you know it!"

One of the FBI men came forward quickly and slammed Fleckenstein back into the wooden chair so hard that it cracked.

Nick was at the end of his rope. A ball of flame was building inside his belly. At this very moment, Rafaella could be dying.

"*Sieg heil, Sieg heil, Seig heil!*" Fleckenstein was laughing.

"How do you sabotage the ships?" Marsh demanded. "Time bombs, incendiary devices? How, dammit!"

"I will never tell you anything! You can kill me! I will never talk! *Heil,* Hitler!"

Marsh turned away. The FBI chief named Baker, who had captured Fleckenstein, came forward and they huddled together. Nick could hear Baker. ". . . it'll take days, but we have methods to break him. Let us take over, Captain."

Days! By that time, Rafaella could be dead! No trace of her! He would never even know what they had done to her. Nick noticed Baker's holstered revolver inside his coat. He had to do something—and right now, he did not care about his own life.

Nick crossed the room, and as he passed the FBI man, he angled out rapidly, fingers closing on the butt of the pistol inside his jacket. With all his might, he jerked it free.

"Hands up!"

Marsh turned, as did the FBI and navy personnel. They stared at him as if this were some kind of a joke.

"I'm *not* fooling, Captain!" Nick screamed.

233

"Put that gun down, Father!" Marsh commanded him. "Have you gone crazy?!"

Fleckenstein was peering at Nick curiously. From the corner, Luciano tried to hide his smile.

"Let's go, up, up!" Nick motioned to Fritz. "We're leaving! NOW!"

Nick threw open the back kitchen door. "You too, Captain Marsh! You're coming along as insurance so I don't get shot in the back!"

Marsh raised his hands. "Drop your weapons, men," he ordered.

The Navy Shore Patrol, who had been hoping for a different kind of command, now reluctantly lowered their carbines.

The other G-men hesitated. "We've got him outnumbered," one said. "We can take him!"

"Don't be a chump!" Luciano was on the FBI in a flash, pulling his .38 from his shoulder holster and throwing it to the floor. "We don't need a bloodbath here! I ain't ready to die!"

Nick was surprised at Luciano jumping to his aid. To his delight, he now saw the gangster wink conspiratorially. Nick grabbed Fleckenstein around the neck and threw him roughly through the open door, then swung on Marsh. The captain stepped outside.

The three of them went down the side of the house and emerged on the brown front lawn. The FBI men, Mafia and the Shore Patrol drew their weapons in alarm.

"Don't!" Marsh screamed. "He'll kill me! Can't you see that?"

Nick pushed Fleckenstein into the front seat of the truck. He told Marsh to drive. Fleckenstein got in the middle. Keeping the men covered in the front yard but being careful to point his weapon well away from the gathering children and neighbors, Nick got in and slammed the door.

Marsh started the truck and they drove off.

Luciano rushed to the front of the house. The navy and FBI were picking up their guns.

"Let's go!" Baker, the FBI chief, shouted, running out. "We can still catch 'em in that slow truck!"

"You're not going anywhere!" Luciano appeared and grabbed away a carbine from a surprised navy guard. He leveled the rifle. "Least . . . not for a couple minutes or so."

55

At Dock 46, the night lights were on. Longshoremen were still loading the *Liberty* in preparation for its departure with over a thousand soldiers tomorrow. Admiral Colditz, at Captain Marsh's suggestion, had increased navy guards on the ship. They were lined bow to stern, wary-eyed and watchful, stopping and checking immediately any unfamiliar faces.

Hulbert and Keller floated the small rowboat with Rafaella beneath the overhang of the huge ship's stern. There in its shadow, beside the gigantic rudder and submerged propeller, the rest of the *Bund* had also gathered. Hulbert pointed down into the water. The men slipped the rolls of copper wire off their shoulders. Fechner, who had the Greek fire welding torch, signaled he was ready and in unison the seven Nazis bent double, kicked over and submerged beneath the vessel.

Hulbert peered over the edge of the boat and saw the fierce eyes of the woman. She did not look scared. It made him wary. This was a dangerous animal, a soldier who, given any opportunity, could kill him. He was glad she was trussed up tightly.

He rolled into the rowboat, took the rope they had used to tow the dinghy and hooked it beneath the woman's arms, then tied a bowline knot beneath her

236

breasts. The coat had hitched up between her legs and he could see goose pimples. She was cold.

Tying the rope around his waist, he slipped off his fins, reached up to the propeller drive shaft and pulled himself up. Carefully he balanced atop the huge shaft, caught hold of the rudder housing and then climbed upward, hand over hand. Keller, still in the water, watched from below.

At deck level, Hulbert crouched before swinging over the stern railing, listening intently for any voices. When he heard none, he untied the rope from around himself, retied it to the railing above, then stood and hopped over it.

A single guard was looking away from him, eyeing the business on the docks below, men loading pallets, swinging them up by crane. Hulbert tiptoed quickly on bare feet. When he was behind the navy guard, he clasped his hand over the sentry's mouth, brought up his two-edged underwater knife and rammed it beneath his right ear. As he lowered the brain-dead guard to the deck, he could feel warm blood across his hand and arm. He pulled the corpse behind a lifeboat.

Now he returned to the stern, untied the rope from the railing and began to pull up the woman. Though she was slender, she weighed a ton. He could not afford to waste time checking his back for more guards. It was hard work and it seemed an eternity before Hulbert managed to catch hold of her coat and swing her up over the railing.

Rafaella, gagged and bound, suffered silently. Even with the excruciating pain the rope caused in tearing at her breasts and muscles, she did not so much as whimper.

Immediately after the Nazi had her aboard, he spun and checked around.

No one had come this way. For a moment, he rested,

close to exhaustion. Then, in the lights from the docks, he caught the woman silently glaring at him.

Rising, he dragged her by the rope across the newly painted metal deck toward the nearest cargo hold. The stern, as he had known, was always the first loaded. He hoped they had not yet locked that hold door.

Crouching behind the raised well of the hold, he tried the door and found it free. The padlock, open yet, swung in its accompanying hasp.

He picked up the alarmingly calm woman, catching hold of the rope to let her down. Lowering her down into the hold, he had no idea how far it was to the bottom of the ship or if he had enough rope. He had not thought that far. Besides, he told himself, it did not matter. Fleckenstein would not care if she died with a broken arm or some other minor mishap.

With less than thirty feet played out, the rope went slack. He knew the woman was resting on something. Dropping in the rest of the line, he closed the hold and padlocked it. Now he would have to rendezvous with his men and help with the sabotage on the *Liberty*. He realized he had begun to shiver badly. But the water would warm him.

Quickly he duck-walked as fast as he could back to the stern. Swinging over the railing, he jumped feet first into the shadows, making only a tiny splash as he hit the water.

56

Nick made Marsh drive fast, giving him directions as they crossed the Brooklyn Bridge—garish even in its dimmed, war-night lights—then off at Lafayette, up to Fourteenth.

"We are heading for the Hudson River?" Fleckenstein, who had been very nervous the whole ride, asked. He could not seem to figure out what Nick was doing. Nick had refused to answer any of his questions, saying only that they "were going to a safe place." But he held the gun tightly, its barrel pressed against Fleckenstein.

At Fourteenth, Nick ordered Marsh to drive past Tenth Avenue and turn left. They were a block from the Hudson, near piers 57 and 56, when Nick told him to stop.

Fleckenstein eyed the oddly triangular, pie-shaped building on Miller Highway warily.

"Get out!" Nick told him.

"What if I won't get out?! Who's gonna make me?! A priest?!" Nick struck his face with the gun, then yanked him out onto the sidewalk. He pushed him forcibly toward the front door of "The Minnow," opened it and followed the stunned Nazi inside.

Marsh, intrigued by what was transpiring, turned toward the bar. The captain knew he should radio for help to stop what was happening. He had a pretty good idea what Father Nick Remington was up to, but instead he threw open the door and stepped inside. The bar was filled with smoke and wall-to-wall longshoremen drinking at tables and a long old wooden bar. The place was covered with hunting trophies.

The bartender, built like the bear that stood on its hind legs behind the bar, now looked away from Fleckenstein and Nick. He shook his head and came down toward Marsh as Nick herded Fleckenstein toward a back room.

"Evenin', Captain Marsh," Marty Sherwood said. "What'll you have?"

The thick crowd of heavily muscled dock workers good-naturedly looked his way. The room had quieted and every last dock worker was watching. Some form of instant communication had taken place. Two of the big men at the bar scooted apart on the long bench.

"Come on, drink with us, Captain," one of them suggested. "Ain't a thing you can do but wait."

Marsh slumped onto the bench.

"Father Remington's gonna hear a confession." Sherwood set up a bottle of bourbon and a glass. "You wouldn't want to stop a man from getting a few things off his chest, would you?"

"No," Marsh said, pouring a generous dollop of the whiskey. "I guess there's nothing in the Geneva Convention rules says a priest can't do that." He swung his eyes toward the back room. "And I hope it's a good confession. Complete and sincere."

Nick locked the door of Marty Sherwood's office, all the while holding the gun on his adversary. He had only minutes. He crossed hurriedly to the alley door, turned the key in that lock and put it into his pocket too.

"What we doin' here, priest?" Fleckenstein demanded.

"We are going to have a little chat." Dear God, could he do this? He was a priest! Holding the FBI at gunpoint . . . kidnapping Captain Marsh . . . bringing this Nazi to the back room of "The Minnow"—he *had* gone insane! His gun hand was shaking badly. He made himself remember Rafaella.

"Sit down!" he ordered.

Fleckenstein suspiciously dropped into Sherwood's desk chair, his eyes alert.

Nick tossed him a ball of industrial twine from a shelf, keeping well out of the way of the Nazi's powerful arms.

"Tie one of your wrists tight!" Nick commanded him. When he did that, Nick said, "Now put it behind your back."

Nick spun the chair around and tied the twine tightly, first around one wrist, then both, finally looping it around the chair and Fleckenstein's thick chest until it was as strong as a rope.

Fritz, feeling his body being constrained, suddenly swung his shoulder up at the gun. Nick danced nimbly back.

"Try it and I'll kill you."

"You wouldn't! You're a priest! I'm calling your bluff right now!" Fleckenstein started wrenching the strands of twine loose and tried to stand.

Nick brought the gun point-blank to Fleckenstein's ear and fired! The cartilage atomized into a spray of blood! The Nazi screamed and fell heavily back in the chair. It was not a serious wound, but the mess and pain were very convincing.

Quickly Nick continued to wrap the string tightly around the Nazi, who sat, every muscle tensed, shaking with fury. But Nick saw in his eyes that he had begun to make a believer out of him. Now could he do the rest?

When the twine was tightly and thickly looped

around Fleckenstein's chest and arms, Nick rolled the desk chair, with the Nazi in it, out into the center of the room.

"Where is Rafaella?"

"Go to hell!"

Nick unloaded the five remaining bullets from the pistol. He reinserted one long cartridge back into the revolver.

"Never! *Heil, Hitler,* priest!"

Nick spun the tumbler. He pointed the gun at the Nazi's right arm.

"I know this game of Russian roulette! I'm not afraid!"

Nick pulled the trigger. To Fleckenstein's and Nick's surprise, it fired! The *Führer* shrieked in pain.

Nick loaded another shell into the gun. He twirled the tumbler. "Where is Rafaella?"

"You fuckin' sonofabitch priest! She's dead! I killed her!"

Nick pointed the gun at Fleckenstein's left arm and pulled the trigger. To both their amazement, it fired again. The Nazi howled in fury!

"You're very unlucky!" Nick shook his head as Fleckenstein roared obscenities.

As Fritz watched, panic building in his eyes, Nick reloaded, inserting yet another silver-cased .38 into the revolver. To the Nazi's horror, Nick grabbed his hair. Jerking back his head, he forced the barrel into Fleckenstein's mouth.

"Where is she?" He repeated the question. When the Nazi did not answer he pulled the trigger. The gun clicked.

"Maybe your luck's improving?" Nick asked. He cocked the gun again. "Here it comes, ready or not!"

Fleckenstein began babbling, straining at the twine, which was cutting into his flesh. The floor around him was pooling with his blood.

Nick pulled the trigger again. As Fleckenstein convulsively jumped, the hammer struck emptily. Nick slowly cocked it again. "Gotta be in here somewhere!"

Fleckenstein's attention was inexorably drawn to the tumbler. He could see the live shell turning toward the firing pin!

"Last chance!" Nick announced, knowing what the Nazi had seen.

Fleckenstein, eyes bulging, mouth working frantically, began to stutter: "Li . . . li . . ."

"What?"

"Li . . . BERTY!"

Nick withdrew the gun barrel from Fleckenstein's slobbering mouth. "Quick! Tell me!"

"She's on the *Liberty!*" Fleckenstein screamed. His mind seemed to have cracked. "In the hold! The stern!" His eyes were rolling wildly.

"How are you sabotaging our ships?!" Nick aimed the gun between his eyes.

"We string copper wire so it trails beneath the ships. It magnifies the sound of their engines so the U-boats can pick them up on sonar!"

"Thank you, *Herr* Fleckenstein." He pointed the gun barrel to the floor, pulled the trigger.

At the roar of that cartridge exploding, Fleckenstein slumped in the chair, his face dissolving into a mass of tears and facial tics as he began to weep.

Nick felt sick. But he had to ask the question that had smoldered inside these past weeks. "Was it you who burned the *Normandie?*"

Behind him, the door was suddenly kicked inward. Two big Shore Patrol crashed inside. Marsh was close behind.

Sherwood pushed his way through. "Sorry, Father. It was either let them through or fight our own."

"You did good," Nick said. "Thanks, Marty."

"Has the convoy sailed?" Nick handed Marsh the

empty .38. The captain was trying not to stare at the bloody ruin of the incoherent Nazi.

"'Bout an hour ago," Marsh answered, over-whelmed at the sight.

"You've got to radio them! Tell them to come back to port! Rafaella is on the *Liberty* and they're all sitting ducks for the U-boats!"

"Let's get to Admiral Colditz! He's the only one who can do that." Marsh started for the door.

"Isn't this priest under arrest?" Baker, the FBI man, demanded as he entered. "He kidnapped our prisoner!"

"He's in my custody," Marsh said, exiting with Nick.

Luciano was out front in his limo, when he saw Nick and Marsh push out of "The Minnow." The priest's hands were blood-splattered and he was covered with pieces of flesh. He stared at him as Nick and Captain Marsh drove away in the navy truck.

Leaving his bodyguard and driver, Luciano pushed through the bar door. Longshoremen stepped respectfully away from the bar when they saw him. Many kissed his hand as he passed through the crowd.

"Mister Lucky," Sherwood said. "What can I do for you?"

"I wanna see the Nazi."

Sherwood led him to the back room where Fleckenstein was being cut free by the Shore Patrol and FBI. His hands and face were bleeding heavily. Several teeth were missing from his mouth.

"That priest's mad as a dog . . . or in love," Lucky said to himself, observing the Nazi's destruction.

Noticing the gangster, Fleckenstein suddenly snapped up in the chair, wild eyes burning with hatred. "That whore of yours, Ruthie!" He laughed insanely. "She spilled all your plans to us! She was the one kept warning me! That's why we were always one step ahead of you bunch of fuckin' guineas! Wop mothafucker!"

The Nazi was led out past an expressionless Lucky Luciano.

The men in the bar glared at Fleckenstein with hatred as he was taken past them by the FBI.

Someone began to sing "Oh, say can you see by the dawn's early light . . ."

In a building roar of approval, the longshoremen joined in.

In the back room, Lucky Luciano was smiling like a fox. It was his trademark when he had decided to kill somebody.

57

"BUT YOU DON'T KNOW for sure!" Admiral Colditz was pacing his spacious, plushly carpeted office on the third floor above the Port Authority Bank. "In my position, I need proof to execute such an order. My whole world turns on proof and if I don't have it, I can't act. If I did, I wouldn't have my job long!" On the floor, in the center of his blue-and-white wall-to-wall carpet was a sterling silver navy anchor with "Don't give up the ship!"

"But Admiral." Captain Marsh was trying to be patient. He was standing with Nick in front of the admiral's dark teak desk since they had not been asked to sit down. "Father Remington even got Fleckenstein to confess how they've been sabotaging the ships!"

"With all due respect to you, Father," the Admiral said to Remington, "the Nazi could have been lying. He's well trained. Besides, who's to say those ships aren't clean? This could be some sort of trap! By alerting the convoy and bringing them back into port, they might be sunk and block all shipping for months. Who knows what these Nazis have in mind?"

"Admiral, will you at least radio the ships?" Nick stepped in. He was trying to hold his temper at this "by the book" officer who, he realized, must have been at

246

the root of the navy's inflexibility at handling the dock problems.

"I will issue a class-two warning. But no more."

"That's not good enough, Admiral!" Marsh's face turned red, his lips pressed so tightly together they showed white. "We need action and now's the time for it. We're in a war, sir! And there are thousands of men on those ships, not to mention our own agent!"

"Proof!" Colditz suddenly planted his palms flat on his desk and faced Marsh. "Logic! Policy, Captain! We haven't had any of that since this whole ridiculous scheme was concocted by you and that superior officer of yours, Commodore Hahn! He got himself killed and all for what? We even had a bank robbery that was nearly a massacre! Granted you've *finally* rounded up the *Bund*—most of them. But don't ask me to go along anymore with this! I won't do it! Not even if the president calls me! This is my command and I've got the rank to make my own choice!"

"You were always jealous of Commodore Hahn." Marsh shook his head angrily at the admiral. "From the very first, you opposed him. Only when he went to President Roosevelt did things get moving. Well, I won't let you stop us now, not when we're so close!"

Marsh strode across the Prussian blue and milky white carpet. "Just what precisely are you going to do?" Colditz shouted. "I demand an answer!"

Marsh stopped, feet planted on the anchor. "I'm going to act like we're at war, Admiral. Even if it means taking off this uniform to do it!" He turned and left.

"You're on your own, mister!" Colditz cried as Nick followed. "You're not acting on *my* orders! I'll have you court-martialed for this! Mark my word! You're a renegade! A misfit! There's no place for you in this navy! I'll see to that!"

58

THE HOLD STANK OF Cosmoline. Thousands upon thousands of M-1s lay packed in their coffinlike boxes. For the last four hours, ever since the ship had gotten under way, Rafaella had been sawing at the rope that bound her wrists, wearing its fibers apart on a corner hinge of a gun crate.

The crates were stacked at least twenty feet high and when the Nazi had lowered her down into the cargo hold, she had helplessly bumped against one case after another, until now she lay wedged tightly between two of them. She felt the rope fray until only one last strand was left. She jerked, but it held. Anxiously she rubbed faster against the metal hinge. The sound of the ship's laboring engines urged her on. There was no time to lose. She knew what the Nazis had in mind for her . . . and the convoy. Death by sinking! She had seen their long copper wires and had understood their use.

Her hands were nearly frozen. It was very cold and damp down here. Suddenly the strand burst and her hands were free. It took her a moment to realize what had happened. A strange sensation. For so long she had been helpless. Now she swung aching arms up, feeling the muscles spasm and cramp.

She pulled off the electrician's tape from her mouth,

then fumbled at the knots around her legs. Bastards! She ached all over. Kicking the rope loose, she tried to stand on the edge of the crate on which she had landed, but her legs would not support her. Fighting to a kneeling position, she reached out, missed her hold and fell.

She hurtled downward, as if in slow motion, waiting for the terrible fall to end. Suddenly her numbed fingers struck something soft, and as her face plowed into the stuff, she realized she had landed in coarse sand. She spat it out of her mouth and struggled to her feet.

In the dim light from the emergency lamp far away in the massive hold, she attempted to focus. Of course. Ballast. She was on the lowest deck. The crates were stacked on sand. In their rush to ready the *Liberty,* she remembered, they had left the ballast normally used to steady a passenger-carrying ocean liner, sacrificing that space for the time they would gain.

Desperately she tried to stop her teeth from chattering. It was so cold! But why? Her breath showed no steam. She wrapped her arms around herself and felt the coat slide across her nakedness. Nazi creeps! Didn't even leave her shoes!

Trying to recall the plan of this deck, Rafaella crawled through the sloppily stacked crates. It certainly had been a hurried job of loading. Many had already tipped over and fallen. She would have to watch that. One of those caissons could crush her.

Working her way through them, she angled toward the weak light, where she knew there would be an emergency exit.

Plowing through the sand, she finally knelt exhausted at the dimly outlined lamp and an oval-shaped door. Only the top part of the door was exposed. The ballast sand had shifted somehow and covered it. For some reason, she felt like laughing. Forcing herself to concentrate, she dropped to her knees and dug frantically at the sand covering the door. Like a dog digging. She giggled to herself.

A handle appeared! She grabbed hold and pushed down on it. She had to warn everyone about what was happening!

The handle would not budge—there was sand blocking it.

In her ferocity and near despair, she clawed a deeper hole, head bent far below her knees. A wave of exhaustion swept over her, making her dizzy. Hypothermia? She found herself for no reason suddenly chortling. Work harder, she warned herself. Warm up! But in her weakened state, she felt her knees slip from the top of the pile. Despite a frantic movement to save herself, she tumbled down into the hole she had created, slipping on her back against the emergency door. The ship rose and fell heavily on a wave. The sand above her collapsed. She was partially buried.

She blew the sand away from her mouth. It was warm under all this weight. She was so cold. But the metal door against her back was somehow strangely colder. She found herself talking. It was nice to have Nick here.

"You still believe in God?" she asked him. "After all you've been through?"

She waited anxiously for his answer. She could not, for some reason, see his face.

"You mean," she heard him finally, "if I were an atheist and didn't believe in the hereafter then I'd be free to do what I wanted with you?"

She found herself giggling uncontrollably.

"And you?"

"What?" She tried to stop the laughter that was hurting her now.

"Do you believe in God, Rafaella?"

"With all my heart. And with all my heart I want you too!"

She began to kiss him. But sand suddenly covered her head. "Nick, don't let me die!" she screamed, realizing. "Not now!"

59

IDLEWILD AIRPORT WAS essentially a military operation. Very few passengers were flying during the war, since the strips were used heavily by transport. At the wheel of the navy truck, Marsh drove through the gate opened by the guards and asked directions to the PBY-5. It was past midnight and he knew it would be grounded from its normal sub-spotting flight searches along the coast.

The guard seemed suspicious, but he directed them to a hangar.

Inside the mammoth Quonset hut, Sergeant First Class Neil McCormick was working on one of the plane's side blisters. The PBY Catalina was an ungainly, insectlike plane with a normal flying-boat hull and enormous rectangular wings on which the plane's twin radial engines were mounted. With the .30-caliber machine gun in a ventral hatch, two more in its nose, plus the .50-caliber guns in its wing blisters, and a wingspan of 104 feet and range of 2,350 miles, the PBY was a favorite among navy fliers. It had the nickname of "Dumbo," after Walt Disney's flying elephant.

"Trouble?" Marsh asked the sergeant-mechanic.

"Pontoons don't lower like they should, sir." He saluted and gestured a greasy hand toward a wing tip.

Marsh noticed that the floats supporting the wing were not retracted as they should be for a landing.

"She fly, Sergeant?"

Sergeant First Class McCormick squinted up at the captain. "Can't go fast's she should."

"We need her. Now."

"You got flying orders, sir?" He wiped his hands on a red rag. His khaki overalls were covered with grime and oil stains.

"We've got an emergency, Sergeant!"

"Past midnight." The sergeant checked his watch thoughtfully. "Pilot boys all at the officers' club. Doubt there's one who could walk a straight line."

"You fly?" Nick asked Captain Marsh hopefully.

"I'm strictly a salt." He shook his head. Then smiled ruefully. "When I get the opportunity."

"Used to do a little crop dustin' before the war," the sergeant said.

"You take this up?"

The sergeant scratched his chin. "A real emergency, you say?"

"All the ships in the convoy that just sailed! The supplies and lives of the men on them!"

"The hell you say," the sergeant agreed. "Sounds like a wartime emergency to me. But don't get me wrong, sir, I'm hesitatin' cause a court-martial's a court-martial!"

Marsh yanked his .45 from its holster. "I'm giving an order. That help you make up your mind, Sergeant?!"

"Yes, sir!" The sergeant saluted smartly, a smile forming on his lips. "An order's an order! Get aboard and watch an enlisted Arkansas hillbilly help win this war!"

As the sergeant swung up to the cockpit of the PBY, the guard who had let them pass at his gate stepped through the tall double doors of the hangar.

"Oh, shit," the sergeant said. "Trouble."

"Just what is going on here, sir?" The guard advanced toward Captain Marsh.

"We've got a mission," Marsh said.

"Well, then, sir, I would like to see some flying orders." The guard stepped back and undid the leather flap on his holster.

Marsh stared at his action. He started to reach for his own pistol, which he had holstered, then stopped. Face reddening, he bellowed, "I'm a captain in the United States Navy, Corporal!"

"Sir," the guard said, drawing his .45 now, "for all I know you *may* be a captain. Then again, with all the spies running around here, you might just be a Nazi too."

Remington looked at Marsh. Every second wasted, the convoy was further out to sea. Closer to the waiting Nazi U-boats.

"Son," Remington said, turning to the young corporal, "we've got something to do and we've got to do it quick! So back off and put that gun away."

"And just who are you?" The guard eyed Nick's civilian clothing. His pants were ripped at one knee.

"I'm a priest, working on the docks."

"Thought you looked suspicious when you entered. Reason I came down here was to check up on you." He flashed his eyes briefly up at the sergeant. "You in on this too, Sergeant McCormick?"

"I believe 'em, Tasy."

"You'd believe shit for Shinola," the corporal said. "You got a rep 'round here for being stupid, Sergeant."

The sergeant tensed and rose to his full height. "Corporal," he said, "you are addressing Sergeant First Class Neil Willard McCormick. And you are holding a gun on a captain of the United States Navy, not to mention this here priest. I'm gonna count to three, then I'm comin' for you. And if you want to shoot, you'd better make up your mind quick-like 'cause when I move for a man, I don't stop. One!"

The corporal lost some of his cockiness and took a slight step back.

"Two!" Something briefly caught the sergeant's eye at the door. Nick and Marsh reacted to the blur too.

"Three!" Luciano shouted from behind the guard. As the corporal spun, the gangster socked him squarely between the eyes.

The guard slumped to the concrete, his pistol clattering away.

Lucky rubbed his knuckles. "Shit, that was dumb! Ow! Shoulda used a wrench or somethin'!"

"Thanks," Nick said, running toward the tall hangar doors and pushing one open. Marsh was shoving at the other, making room for the PBY to exit.

"Who're you?" the sergeant asked as he slid through the open cockpit window.

"Just somebody who needs an alibi." Luciano pulled the chocks from the wheels of the plane.

60

KLAUS ZIMMERMAN PULLED off his headphones he had been listening into for the last hour and shouted: *"Hier, Kapitän!"*

Kapitän Melker was not only in charge of this U-boat 112, but of the entire underwater fleet of thirty-six submarines. They had been waiting since midnight, having formed a line a mile wide in the Atlantic, tensed for the first sounds of the approaching convoy. "Designation?" the captain requested.

Zimmerman, the sonic operator, rolled the compass until the sounds were loudest. "One hundred ninety-two degrees!"

"Pinpoints?" bearded *Kapitän* Melker demanded. "Are they working?" The captains had initially argued among themselves about the effectiveness of the new sabotage installed by the *Bund.* Would trailing thin wires really silhouette the most important ships in the convoy as promised? It had so far.

"Ja! Ja!" Zimmerman listened once again as sweaty sailors, men who had not seen their homeland since the war had started, filled the compass room. Most knew that after this mission, they were to pick up the head of the *Bund, Herr* Fritz Fleckenstein, and return home to Germany for a well-deserved furlough. Success of the sonar experiment meant they were on their way.

But the captain checked the headphones for himself. There were "pinging" sounds just as he expected but when he spun the compass ever so slightly, the "*pings*" reverberated louder. He knew he was listening to the trailing antennae on the specially chosen ships! His eyes stared unseeing at a wall calendar. Someone had circled today, March 17, feast of St. Patrick.

"Good! Good! Good!" he shouted, ripping off the headset. The *Bund* had successfully rigged this convoy! It would be easy.

The crew of Germans cheered wildly. Their last convoy! Total obliteration. Commendations from the *Führer* himself, perhaps.

"Periscope!" *Kapitän* Melker ordered.

Immediately the long tube whined upward, lifted by its electric motor. The captain brought down the handles and pressed his eye to the rubber-protected lens.

For a long moment he stared.

Behind the escort ship, a heavy cruiser, there were hundreds of vessels lit faintly in the calm night. He could make out small smoking lanterns, slitted wardeck lights that permitted sailors to move about the decks. Even at this distance, one in particular stood out. A large ship with three exhaust funnels. Racking up a larger Zeiss, he stared through the 250mm lens. It was a big ship all right. And through the high-powered lens he seemed right on top of it. In the moonlight, he thought he could even make out the name.

"One eight seven niner." The captain shouted its compass bearing to his radio man.

Zimmerman swung his sonar compass dial. A super "*ping*" made him yank off his headset in sudden pain. It was all the captain needed. He had been watching and smiled.

"Radio the other U-boat captains," he ordered, turning back to his periscope. "Tell them we will take the third ship from the Western perimeter, large configuration, three funnels, a transport perhaps, multiple decks." He stepped away from his periscope. "Each U-boat is to select its target by sonar evaluation and radio to coordinate."

"Jawohl, Kapitän!!" Zimmerman saluted and sent the message by code.

The fleet of U-boats swung out of line and picked their ships. A semicircle of sea wolves now waited for their prey. In a bit, radio silence was strictly enforced. The convoy advanced.

Aboard U-boat 112, Zimmerman said softly: "Ten thousand meters and closing. Ninety-nine . . ."

The captain peered back into his periscope, sighting carefully on his big ship. Normally they would fire their fish at less than three thousand meters. But no need for that tonight with the targets so easily identified.

Up front, in the narrow nose of the battery-driven submarine, eight muscled sailors slid an electric torpedo into its tube, then locked the sea-door behind it, spinning the wheel tightly into place.

"Fire!" *Kapitän* Melker whispered.

Even in the dark the electric-powered torpedo was visible as it shot from the nose, stirring up the phosphorescent water, its whirring propeller thrusting it forward toward the convoy.

Petty Officer Navarro, a wiry Puerto Rican, had the watch on the starboard bow of the *Liberty*. He was due to be replaced in two minutes. He was cold in the raw Atlantic winter, wet from the rain they had passed through just outside Delaware, but what he saw traveling beneath the surface of the water made him forget his discomfort. Quickly he raised his binoculars and tried to focus on it. It was not easy with the ship's movement. Something like a small whale was streaming green fireworks as it plowed toward them. At first he

258

thought it was a steam torpedo, a German 21-inch G7a, since it was showing bubbles.

"Torpedo off starboard, 6,000 meters!" he cried up.

All along the deck other watchers swung their glasses on it. A lieutenant in forward control sounded the alarm. At the same moment, the captain in the wheelhouse got the message and ordered the ship hard to port.

As the captain desperately clenched the blast bar behind the cockpit windows, he saw the torpedo streak toward the *Liberty*'s nose as she swung with agonizing slowness to the left.

At the bow, Navarro stared at the torpedo closing on the *Liberty*. It was too large to be steam-powered. He knew the wake was an oceanic phenomenon and that this was a big electric bomb, honing in! As it drove at the bow, the *Liberty* swung away by mere inches!

Navarro had just grabbed the railing to brace himself when he saw the huge torpedo miss and go by unimpeded. The dreaded explosion had not occurred. He stepped back and was about to yell up "All clear" when he spotted three other torpedoes at midship. The Germans had merely decoyed them!

In the quick triple blasts that followed, Navarro felt himself heaved into midair. He saw flashing, buckling decks below just before he sailed downward into the cold seawater of the Atlantic.

61

In the PBY, Remington anxiously peered through the scattered clouds that glowed white in the moonlight. He could see the Atlantic farther below, clear and calm. Desperately he tried to catch sight of the convoy.

"We should be coming into radio range," Sergeant McCormick shouted from the pilot's seat. In the co-pilot's chair, Marsh flipped the dial to the military frequency allotted to the convoy and began trying to make contact.

"I know you love her," Luciano said as he stood beside Nick in the cockpit doorway, smoking his cigarette.

Nick spun, momentarily tearing his eyes away from the ocean below. In the dim light of the cockpit, he saw Luciano wink.

He turned away, grateful for the lack of light, aware only of his violent blushing and flushed cheeks. Was it true?

Suddenly, forty miles ahead and below, all 167 ships of the convoy came into view. In addition, twenty-three heavy cruisers and destroyers surrounded them. The giant phalanx, steaming in the moonlight, was leaving bright green phosphorescent wakes.

"There!" Nick pointed.

Captain Marsh spun the directional antenna and grabbed up the mike. "Mayday, Mayday, U.S.S. *Roosevelt.* Message to Admiral Norman Westbank!"

"Westbank here," a crackly voice shouted after a second. "We are under strict radio silence! Who the hell is this?"

"Captain Marsh here, sir! We are flying behind you, sir! You are about to be attacked by U-boats! You are being identified by copper wires trailing from beneath your ships!"

"What?! Just what . . ." The sound was lost in sudden static.

In the distance, three explosions ripped the night! A large ship began to burn!

"We're too goddamn late!" McCormick cried.

Rafaella lay covered by the ballast sand. The blast of the first torpedo popped her out of her hole. The second flung her back against the gun casings.

In the explosion, many of the boxes split open and spilled out their grease-coated rifles. Icy salt water poured through the holes ripped in the steel plates of the ship. As the sea gushed into the *Liberty,* Rafaella clung to a gun box that had remained sealed. She was swirled violently around in the tempest, banged nearly unconscious against black things she could not see. All she had to do was let go of the crate and the horror would cease. Yet she clung on, bobbing wildly in the black bowels of the ship as the water rose.

Inside the submarines, the German captains fired more torpedoes which found their targets. Ship after ship in the convoy began to blow. In the periscopes, the captains could see small figures leap for the safety of the water amidst the flames. Taking this convoy was like shooting fish in a bathtub.

Sonar radiomen continued to lock in on trailing antennae and expertly guided torpedoes to the most valuable ships. The Wolf Pack, as the submariners chose to call themselves, stood safely far from the convoy and cheered as one fiery eruption after another burst the ships apart. Another successful mission. The *Führer* waited with open arms and laurels.

Aboard the U.S.S. *Roosevelt,* Admiral Norman Westbank had just ordered his attack force of fast, specially-equipped destroyers to locate the Nazi subs when he stopped in midsentence. His junior officers stared at him.

"Sir?" a captain asked.

The admiral, seeing a nearby cargo vessel burn, remembered the strange, partially received message he had heard from a certain Captain Marsh. "I want crews on every ship in the convoy to drag bottom," he announced.

"Maintenance? Now?" another officer asked. Was the admiral going mad?!

Westbank roared: "You won't find barnacles, dammit!"

In less than a minute, that order had been broadcast to the entire convoy. As ships desperately maneuvered in their defensive zigzag fashions, crews lowered weighted cables over bows and, pulling them along beneath the lengths of their ships, found to their surprise thousands of feet of thin, tangled copper wire.

Kapitän Melker spotted the approaching destroyer. Quickly he asked the sonar man for other targets. Immediately Zimmerman identified two transmissions from big ships in the convoy. But as he spun his compass to select the fattest prize, he blinked in amazement.

"Pinpoint, hurry!" Melker screamed.

"The ship . . . it is . . . disappearing!" Zimmerman shouted back, confused.

"Impossible!" Melker grabbed the headphones and listened.

Zimmerman spun the compass frantically but suddenly a violent explosion rocked the sub. "Where did that come from?" he cried, stunned.

"Take her down, down!" Melker ordered. Cursing the sudden and mysterious bad luck, he braced with his crew for the depth charges! But they should not have come this soon!

Inside the other thirty-five U-boats, other captains were surprised also. They dove in their boats and fought to understand the disappearance of their target. The seasoned crews on the submarines were used to this evasive strategy. On nearly every attack of a convoy, they expected to sit on the bottom for a while after the kills, waiting for the depth charges to stop. But something else was happening this time. All around them unusual blasts began to fill the ocean.

Kapitän Melker, aboard 112, heard strangled cries for help from sub 120.

"What is it?" Zimmerman cried, ripping off his headphones. "These are not ordinary depth charges!"

Suddenly multiple bursts popped like firecrackers against their hull.

The crew of 112 held their ears and tried to keep their sanity as the thousands of explosions deafened them.

Aboard the U.S.S. *Charleston,* an escort destroyer of the long-hull Buckley class, the ship's captain watched as "The Hedgehog," the new navy weapon, began to pour 7.2-inch depth charges in a pattern of twenty-four nearly a half-mile ahead of their bow. In addition, standard depth charges were being fired overboard.

But it was "The Hedgehog" that was showing what

was below. The sea in front of them was boiling up submarine paraphernalia—anything that floated.

"We're in the middle of 'em!" Captain Boyd could not contain his excitement over the effectiveness of the first run of his "Hedgehog." There were subs everywhere and they were sinking them!

62

FROM THE AIR, NICK, in a fit of growing panic at the slowness with which they were approaching the convoy, saw the first faint ridges of dawn glimmering along the horizon. Below, less than a mile or two away, at least a dozen ships were burning. Anxiously peering through the PBY's ventral hatch, he again gazed at the *Liberty,* in the center of the convoy. On fire, listing badly, it had stopped in the water and soldiers were jumping from its flaming decks.

Impulsively he pushed down from the viewing hatch and scrambled forward through the fuselage. He wanted to tell Sergeant McCormick to land in the water, realizing at the same instant that he was demanding certain suicide for everyone on board. Yet somehow he had to help Rafaella.

As he pushed through the forward compartment, his hand closed on a parachute. There was a pile of them, stacked neatly on the floor. He lifted one and stared intently at it. Then he pulled it on.

"Whatcha doin'?" Luciano had turned from the cockpit.

"Tell the sergeant to make a low sweep over the *Liberty*'s decks!" Nick shouted.

McCormick, who had heard him, turned. "You're fuckin' crazy, Father! You can't jump!"

Nick ignored him. As he finished cinching the groin straps, he saw that Luciano was grinning.

"Amused?" Nick hated that smirk.

"Remembering," Luciano said. "Uncle Joe had me bring Rafaella over from Sicily."

"She owes you nothing."

"I ain't never asked for nothing." Luciano grinned wider. "Wouldn't done any good with that one."

He reached down and picked up a parachute and pulled it on. "Trouble is, bring somebody over from the old country, you become responsible. That's the law."

Nick stared in amazement. Luciano was jumping too? He reached out and clasped him apologetically. "For a long time I've thought you had something to do with the sabotage—you know, using it somehow to make a better deal for yourself with the government. You're a good man, Lucky Luciano. Forgive me for doubting you."

"You don't know me at all, Father." Luciano's grin vanished. "I ain't no hero. It's just I couldn't go back if I didn't help my *famiglia.*"

"Here she comes!" Captain Marsh screamed as the plane plunged downward. He rushed back and cranked open the side door himself. "Since you're both crazy enough to try this, the sergeant here's gonna give you the best chance he can!"

"Get ready!" McCormick roared at the controls.

"Find her!" Marsh begged Nick.

The PBY leveled out and skimmed low over the water. McCormick kept the altimeter at just above 500 feet. Just enough time for a parachute to open.

He pulled up on his wheel, thanking God for the PBY's broad wings and easy maneuverability, and floated toward the burning vessel. It was a piece of cake flying her after some of those junky crop-dusters! The bow of the *Liberty* was the only spot not on fire.

266

"Now! Jump!" he shouted as they loomed over the vessel.

Nick went out first. As Luciano dove, he said to Marsh, "The things I do for myself!"

Nick hit hard on the *Liberty*'s riveted deck and since she was listing, rolled down the incline. Grabbing hold of a capstan, he realized he had landed far back from the bow. In the roiling smoke and darkness, he saw Luciano float over him, miss the ship entirely and plop in the ocean. Nick tore off his billowing parachute. Several soldiers who were skidding down the deck to jump into the water looked at him in amazement.

"What you doin', buddy?! You're supposed to get the hell off!" one yelled, engrossed even in this emergency with the man who had just dropped from the night sky.

"You a Nazi or somethin'?" another accused him. Instead of stopping to explain, Nick pushed the soldier off the deck into the sea, then went to help Luciano. But he saw the gangster hoist himself from the water on a broken cable.

"I'll take the stern," Nick screamed to him. "Rafaella's somewhere on the lowest deck!"

Luciano signaled he had heard.

Nick fought his way through the twisted remains of the fallen superstructure.

Ghostly wraiths of catwalks, twisted funnels and crumpled iron stairs lay strewn about middeck. Pushing toward the stern, Nick spotted an intact stairwell disgorging soldiers from below. The smoke was thick, but he could see no other way down. Suddenly that old terror of being trapped in his boyhood cave swept over him. He could not go! Then Rafaella sprang to his mind.

Shielding his eyes and nose with a raised arm, he forced himself down past the panicked men fighting to escape upward.

It must have been like this when Rafaella came down in the *Normandie*. Now, ironically, he was in the same situation, but he was not at all sure he could pull it off. It was such a big ship and it was sinking fast. Even the stern hold in the *Liberty* would be huge. Where to start? And how did he know the Nazi was telling the truth about "the stern"?

Arriving at the lowest level after walking forever in thick smoke, he found himself hip deep in water. The flow of men had diminished as he had gone down. Now the ship was nearly evacuated.

Quickly he waded past watertight cargo compartments. Several doors were leaking water, spewing it out through the cracks. The pressure behind those doors was threatening to force them open. How long would they hold? If Rafaella were behind one of these, it was already over.

At Compartment 117, he stopped. He was in the deepest recess of the stern.

One seventeen's steel door was also leaking seawater, but it did not seem to be filled to the top like the others he had passed. He tried its wheel but it was jammed. How to get it free?

Suddenly the ship lurched, tilting farther to starboard. He caught himself as water in the hallway sloshed over him. Time was running out.

Backtracking, he found a door with ORDNANCE stenciled in black letters against its gray metal. He tried the door. It was locked. Quickly he yanked a fire axe from its emergency station and hacked at the metal door until a hole about waist high, the size of a football, gradually appeared. Sticking his face up to it, he could see the floor inside was covered with water. Mortar and artillery shells for land warfare were stacked in long rows on sturdy metal shelves. Next to them were boxes of hand grenades. As he reached his hand desperately through the small hole, the lights in the ship momentarily failed and he was thrust into darkness. Then fitfully, they sputtered on again. How long before they went?

Grabbing a small, heavy crate, he dragged it close to the door, opened its metal lid and managed to scoop out three grenades from the sawdust inside. He eased them through the hole. Then, as quickly as he could through the mounting water, he lodged a grenade inside the wheels of the final three doors in the stern. If Rafaella was not inside one of these, he would never find her. There was no time for further search.

Pulling the pin on the first door, he swam furiously to the second, pulled that one, then the third. Just in time, he ducked beneath the water as the first grenade detonated. He waited for the second and third to blow, then stood up.

In a cloud of cordite, he saw that the first door was still intact. Dismayed, he turned to the next one. The second door was pouring out water and sand as its hinges gave way under the tremendous pressure. The third door looked ready to collapse too.

Half-swimming, half-wading against the increasing tide, Nick fought toward the second door. Bracing himself beside it, he peered inside. But all he was facing was darkness. Suddenly the door flew off as thousands of gallons of seawater and tons of sand roared into the hallway. He caught hold of the ceiling pipes and pulled himself up out of the torrent.

"Rafaella!" He screamed her name.

A loud cracking noise made him turn. The bolts of the third door were being ripped from their hinges! With a gigantic blast the third door blew out, hurtling within inches of his head. Gun cases, sand and a river of water gushed past him.

A crate struck him in the chest and another in the legs. In that same instant, the lights in the corridor died.

In total darkness, he felt himself cruelly swirled

around and around. The crates pounded him. The mighty force of the released water rolled him over and over, squeezing the air from his lungs. He had never felt more alone and out of control. Claustrophobia threatened to overwhelm him. Mercifully he felt unconsciousness sweep over him.

Then miraculously, in outstretched hands, he felt flesh. He thought he was imagining it but it was not the hard wall or the crates or even separate rifles that had come to him—it was a soft, giving, yielding human. He clutched it, pulled it toward him. And somehow, even in his blindness, he knew it was not the corpse of a seaman. It was she—his beloved! She, against him. Her arms and legs moving with the flowing seawater. But lifeless? Cold flesh? Unbreathing nakedness? He felt his feet brush the bottom of the corridor and with all his might he pushed up to ascend.

His head struck a floating crate. In his pain, he shoved at it, swam around it. He was aware his lungs were burning. The water streamed downward past them. They were going up, upward.

When they broke the surface, which was inches from the ceiling of the corridor, he gasped in a great gulp of air. It was dark; he could not see. The lights must have gone out. He held her close. For a terrifying moment, he was back on the *Normandie*—back in the collapsed tunnel, suffocating in dark mud.

He stumbled and fell. But he could stand here—he had found the steps!

At the third level, he lost his way. As the ship lurched farther to starboard, he fell heavily against a gunwale and hit his head. But in a moment his eyes cleared, the weight of Rafaella reminding him of his duty.

Suddenly he saw light. Boldly, with the last of his energy, he strode forward.

In the clearer air on deck, aware of the sea below and the crazily tilted ship, Nick held Rafaella.

"We have to jump," he heard himself say. He saw that her eyes were shut, her face sweet, composed, beatific. She seemed so still!

"Rafaella?" He called her name. He kissed her cold lips. At that moment, the ship rolled completely over, belly up. Panicked, clutching her tightly, he tried to leap clear.

He held her face above the oily, flaming water. The sea was picking up. Men around them were shouting, slipping under, drugged by the cold. A rubber raft appeared, filled to overflowing with survivors. Nick fought for a place against its side and held fast, Rafaella in one arm.

A fight broke out. There were too many soldiers who did not know how to swim and were exhausted. They swamped the boat with their weight, struggling maniacally for a place. Someone slammed one of the raft's oars down on Nick's head. He remembered his struggle to resurface. But when he did, no matter how he groped and dove in the vast sea, he could not find Rafaella again.

III

PARADISO

A great flame follows a little spark.
—The Divine Comedy
Paradiso, canto I, 1.34

63

The TOTAL POWER THE Nazis had held over shipping from the Eastern seaboard was finished.

On that night and early morning of March 17, although 43 ships were sunk or heavily damaged, the United States Navy counted four "certain" kills of Nazi U-boats and seven "probables." The fortunes of war had turned. From now on, without the help of the *Bund,* the "Wolf Pack" was on equal footing and would have no advantage. Even though 1,000 ships would be lost by July and another 675 by the end of the year, the Atlantic was a fair war.

"Operation Underworld" was declared a success. Though its existence was not revealed until after the war (and then only in dribbles as it was "declassified" from its Top Secret "red letter" status), word quickly got around the streets of New York that Charlie Lucky had single-handedly routed the German saboteurs. He became even more of a mythic figure than before and his stature grew into legend. Everybody agreed Lucky Luciano should be freed as quickly as possible for his services to his country.

Nick had been picked up by the U.S.S. *Wyoming,* along with nearly 800 other survivors of the *Liberty.*

He had been told by the ship's nurses that Lucky had located him in the water and held his head above the waves until they were rescued. It confirmed his belief in the gangster. All the doubts and suspicions Nick had held about his participation in "Operation Underworld" had disappeared forever. Luciano might be conniving and devious, but when it came to fighting Nazis, he had done a virtuous deed. He had proven himself.

Taken back to New York City, Nick was first placed in the Bird S. Coler Hospital on Roosevelt Island, but then by some mysterious order moved to St. Clare's on the corner of West Fifty-second and Ninth in midtown Manhattan.

The nuns in their white-coiffed, buttresslike bonnets swept about efficiently and attended to his wounds, which were many. Hypothermia, a broken collarbone, assorted gashes and burns filled the list. Still, he was able to walk about the hospital and he asked every survivor he met the same questions: Had he seen a woman? He described her unmistakable copper-red hair. Were there any other boats picking up survivors? The results were all the same—sympathetic "no's" or vacant stares at this obsessed man.

Captain Marsh came to say goodbye. He had been given his command. His orders were to run "Hooligan's Navy," which consisted of more than 500 volunteer civilian yachts patrolling the coastal waters, spotting subs. They carried small arms and depth charges. Ernest Hemingway was a participant.

"It's not the front," Marsh shrugged. "But if I do this well, who knows?" He was dressed handsomely in a new navy blue suit and captain's bars gleaming, looking well and fit.

Nick listened quietly, nodding. Then when the silence had grown too long, he asked, "Is there any word?"

Marsh walked to the window and peered out at the rain drizzling down on New York. "Lieutenant Massaro is still listed as missing in action."

"That's not what I asked."

"There's no word, Father. Sorry. I liked her as much as you did."

"No, you didn't." Nick surprised even himself.

"Well." The captain suddenly reddened. "Hey, you know it was that gangster Luciano who found you and kept you from drowning?"

"So I've been told. He's back in prison?"

"Dannemora. Word is he'll be paroled soon." The conversation died and then Marsh said: "I don't know how to tell you this. I wasn't going to. But since you . . . cared for her, you should know. Rafaella was hurt by the *Bund*. Fleckenstein boasted about it to us."

"Hurt?!" Nick sat up in his bed. "How?"

"They . . . raped her."

Nick lay back, closed his eyes. "I should have killed that Nazi when I had a chance," he said.

Marsh never expected that from a priest. "There's still a chance she was found by another ship . . . one that continued on in the convoy. They can't break radio silence, you know."

"Did you know hypothermia sets in after fifteen minutes in a cold sea?" Nick opened his eyes.

Marsh nervously checked his watch. "Well, Father, I . . ."

"You gotta go." Nick stuck out his hand. "Good luck."

"Maybe when I get back, a bishop can take a lowly captain to lunch?"

"A bishop?"

"Oh, Cardinal Spellman let it slip. He's very pleased with the success of our operation. It was him who got you moved here."

Marsh left after saluting emotionally. Nick thought it

was all dried-out bullshit. With Rafaella gone, he felt he had no reason to go on living. Becoming bishop again, a dream he had held for so long, now lay sour and unwelcome in his gut. He tried to picture himself as a bishop but every time he tried, he wound up thinking only of Rafaella.

He had dozed off in the small room he shared with three other civilians when someone shook him. Awakening, he saw before him in the light from behind his bed a small, red-haired man in a shocking green suit, black hat in his hands. Outside, it was dark.

"Father Remington?" the man, with a strong Bronx accent, asked.

Nick stared at him.

"I'm Meyer Lansky," the little man said. "I gotta show ya somethin'."

"You're a friend of Luciano's?" Nick remembered him from the farmhouse. It seemed so long ago.

"Friend . . . by business." Meyer grinned. "Me, around those wops, I'm nothin' but a faggoty little Jew who's got to prove himself. I don't mind. They think I'm smart, so there. But don't tell no one, 'cause secretlike, I feel I'm dumb." He laughed ingratiatingly.

Nick smiled. "What time is it?"

" 'Bout two in the mornin'. This won't take long. Can you walk? We just gotta go down to the basement."

Nick swung out of bed, pulled on his robe and slippers and followed the gangster. As they neared the desk, he slowed. Patients weren't allowed beyond this point.

Lansky caught his hesitation and motioned him forward. "Don't worry, Father," he said, "everybody's been greased."

There were no nuns around. Only the night nurse, and she waved merrily as they passed.

They rode the elevator down to the hospital morgue.

Several of Lansky's men were standing inside the long, narrow refrigerated white room that held the corpses on their metal tables. For a brief instant as he approached the cadaver, he felt sick. Was this Rafaella? But when he pulled back the white sheet, Ruthie, Luciano's girlfriend, lay there.

"We brought her over special from the city morgue. Wanted you to see."

"What happened?" Nick asked, relieved and yet horrified at the sight. There were bullet holes in her upper chest and shoulders.

"Far as we're concerned here, Father, this here's Jane Doe, number 5. Says so right on her big toe, okay?"

Nick shook his head, agreeing.

"Seems this certain Jane double-crossed a big-time Mafioso. Was her who gave info to the Nazis so they could keep one step aheada you."

"So that was how Fleckenstein always knew! But why did Ruthie do it?"

"This big-timer forced Jane Doe into whorin' when she was a young thing." Lansky's eyes were riveted to her face. "She hated him for it. He never knew that." He let the sheet fall.

"And so she helped the *Bund?* I don't understand. How would that hurt Luciano?"

"She wanted to stop the big-timer from gettin' out of the slammer! Because you see, Father, he went too far!" His voice rose into a quick, emotional falsetto. "Ask the King of Kingpins who torched the *Normandie.*"

Was it possible?! Had Luciano himself set fire to the *Normandie?* A strategy to force the U.S. Government and the navy to make the deal he wanted? A deal that would not only commute his fifty-year sentence but make him a national hero? It was ingenious . . . and as heinous as any crime ever committed. If this were true, Lucky Luciano had suckered everybody . . . including Nick.

"Then the *Bund* was only successful because the Mob *let* them sabotage ships?" Nick pressed.

"I ain't sayin' nothin' 'bout that," Lansky said. "I told you who to ask." He let his eyes wander back to the sheet and momentarily they filled with a raw, aching hunger.

"You . . . liked her?" Nick asked.

"Yeah. She didn't feel a thing. I swear."

Nick felt his face tingle in shock at Lansky's admission.

"Big man don't do his own jobs, Father. It was business. Nothing personal," Lansky said. He seemed mystified that this priest could not understand so elemental a law.

"What do *you* want, absolution?" Nick suddenly exploded.

"Me? I'm a Jew, Father." Lansky motioned his men to take the body out of the cold room. "Maybe what I want is to get even a little. Make me sleep better." He went out the door, following Ruthie.

"I've been an idiot! A fool!" Nick shouted even as the door closed. "All of you are scum! Murderers!"

He stalked angrily back to the elevator. When he was in his room, he dressed quickly, borrowing a wooden cane from one of the sleeping patients. Then he hobbled out past the main desk.

A nun emerged from the prescription room just as he passed. "Where do you think you're going, Father?" she demanded.

"To meet the devil himself, Sister!" Nick got on the waiting elevator.

64

Lucky Luciano MADE HIMSELF comfortable in the warden's wooden rocker. He was back at Dannemora, living in luxury. Right now Lucky had chosen to meet Governor Tom Dewey in the warden's own house. It was a small cottage, just large enough for the warden, his wife and two children. The point it made on the governor was calculated. The house sat outside the prison's walls.

The governor, who had arrived alone that morning at the behest of President Roosevelt, sat on the divan by himself, listening to Abraham Polakoff, Luciano's attorney, read the brief that he had prepared. Frank Costello stood near the window, drinking coffee. Tight-lipped, Dewey had politely refused any refreshment. He stared balefully with his black eyes as Polakoff finished.

". . . all sabotage has ceased on the docks of New York. All waterfronts, as promised, on the entire East Coast are quiet. Supplies flow smoothly to our men fighting overseas. 'Operation Underworld' is completed." The lawyer paused as he turned the page. Dewey stiffened, knowing the demands were coming now.

"Therefore, for his participation, Mr. Charles Luciano wants to be pardoned immediately. And second: that the waterfront be left in the hands of those who run it . . . in perpetuity." Polakoff closed the legal document and looked at Dewey.

"The Mob wants to run the docks?" Dewey sneered. "I deny that second request emphatically!"

Polakoff started to protest, but Luciano motioned him away. "Don't matter. What can anybody do about us?"

"As for the pardon, Governor?" Costello spoke up from the window.

Dewey sank back on the couch. He knew that President Roosevelt had acknowledged the debt owed Luciano. But secretly he knew also it was a smart political move. Dewey was touted as Roosevelt's Republican opponent in 1944. To pardon the gangster would blot Dewey's character. The very criminal he had sent to prison and on whom he had built his political career would destroy him with the voting public. But what could Dewey do?

"As for your first demand, Mr. Polakoff"—Dewey chose to ignore Luciano and speak directly to the attorney—"the president will pardon this criminal."

"Governor," Polakoff corrected him, "it is you who will pardon Mr. Luciano, is it not?"

Tom Dewey rose angrily and crossed the room to exit.

"Governor," Luciano whispered between clenched teeth.

Dewey paused at the door which led outside to his waiting limousine.

"Since you framed me to get to be governor, I am revenged."

Dewey shot outside, calling for his chauffeur to take him home.

Uncharacteristically, Luciano sprang from the rocker

and did an exuberant dance. Polakoff immediately shook his hand in congratulation.

"You did it!" Polakoff cried. "You're a free man, Charlie Lucky!" They embraced.

"I beat 'em!" Luciano growled. "I beat 'em good, didn't I!"

"We're gonna have a party for you the likes nobody in New York's ever seen!" Costello promised, patting his back. "We're gonna celebrate big, Lucky! You too, Abe!"

"I'll be there," Polakoff promised, elated.

The walk back to the prison was a short one. The warden joined them and stayed a little ahead of the group. Luciano was so excited he jabbered away and did not see the taxi pull up in front of Dannemora or Nick Remington get out.

Lucky was feeling as he had in the old days. A huge weight had been lifted from him. He was a free man! It did not matter he was going back to his cell now. The future was his—won by a bold stroke. He had lived up to his name of Lucky once again.

Nick blocked the narrow, icy sidewalk. The men, clapping one another's shoulders and dancing about like adolescents, approached. When Lucky saw Remington, he came forward and threw his arms around him.

"Hey, hey," he laughed, "you're lookin' good, Father!"

"He should be, after you pulled him out of the water!" Polakoff attempted a joke.

"What is it?" Lucky asked, concerned. "You get bad news about Rafaella? What, tell me?" His voice was solicitous, warm.

"Did you . . . burn the *Normandie?*" Nick demanded.

Luciano studied the big man before him. The black wool topcoat made him seem even bigger.

"As your attorney, Mr. Luciano, I advise you not . . ." Polakoff interjected.

"It's all right, Abe," Luciano said. "Bishop Remington here deserves an answer to his question. Right, Bishop?"

Nick had to admire the man. Luciano was reminding him of his own payoff. What could the gangster have achieved if his life were not twisted and evil? He *was* brilliant.

Not rising to the bait, Nick repeated: "Did you . . . burn the *Normandie?*"

Luciano grinned suddenly, swung an affectionate arm around Nick and tried to lead him off. In a flurry, Nick flung him away, his elbow striking Luciano in the nose. The gangster fell and rolled heavily off the walk to the frozen ground.

Immediately Polakoff, Costello and the warden rushed to him. Luciano waved them away and rose on his own. He walked off several feet, wiping the blood away, and beckoned to Nick. "C'mere," he said coldly.

Nick, realizing Luciano would not speak in front of the warden, went out and faced him.

"Why deny it? I got what I wanted."

"It's true then?"

"Shit, it was a banana race. I even let the Nazis do all that crap, sinkin' ships and everything! How else could they have pulled it off with us controllin' the docks? Though I'll admit it did get outta hand. Those fuckin' Nazis! But I needed somethin' to get the attention of the president! Somethin' big, see? Yeah, I torched the *Normandie.* Or two of my boys did. Even wore blond wigs to make 'em look German. But it was all my plan!"

Nick leaped for him. "You killed Joey!" He grabbed

284

the gangster's throat, knocking him down to the ground. "You murdered my best friend!"

Polakoff, the warden and Costello roughly pulled Nick off. Luciano jumped up and kneed him hard in the groin. Nick fell, dry-retching.

Luciano, bruised but otherwise unhurt, shook his head at him.

"Che va piano, va sano," he spoke, his eyes dead, face expressionless. "We have a sayin' on the docks. It means 'Go slow, stay healthy.'" And with that, he walked away, not looking back.

"I'll tell everybody what you did!" Nick shouted after him. "Arson and murder will keep you inside prison! Murderer! You killed Ruthie too!"

The massive iron gates of the prison opened for Charlie Lucky and closed behind him. Luciano did not look back. Polakoff and Costello walked away to their own waiting limousine.

Nick, fighting off the black pain that swelled up from his groin, rose and limped back to the waiting taxi and the driver, who was looking scared.

65

AT NICK'S REQUEST, THE hack took him to the water-front on the Hudson.

"This it?" he asked when he stopped his taxi at the address Nick had given him. They were idling in front of "The Minnow" bar.

Nick seemed to awaken from a distant dream as he turned his eyes from something only he was seeing and stared at the familiar front of "The Minnow." Inside he could picture his friends sitting on the worn moleskin bench in front of the long bar. He could almost taste his first of many drinks.

"Something I gotta do first."

"Listen, buddy"—the driver swung in his seat—"I don't like what you did back there! I mean, I recognized who that was! Plus, there's a war on and gas don't grow on trees!"

"Fifty-first and Madison," Nick said.

The cabbie parked at 452 Madison Avenue, in the rear of St. Patrick's Cathedral, in front of the rectory. Across the street in a high-rise was the Archdiocese of New York's chancery offices.

Nick climbed out and started up the sidewalk.

"Hey," the cabbie yelled, "this finally the end of the line?"

"Why, yes." Nick turned, confused.

"Then pay up!" The cabbie, double-parked, got out. Nick dug in his pockets.

"Don't tell me you got no money, for Chrissakes!" the cabbie suddenly groaned. "Don't tell me that! I gotta come up with it if you don't!"

"Somebody here will give you money. Don't worry!" Nick said.

"Fuck this, buddy!" the cabbie screamed. "I'm gonna get a cop! Don't you move!" He searched up the street. At the corner of Fiftieth, as he had remembered, a traffic officer stood in the intersection, waving through cars. The cabbie sprinted toward him.

Nick crossed the sidewalk to the rectory stairs and went toward the ivy-covered brick wall. He pressed a small inset white buzzer. In a moment a peep door was slid back and the housekeeper appeared.

"Father Nick Remington," he identified himself.

"Do you have an appointment, Father?" She eyed his disheveled appearance.

"Please," he said. "I've come to pray in the cemetery for Father Stumpo."

She hesitated, then pressed her inside buzzer, which released the large iron gate's latch. Nick pushed inward, leaving the gate ajar.

He walked down the quiet, sheltered brick path of the priests' cemetery. Here, beneath low tombstones, hundreds of former pastors, bishops, archbishops and even a cardinal or two lay in eternal repose, all equal in death. It was a special place. Reserved for those who had somehow contributed their lives to the good of the Archdiocese of New York.

He found Joey by the church wall. Spellman had kept his promise. His gray granite tombstone said: "Father Joseph Aloysius Cornelius Stumpo. 1902–1941. R.I.P."

"Hello, Joey," Nick said as he knelt at the grave.

The cop and the cabbie burst into the cemetery.

"There he is!" The hack pointed. "The deadbeat hisself! Runs me all over the fuckin' country! I want him behind bars!"

"All right, all right," the cop said. "I'll handle this."

But as they started down the walk, a side door on the rectory opened and out stepped a purple-robed prelate. The cop immediately recognized him as Archbishop Spellman.

"What's the trouble here?" he asked, after spotting Nick kneeling nearby.

The cabbie explained. Spellman wordlessly dug in the deep pockets of his cassock and gave the man a hundred dollars. "Keep the rest for yourself," he told him.

"That do it?" the cop asked the cabbie, relieved he did not have to haul anyone downtown.

"It's wages," the cabbie grumbled and went off, counting the money again.

"You want that guy out of here, Holiness?" the cop asked Spellman.

Spellman smiled at the appellation. " 'Holiness' is for the pope," he said. "I'm just a bishop, Officer."

"Well, I ain't Catholic," the cop said. "No offense meant."

"None taken." Spellman turned toward Nick. "As for that guy, he also is a bishop of the Holy Roman Catholic Church. Or will be."

"Well, nothin's like it seems these days." The cop shook his head. "Good day, Bishop." And he went out of the cemetery.

Spellman knelt beside Nick and prayed for some time in silence.

"It was Luciano and the Mob who sabotaged the *Normandie*," Nick whispered brokenly. "He told me himself. 'Operation Underworld' was a hoax devised by Luciano!"

288

"Can you prove that?" Spellman asked, as the shock registered on his round face.

"I don't know . . ."

Spellman nodded in resignation, then stood. He reached into his cassock pocket and handed Nick a telegram.

"This came for you. I guess they didn't know where else to send it."

Nick rose, took it with trembling hands and tore it open. It was from London High Command. "By Captain Robert Marsh's request, we are informing you Lieutenant Rafaella Massaro DID NOT arrive with convoy. Therefore, she is officially listed as a CASUALTY. Signed, Commander Lee Holtz, U.S.N."

Nick lowered the yellow telegram. It hung like a dead bird from his hand. Spellman took it and read it.

"I'm sorry," he said. "I will pray for her."

"Thank you."

"I know this may not be the time, Nick," Spellman said. "But you have a future. And frankly, the Church needs you."

"Why is it just when you don't want something, you get it?" Nick asked, watching a pigeon spring from the cathedral wall and float out over the cemetery and the streets beyond.

"Because it doesn't matter what we want," Spellman answered.

"You sound so certain."

"I have to be. What I get paid for." He put an affectionate hand on Nick's arm. "Take some time for yourself. I have a house on the beach. Pray there. Get your wounds healed. Call me when you're ready."

"Excellency," Nick said, "I was . . . in love with her."

"In love." Spellman rolled the phrase thoughtfully over his tongue. "I suppose you made love to her?"

"No. Though I wanted to."

"You at least kissed her then?"

Amazed, Nick had to shake his head. "No." Was *that* possible? The only time their lips had touched was when he kissed her, unconscious in his arms, on the *Liberty*.

"L'amour est un rêve. Mais un baiser peut en faire une realité."

"I don't speak French."

"An old saying. 'Love is a dream. But after one kiss one awakens to find the truth.'" Spellman squeezed Nick's arm tightly. "You never even had that chance. She's dead. Trust this reality, Father," he begged. "It's God's will. He wants you back."

66

To Nick's surprise, Archbishop Spellman's house in Mastic was not a mansion, as he had expected, but a small beach shack. The iron-gray wintry Atlantic lapped at its pilings below the wood decking and pounded angrily on the beach. Sea gulls were his only company, except for an occasional weekend visitor who appeared to paint a nearby house or walk the empty stretches of sand.

He heard about the progression of the war on an old brown Victrola wooden radio. Ten thousand men had surrendered at Bataan, then many of them had died on the infamous "Death March." He cheered when on April 18, Lieutenant Colonel James Doolittle took off from the carrier *Hornet* and led sixteen B-25s to bomb targets in Tokyo, Yokohama, Hokosuka, Kobe and Nagoya. In May, Corregidor surrendered and the Germans attacked Russia in the Kharkov offensive. But the RAF sent 1,000 bombers in a night attack on Cologne, devastating that city.

So it went, with both sides trading blows. America yet taking it on the chin, but getting in some licks. Her allies valiantly were fighting back on half a dozen different fronts, but the war generally was going against them. Still, the determination of the Allies was apparent and Nick felt proud to be an American.

The war became an obsession for him. He followed the nightly radio reports by Edward R. Murrow from London and awaited eagerly the fireside chats from President Roosevelt. But he knew all this activity was nothing more than an attempt to deny Rafaella access to his memory.

In numerous nightly dreams, he saw her peck him on the cheek while they rode the train back to New York. Two human beings who had barely survived together. Painfully he saw her flee from him in his apartment that night. Then he had played the cuckolded husband and ordered Fritz Fleckenstein from her room. In nightmare after terrifying nightmare, he relived the horrible moments in the hold of the *Liberty*. He would awaken from the terrible dreams, screaming her name, seeing her drown again and again.

To keep from dreaming, Nick forced himself to stay awake into the wee hours of the morning, spinning the radio dial for any bits of news or music he could find. Then finally, exhausted, he would sleep for a time, only to awaken from another dream of Rafaella.

He found that he could not accept her death. It was ironic. How many bereaved had he comforted and sympathized with over their losses? He found he had understood nothing, had no idea of how it hurt. Rafaella's loss was physical.

Slowly, in long, cold walks on the beach, Nick forced himself to open up to his grief. The more he allowed himself to think about Rafaella, the more he marveled at such a woman. She had been extraordinary! How did she call up such deep reserves of strength after what the monks of Mazzarino had done to her? How did she have the wisdom to understand that Nick could love and heal her? A lesser woman would have continued to hate.

All his life he had thought of men as being stronger

than women. Now he wondered. If all that had happened to Rafaella had been visited on him, he would have snapped like an oak tree in a hurricane. But Rafaella, supple as a reed, had merely bent over, then straightened up after each storm had passed.

And so in his meditations, he grew to love Rafaella deeper and miss her as a part of himself that had been amputated. But in his thoughts and dreams, he found himself growing agonizingly obsessed over her final hours on this earth. It had been a terrible time about which he could know nothing.

He was sure she had somehow survived the final attack by the *Bund*. He hoped her strength would have come from being an officer at war. But what had she experienced *after* she had been so brutally used? After all the old wounds caused by those monks reopened. And in that terrible loneliness, suffering through all her reawakened agonies, she had died.

Had she even felt him carry her up from the hold of the *Liberty?* Taken some small comfort from his kiss? Or had she been dead even then? At the memory of her pitiful nakedness beneath the torn and stained overcoat, his throat ached and fresh tears flowed from his eyes.

It was in the second month of his hermitage that he found himself itching to get back into the war. Yet he had begun to feel certain it would not be as a cleric.

He wrote long letters to Spellman, attempting to sort out his feelings. Each wound up with the same conclusion: "My becoming bishop is built on sin: the murder of Father Joey. On a hoax: the campaign called 'Operation Underworld.' It is a lie and I cannot bear to profit from it. Therefore, I feel conscience-bound to return to my former way of life."

Each letter was returned, opened, usually with a

293

note. "Archbishop Spellman in Rome . . . in Africa . . . in Philippines. Will answer soon." It was always signed by Monsignor Michael Dolan, Spellman's personal secretary. Nick suspected the archbishop saw his letters, but it was his way of saying: "I don't accept your decision."

67

June 12, 1942
New York City

MONSIGNOR DOLAN WAS STANDING in the archbishop's rectory office behind St. Pat's, holding the mail that had collected since his last trip abroad. "Oh, two more from Father Remington," he said.

Spellman yawned from behind his desk. He was bone tired from the twenty-hour flight from London. "Same broken record?" he asked.

"He seems to have made up his mind, Excellency."

"Nonsense. I know what's best for him."

"There's something else, Excellency." Monsignor Dolan picked up a manila envelope. On its front were the military markings of the U.S. Navy.

"What's this?" Spellman asked.

"Received from Liverpool yesterday."

"Liverpool? I was just there two days ago. Dreary place."

"No, Excellency. Liverpool, Nova Scotia. Four hundred ninety miles off New York. I looked it up. The letter's open."

Spellman eyed the envelope closely a moment, then upended it on his desk.

"No!" Spellman cried as its contents spilled out. "Dear, dear God!" He was facing an 8 × 10 official photo of Lieutenant Rafaella Massaro, head bandaged, propped up in her hospital bed. "It's her!"

"A militarized trawler from Liverpool, one of a fleet responding to the May Day sent by the convoy on March 17, helped pick up survivors," Monsignor Dolan recited from the dispatch by memory. "Of the six scooped from the water, two survived. A man and a woman."

The archbishop tore the photo in half. "As far as we're concerned, she did not survive." He shoved it and the dispatch back into the envelope and threw it in his wastebasket. Looking up, he saw the shock registered on the young monsignor's face.

"The Holy Father himself wishes to reward and consecrate Nicholas Remington. And President Roosevelt is going to throw a luncheon for him!" Spellman stood. "Believe me, Mickey, it's the best for everyone."

"But he'll find out someday," Dolan protested. "Then what?"

"By then Remington will have come to his senses. Right now he's acting like some lovesick moralist! Somebody's got to bring him down to earth. There's work to do and he's needed. That's all, Mickey."

The monsignor bowed and started to exit.

"Oh, Mickey," Spellman said. "Pope Pius XII wishes to consecrate our American hero in a week's time. Take care of that, will you?"

The monsignor closed the door.

Spellman leaned wearily back in his red leather chair. He had to appear tough for everybody. For the entire armed forces, which were under his spiritual command. For the massive Archdiocese of New York. For everybody. He wished his mother were still alive so he could sit and cry with her now that he needed it.

He stood to go upstairs to bed. Momentarily his eye

was taken by the navy envelope lodged in the wastebasket.

Leaders were guilty of different sins than mere mortals, he told himself. Still, as he shut off the light and closed the door to his office, he hesitated a brief moment. "Forgive me," he said to the darkness behind him.

68

He was packing when the Packard pulled up on the sandy road that led off the main highway. To his surprise, Monsignor Dolan emerged, his lanky, ascetic frame unfolding from the driver's seat. Nick greeted him at the door and let him enter.

They stood facing each other awkwardly in the small living room that looked straight through the kitchen and out onto the white-capped water.

"Going somewhere?" Dolan asked, spotting the two suitcases lined up.

"There's a war on, Monsignor," Nick said.

"Yes, I know." He seemed to study the suitcases intently.

"Can I get you some coffee, something?" Nick remembered his manners.

"No, thank you. I've got to get back to the city. Perhaps I could give you a lift?"

"Save me bus fare."

Monsignor Dolan noticed Nick was dressed in wool slacks, a thick Pendelton lumber shirt—civilian clothes. "I suppose you want to know why I'm here," he said. He opened a small square white box which Nick had noticed him holding. Inside was the purple hat of a bishop. "Pope Pius XII wants to consecrate you himself. Reparation for the injustice done to you."

"The archbishop doesn't miss a trick, does he?" Nick said, gazing at the hat.

"He won't take no for an answer. You know him," Monsignor Dolan said. "Neither will the Holy Father."

Nick breathed out a long, exasperated sigh.

"I understand Pope Pius did not want to be pope," Dolan offered quickly. "He begged to be let off the hook after his election, Excellency."

"Don't call me that," Nick said. "I'm not a bishop." He picked up his bags and said: "How about that ride you offered?"

"Are you sure?"

"Tempted."

"Then take it!" Dolan held out the purple hat.

Nick shook his head. "You heard about what happened?"

"We're very proud of you in the archdiocese."

"Everything comes with a price, Monsignor. I'm somebody else now. A man who's still in love with a woman. I'd kill for her if I had to. Not real good material for a bishop."

"All sins are forgivable by God."

"That's just it," Nick said, going out the door. "I'm not sorry for the way I feel."

They rode in silence through the small towns of Patchogue, West Islip and Bellmore. Monsignor Dolan stared, frowning, as he drove, seemingly enmeshed in his own tangled thoughts. When they crossed the Brooklyn Bridge, he suddenly turned and asked: "Was Lieutenant Rafaella Massaro the one you loved?"

"Even in death."

The monsignor turned again to his own thoughts.

The Packard dashed along the New York Expressway. A sign flew by the windows: "Idlewild Airport."

"Quick!" Dolan spun to Nick. "Tell me! Do you

have any doubt, any slightest wavering at not accepting the hat of bishop?"

Nick shook his head. "A different man wanted that."

"Then, God forgive me. Archbishop Spellman will probably kick my behind down to an assistant pastor in Harlem . . ." He agitatedly crossed himself and swung the car off at the airport exit.

"You're going to Nova Scotia!" Dolan told him.

"Nova Scotia?" Nick asked, puzzled.

"To see the woman you love. She's alive."

69

Through Monsignor Dolan's efforts, Nick was allowed on a Civilian Flying Corps cargo plane. Flying old Douglas Bolo B-18s and DC-2s, the Corps' main duty was to ferry hospital supplies across the Atlantic, stopping to refuel either in Gander Airport, Newfoundland, or Reykjavik, Iceland, finally to land in London, England, or hiphop onward to such distant fields as Casablanca and Marrakesch. To succeed in getting the Corps to cooperate, Monsignor Dolan quickly crossed himself again and signed "By Order of Archbishop Spellman," together with his rank of Military Vicar of Armed Forces, equivalent to that of a general.

Sitting inside the DC-2, tucked in between a long row of surgery lamps and metal hospital beds, Nick waved goodbye as Monsignor Dolan exited onto the boarding stairs. The winter wind whipped his cassock up so he had to hold it down.

They flew north over New Bedford and then out into the Atlantic. Nick had said nothing. The shock had been too great for his system. At first he had thought it was some sort of bad practical joke. But then he realized it was real. Rafaella *was* alive! Monsignor Dolan would not dare tease or kid about such a thing.

"Java, Father?" One of the crew members, a

301

nineteen-year-old tailgunner, offered him a cup of steaming coffee. It was very cold up here and he was not properly dressed. The coffee tasted good. He smiled up after sipping it. Somehow it brought with it reality.

The plane landed at Halifax, an airport sixty miles east of Liverpool. Nick jumped down from the door onto the macadam as the crew waved goodbye and bid him good luck.

An old farmer picked him up on the island's only road. He was driving a rusted Model-T Ford truck. The farmer did not speak a word the entire way to Liverpool. When he stopped in the tiny fishing town on the south shore of Nova Scotia, he said, "Here."

Nick got out. "Where's the hospital?"

"Ain't none," the farmer said. "Used to be, but storm blew it down in '36." He motioned to a low, squat, cheerfully white building halfway down Liverpool's only street. "Clinic there." And he drove away without giving Nick even the chance to thank him.

Feeling suddenly naked, Nick hefted his two bags of luggage. He strode down the steep, cobblestoned street and stopped before the white building. "Liverpool Medical Clinic," the sign stated, with the name of the local doctor below.

A plump nurse answered his knock. She was young, and her eyes and her voice were merry. "Yes? Can I help you, sir?"

"I'm looking for . . . Rafaella . . . Lieutenant Massaro," Nick added when the nurse smiled knowingly.

"She's not here."

His heart sank. Was he to be deprived of seeing her even now?

"Oh, not to worry," the young nurse laughed at seeing his dismal expression. "She's just on the docks there. Taking some fresh air. Shouldn't be. Told her that. But she's stubborn, a willful soul. Anyway, she's

there. Do you want to come inside and wait for her
return?"

"No," Nick said, turning down the street and straining to catch a glimpse of Rafaella. "Can I leave my bags
here?"

"No one will take a thing. But I'll bring them inside
myself." The nurse lifted the luggage into the doorway.
"Would you be Nick then?"

"How did you know?"

"She asked incessantly for you in her delirium." The
nurse paused, a cloud passing over her bright, ruddy
face. "But after getting better, she's become with-
drawn. Won't talk. Refuses to let any of us even touch
her."

Unable to hear more, Nick spun away. He ran along
the cobblestones, down toward the docks.

The nurse, at first startled, understood and smiled
hopefully.

Rafaella was standing near a dock piling, gazing out
at the windblown, churning Atlantic. Her back was to
him. She was wearing an army-issue wool coat and a
funny little brown wool watch cap with a bill. He stood
beside her and tried to say her name. It was difficult to
believe he was even looking at the same woman who
had haunted his memories and dreams. And not dead
but living! Really, truly alive!

She was looking fixedly at the turbulent green-gray
sea. Her wonderful laughing, mocking eyes were list-
lessly staring at something. He wanted to reach out to
her. But he sensed something was going on, something
more powerful than he could offer. Was he too late?
Had the reed finally broken?

"Rafaella?" Nick whispered. It was all that he could
manage.

She slowly turned her head to him. Her green eyes
were vacant, dull, showing no recognition. A woman
viewing a stranger.

He could think of nothing but wanting to hold her. He opened his arms.

"You?" she asked.

He nodded, tears burning his eyes.

She stepped into his arms. "Oh, Nick," she cried, "it is you!"

"Darling," he spoke between half-sobs and laughter that were forcing their way from his throat.

Crying, she clung to him as though he were life itself.

He held her and they stood there, the warmth building between them.

And then they kissed. And he knew, more than himself, his life, his soul . . . he loved her.

Epilogue

AFTER THE WAR, Fritz Fleckenstein was deported to Germany and was forced to stand trial for his Nazi war crimes. Lulu, his wife, joined him there with the children. After serving ten years in prison at Spandau, Fritz was released in 1956, a broken man.

At Nick's urging and because of his own political future, Governor Tom Dewey delayed Charlie Lucky Luciano's parole until after the war. And then, to Luciano's chagrin, the governor had him deported straight to Sicily.

Meyer Lansky's power in New York grew. His own gang flourished. After the war, Vito Genovese, Lucky's old partner, returned from Italy and absorbed Luciano's family. Frank Costello retired.

In 1946, Luciano attempted a comeback in the United States by setting up shop in nearby Cuba. But with the threat of aid being cut off by the U.S. Government, Batista deported him back to Italy. Luciano lived there in exile until his death from a heart attack at the Rome airport in 1962. He was meeting a motion picture producer who wanted to make a movie of his life.

Tom Dewey, in delaying Luciano's parole, did little good for himself. He ran against Franklin Roosevelt in

1944 and was defeated. He lost again in 1948 against Harry S Truman.

Archbishop Francis J. Spellman was elevated to cardinal by Pope Pius XII in 1946. In a strange coincidence, Sister Pasqualina, the pope's powerful housekeeper, crusaded personally to bring the Mafia monks of Mazzarino to trial. But Spellman, fearful of a scandal on this explosive issue, urged Pope Pius to stop the prosecution of the Franciscans. It was only in 1964, during the reign of Pope Paul VI, after the monks had been exonerated for their crimes, that they were retried. This time, they were found guilty of murder, extortion, rape and mayhem. Each monk was sentenced to thirteen years.

Later it was revealed that Nick Remington, then a prominent correspondent for CBS, had been greatly responsible. Through the reigns of Pope Pius XII, Pope John XXIII and Pope Paul VI, Nick had kept pressure on the Vatican and would not let the issue be forgotten.

Lieutenant Rafaella Massaro retired a lieutenant-commander in the United States Navy. Her distaff branch of service, the SPARS (from motto "Semper Paratus" of the Coast Guard), was dissolved after the war. Its members were reinstated under naval jurisdiction.

Nick and Rafaella Remington today live in Manhattan on Park Avenue. Parents of three children, all boys, they have seven grandchildren, all girls.

Bibliography

Anslinger, Harry O., and Oursler, Will. *The Murderers*. New York: Farrar, Straus, 1961.

Campbell, Rodney. *The Luciano Project: The Secret Wartime Collaboration of the Mafia and the U.S. Navy*. New York: McGraw-Hill, 1977.

Carlyle, John Aitken. *The Temple Classics,* translation of *The Divine Comedy*.

Dolci, Danilo. *Report from Palermo*. New York: Orion Press, 1959.

Falconi, Carlo. *The Silence of Pius XII*. Bernard Wall, trans. Boston: Little, Brown, 1965.

Flynn, George I. *Roosevelt and Romanism: Catholics and American Diplomacy*. Westport, Conn.: Greenwood Press, 1976.

Gage, Nicholas. *Mafia, U.S.A.* New York: Playboy Press, 1972.

Gannon, Robert I., S. J. *The Cardinal Spellman Story*. New York: Doubleday, 1962.

Gosch, Martin A., and Hammer, Richard. *The Last Testament of Lucky Luciano*. Boston: Little, Brown, 1974.

Greeley, Andrew M. *The American Catholic: A Social Portrait*. New York: Basic Books, 1977.

Johnson, Paul. *Pope John XXIII*. Boston: Little, Brown, 1974.

307

Katz, Leonard. *Uncle Frank: The Biography of Frank Costello.* New York: Drake, 1973.

Leckie, Robert. *American and Catholic.* New York: Doubleday, 1970.

Lewis, Norman. *The Honored Society.* New York: Putnam, 1964.

Murphy, Paul I., with Arlington, Rene R. *La Popessa.* New York: Warner Books, 1983.

Pallenberg, Corrado. *Inside the Vatican.* New York: Hawthorn Books, 1960.

Teresa, Vincent, with Renner, Thomas C. *Mafia.* New York: Doubleday, 1975.

Toland, John. *Adolf Hitler.* New York: Doubleday, 1976.

Wayman, Dorothy G. *Cardinal O'Connel of Boston.* New York: Farrar, Straus and Young, 1955.

Time—1939–1947

The New York Times—1939–1947